Praise for

"*Bees in June* is the kind of novel that wraps itself around your heart and doesn't let go. Elizabeth Bass Parman has created a world so rich with charm and quiet magic that you'll want to pack your bags and move straight to Spark, Tennessee. The characters—especially Rennie—are beautifully real, and the story glows with warmth, resilience, and the kind of hope that stirs your soul. This book is a heartfelt reminder that healing can be found in unexpected places and that sometimes, if we listen closely, the bees might just lead us home."

—Jennifer Moorman, *USA TODAY* bestselling author of *The Vanishing of Josephine Reynolds*

"Your heart will grow after reading Elizabeth Bass Parman's sweet and tender sophomore novel, *Bees in June*. Rennie is the kind of character you can't stop rooting for, and I read with a mix of tears and joy until the final breathtaking finale. A tribute to the human spirit and one woman's desire to remake herself, this novel should be on everyone's TBR list."

—Brooke Lea Foster, author of *Our Last Vineyard Summer*

"First-time novelist Parman delivers a twisted tale of small-town drama. Fans of gothic tales or Southern novels will enjoy this."

—*Library Journal* for *The Empress of Cooke County*

"Parman superbly teases out the good and bad sides of people . . . This novel effectively combines very human foibles, hilarious circumstances, and honest yearnings of the heart with page-turning endings. Highly recommended."

—Historical Novel Society for
The Empress of Cooke County

"Get ready to laugh! Elizabeth Bass Parman is a true Southern storyteller. I couldn't have loved *The Empress of Cooke County* more."

—Fannie Flagg, *New York Times* bestselling author

"Funny, fast-moving, suspenseful, with unforgettable and deeply drawn characters, *The Empress of Cooke County* will rivet readers."

—Lee Smith, *New York Times* bestselling author

"You won't simply read *The Empress of Cooke County*, you will fall into a world we all long for: sizzling small-town life in the American South with its secret history, vivid characters, and juicy dramas. If the complicated Jezebel and the feisty women of *Steel Magnolias* had a baby, it might be Posey Jarvis. Put on a pot of coffee, cut yourself a wedge of chess pie, and dive in."

—Adriana Trigiani, *New York Times* bestselling author of *The Good Left Undone*

"*The Empress of Cooke County* gives you a juicy taste of small-town Southern life at its best! Be prepared to laugh out loud as you race through pages full of secrets, high drama, and an unpredictable ending!"

—Lisa Patton, bestselling author of *Whistlin' Dixie in a Nor'easter*

"*The Empress of Cooke County* is, at its core, a tale of connection. Parman examines both the small acts of kindness that nourish connection and the selfish impulses that starve it. You can't help but root for this tender celebration of community, would-be empresses, and big dreams."

—Mary Liza Hartong, author of *Love and Hot Chicken*

"Elizabeth Bass Parman dazzles in *The Empress of Cooke County*, a lush, 1960s Southern charmer brimming with wit and whimsy. Join the unforgettable Posey Jarvis and her daughter as they navigate the twists and turns of small-town Tennessee with gin-soaked escapades, a possum-infested mansion, and enough peach cobbler to make your mouth water."

—Hope Gibbs, author of *Where the Grass Grows Blue*

"As someone who often fantasizes about a simpler way of life, stepping back in time to Queen Bee Posey Jarvis's colorful world was a slice of literary heaven. A delightful 1960s Southern charmer on every level. What a stunning, poignant debut."

—Rea Frey, #1 bestselling author of *Don't Forget Me* and *The Other Year*, for *The Empress of Cooke County*

Bees in June

Also by Elizabeth Bass Parman

The Empress of Cooke County

Bees in June

a novel

ELIZABETH BASS PARMAN

Bees in June

Copyright © 2025 by Elizabeth Bass Parman

All rights reserved. No portion of this book may be reproduced, stored in a retrieval system, or transmitted in any form or by any means—electronic, mechanical, photocopy, recording, scanning, or other—except for brief quotations in critical reviews or articles, without the prior written permission of the publisher.

Published by Harper Muse, an imprint of HarperCollins Focus LLC.

Scripture quotations are taken from the King James Version. Public domain.

This book is a work of fiction. The characters, incidents, and dialogue are drawn from the author's imagination and are not to be construed as real. Any resemblance to actual events or persons, living or dead, is entirely coincidental.

Any internet addresses (websites, blogs, etc.) in this book are offered as a resource. They are not intended in any way to be or imply an endorsement by HarperCollins Focus LLC, nor does HarperCollins Focus LLC vouch for the content of these sites for the life of this book.

Without limiting the author's and publisher's exclusive rights, any unauthorized use of this publication to train generative artificial intelligence (AI) technologies is expressly prohibited.

Library of Congress Cataloging-in-Publication Data

Names: Parman, Elizabeth Bass, 1961- author.
Title: Bees in June : a novel / Elizabeth Bass Parman.
Description: Nashville : Harper Muse, 2025. | Summary: "Uncle Dixon always told Rennie to tell the bees everything, but somewhere along the way, Rennie forgot. Now, with her life at its lowest, she begins to see the bees in a new light. Will she believe again in the magic of the hives, and will she listen as the bees try to guide her home?"—Provided by publisher.
Identifiers: LCCN 2025006141 (print) | LCCN 2025006142 (ebook) | ISBN 9781400342600 (trade paperback) | ISBN 9781400342617 (epub) | ISBN 9781400342624
Subjects: LCGFT: Novels.
Classification: LCC PS3616.A75698 B44 2025 (print) | LCC PS3616.A75698 (ebook) | DDC 813/.6—dc23/eng/20250320
LC record available at https://lccn.loc.gov/2025006141
LC ebook record available at https://lccn.loc.gov/2025006142

Printed in the United States of America

25 26 27 28 29 LBC 5 4 3 2 1

This book is dedicated to my mother, Clara McDonald Bass, who taught me to cherish strength, resilience, and joy.

Bees in June

A swarm of bees in May
Is worth a load of hay;
A swarm of bees in June
Is worth a silver spoon;
A swarm of bees in July
Is not worth a fly.

—Seventeenth-century beekeepers' poem

PROLOGUE

HIS HEART IS STILL BROKEN.

Could we have prevented this?

Who among us was strong enough to fly that vast distance? Even if we could have managed such a feat, a man in love is not likely to listen to reason, no matter how sage the advice.

It's been years in human time, and he is no stronger. He has ignored every sky-swept sunset and even the most intoxicating rose. We fear his wounds will never heal.

He is so earthbound now, keeping his eyes downcast instead of among the stars that used to leave him wonderstruck.

It all seems so cruel. There must have been a gentler way to redirect him to his true path.

Life for humans is rarely gentle. Experiencing the sting of betrayal will allow him to understand how sacred the balm of true love is when he finds it at last.

The lessons are so hard.

True, but the rewards are so great.

May we tell him?

Yes, it is time. We must construct a premise more compelling than even our most magnificent honeycomb so that he can reach only one conclusion. The sooner he gets to Spark, the sooner his shattered heart will begin to knit back together.

What about her heart?

It grows colder every day. If he does not hurry, though, more than her heart is at risk. Her very life depends upon our success.

Is he going to save her?

No, something even better is afoot. She's about to realize she must save herself.

CHAPTER 1

Spark, Tennessee
June 1, 1969

SUNLIGHT FLASHED AGAINST A BIT OF SILVER CLASPED in the enormous crow's beak. The bird, black as a moonless night, soared in a lazy semicircle over the newly sprouted tobacco. A soft breeze stirred the oak leaves and ruffled the white blossoms on the climbing roses that had grown against the small farmhouse for the last fifty years. The bird landed on the porch with his offering of a can's pull tab encircling his chipped beak like a ring. As he dropped the metal onto the enamelware plate, he cocked his head to eye Rennie Hendricks. She reached over her sleeping dog, picked up the ring, and deposited the scrap of metal into a mug filled with paper clips, bent nails, and foil gum wrappers.

"Thank you, Poe." She set aside the worn copy of *Jane Eyre* she was reading and pointed to the enamel plate. "Some pumpkin and sunflower seeds and near the last of the peanuts today. I should have had all three planted at least a month ago. The sunflowers and pumpkins will catch up, but peanuts need time. Maybe—"

Shrieking in protest, the crow flew off in a rush of wings

and feathers as Rennie's husband, Luther, stepped onto the back porch. "Takin' this to the barn," he said.

Rennie's eyes fell to the wooden cradle in his hands. "I'm not ready yet, Tiny. Please put it back in the nursery."

"We don't have a nursery, same as we don't have a baby." He set the cradle on the worn wooden boards of the porch. "It's been almost three weeks. Time to get back to life."

Rennie's voice trembled. "Tiny, please. Try to be understanding."

"Staring at an empty cradle all day isn't gonna bring him back. Our son is gone—dead and buried. I've *tried* to be understanding, like when I drove you out to the cemetery yesterday. I thought you'd cry a little and say one of your prayers, but what do you do instead? Pull out a blanket and tuck it into the dirt around his grave. He's not cold, the same way he doesn't need *this*." Tiny grabbed the cradle. "What if someone saw you singing that crazy lullaby about the moon and stroking the blanket you put over a mound of dirt? They'd be callin' Doc Grisham and tellin' him you've gone loony."

Rennie's voice shook. "Please put it back." Losing Gabriel had devastated her, but after the funeral, Tiny had returned to his routine like nothing had happened, while she lingered in a gray pit that made even the smallest of tasks daunting. "I need more time."

His jaw tightened, and without a word, he went back inside with the cradle. When he returned, he said, "It's tough on both of us, but moping on the back porch all day isn't doing any good." Running his enormous hands through his sandy hair, he added, "How about cooking us a nice supper or mending that shirt I tore on the fence last month?" He stepped off the porch but turned around to add, "Maybe think about focusing on me for a change now that you're not gonna be a mama."

She swallowed her protest. She *was* a mother, and always would be, even if her child was already in heaven, and he was wrong to say otherwise.

Tiny glared. "You hardly even look my way these days, but if you did, you'd see I'm struggling too, losing my son and trying to farm this godforsaken land. Almost everyone we graduated with makes their living off tobacco, but I swear I don't know how any farmer survives. Beb White says it takes a thirteen-month year to turn a profit in tobacco, and he's right." He looked at his wife. "I could use some encouragement and maybe a little appreciation while I'm out here working like a dog, trying to keep us fed and coming up with the damn rent my own parents are chargin' us."

Rennie had been expecting the topic of money to come up. It worked its way into every one of their numerous fights, and with what had happened a few days ago, the topic was overdue.

Tiny's father had crossed the field that connected the two houses earlier in the week, letting himself into the kitchen without so much as a knock, demanding to see Tiny. "Where's that bastard son of mine at?" Wayne Hendricks had snarled. "He owes me a hunnert dollars rent. Said he'd bring it by this morning, but of course he didn't."

"He's in Nashville getting supplies for the farm."

"Is that what he calls his liquor store runs? Tell him to pay up or you and him both will be out on your sorry asses." On his way out, he added, "How does it feel to be married to a loser?"

When Tiny had returned, she dreaded delivering the message, knowing it would result in a fight that would end with Tiny driving to Putney to drink away whatever was left of the day or night at the Moonshine Lounge in nearby Caldwell County. She was right, even with leaving out the part about being married to a loser, and Tiny didn't return until almost noon the next day. He was feeling the pressure, and so was Rennie. The farm wasn't much, but it was the only home she had. She surveyed the small house she had lived in for the last four years, with its faded white paint and shingles curled enough from decades of sun and rain to flap like bird wings whenever the wind blew.

She had barely survived the last three weeks. Her body insisted she had an infant to feed, producing milk for a child who would never nurse. Her mind heard Gabriel wailing for her, and she spent the first few nights home roaming the house, searching for him. Her brain eventually comprehended Gabriel was gone, but her heart only wanted to crawl in a grave of her own beside him. "I feel so left behind," she had sobbed to Tiny, who had no way to cope with his wife's cavernous emotions beyond awkwardly stroking her hair.

She slowly rocked, thinking over their money troubles. What if she found a job? She could help ease some of their financial stress, and having something to do, somewhere to be, might distract her, get her back onto a path that could lead her to a semblance of normalcy.

The crunch of gravel on their rutted driveway made them both look up. Tiny grunted. "Here comes May Dean. Why am I not surprised? I told everyone to stay the hell away from us and let us mourn in peace, but your idiot cousin never thinks the rules apply to her." He grimaced. "Need to check something in the barn."

May Dean Bradford parked a shiny red convertible in the side yard and pulled a Castner Knott shopping bag from the back seat. A gust of wind blew her blonde hair across her face and swirled her flowy green dress. "I know Tiny said no calls or visits," she said from the driveway, "but I couldn't stay away a minute longer." After climbing the three steps onto the porch, she gestured to the bag. "I've brought you some food." She smiled at the sleeping dog. "I'm glad to see you, Spot." May Dean nodded to the bag. "Some of my pot roast, mashed potatoes, and coleslaw, plus some Jell-O salad. Of course, I'm not as good a cook as you, but who is?" May Dean pecked Rennie on the cheek and frowned at her pale face. "I'll put all this in the fridge and fix us some lemonade." She lifted a jug from the bag. "I just made it this morning."

"Thanks. That'd be nice."

After a couple of minutes, May Dean popped the screen door open with her hip and handed Rennie a glass that glistened with beads of condensation. "I've missed you these last three weeks. How've you been feeling?"

"Tiny's ready for me to get back to normal."

"I asked about you, not Tiny."

Rennie sighed. "Not too good. I don't have the strength to do much past sit on this porch and watch the world go by." She glanced toward the barn where her husband was hiding from May Dean. "But I'm thinking of looking for a job, something to occupy my mind."

"Don't rush into anything too soon. Your body needs time to heal." She handed Rennie a small box. "I was doing some shopping yesterday and saw this. I thought of you right away. It's a fancy barrette." As Rennie opened the gift, May Dean nodded toward the convertible. "Come for a ride with me. You can pin back your beautiful auburn hair, and we'll see how fast my birthday present will go."

"Some other time." A flash drew her eye to the porch railing. *Why would a lightning bug be out in the middle of the day?* She looked closer. The sparkle came from a bee, not a lightning bug, and it was stalking up and down the porch railing. Was it glowing? She shook her head. *It must be the sun reflecting off its wings*, she thought, but the vibrance told her she was wrong. *Bees don't shine.*

She turned back to her cousin. "And my hair's mouse brown." A slight smile crossed her lips. "Remember when you took me to that fancy beauty shop in Nashville and that snooty stylist said he'd never seen actual mouse-brown hair before? I've never forgotten it." Odd that the bee was ignoring the fragrant roses blooming just a foot away, and the sun was *still* reflecting from its wings, even though it was in shade. A memory stirred in her brain—she'd seen that light before.

"He was just jealous because his own hair looked like dishwater after an all-you-can-eat buffet." May Dean followed Rennie's gaze and immediately slipped off a shoe. "I'll kill it, what with Tiny being so allergic and all."

Rennie lifted her hand in protest. "Never kill a bee, especially in June. Uncle Dixon taught us, remember? 'A bee in June is like a silver spoon.'"

Putting her shoe back on, May Dean frowned at her cousin. "I thought that poem was about how bees stop swarming by July 'cause they're all dead as a fly."

Rennie shook her head. "It's about how bees help the earth.

And June bees are the best of all. They pollinate the plants and ensure the farmers will have a good crop."

"I'm glad one of us was payin' attention. Sometimes Uncle Dixon's stories seem too much like school." She brushed her hair off her shoulders. "It's forty-nine days till the moon landing. Ev and I have a countdown calendar on the fridge, and I took one over to Uncle Dixon too. Ev says it's science and American know-how that'll get those brave men to the moon, but *I* think it's magic and prayer." She tugged at the hem of her dress. "My parents' first date was to hear this new thing called a radio, and here we are, talking about a man walking on the moon. Do you and Tiny want to come over and watch the landing at our house?"

"Tiny thinks the government's faking the whole thing, that they're going to film it all out in Hollywood to fool the Russians." Rennie paused. "But I'd like to see it."

"Great. We'll plan something."

Rennie rocked gently while May Dean shifted in her chair, her face flushing as she spoke. "I met the man who bought the old Sawyer place next door to Uncle Dixon. He moved in about two weeks ago. His name is Ambrose Beckett, and he is *so* handsome. I'm guessing he's about thirty. Black hair and the biggest green eyes. And no sign of a wedding ring. You should take him one of your famous pies so you can meet—"

"You're babbling, May Dean. When you talk this fast, you've got something you're afraid to say."

After a tense moment of silence between the two women, May Dean whispered, "I'm scared to tell you."

"Maybe I can do it for you." Rennie took May Dean's hand. "You and Everett are expecting."

Words gushed from May Dean's lips. "How did you know? I didn't want to say anything because your pregnancy was so hard, and then, well, I mean . . ."

"Gabriel died. You can say it." Her voice was barely a whisper, and the words sliced like knives as they crossed her throat. "My baby came too early to survive on his own."

May Dean hung her head. "I'm so sorry, Rennie."

Rennie pasted a smile on her face. "Listen to me. You can be sorry my son died, but don't you *ever* be sorry about your baby." Her voice quavered as she softly added, "I'm happy for you."

May Dean's face flooded with relief. "I hated keeping it from you."

That shiny bee was *still* marching up and down the railing, mesmerizing Rennie. Chill bumps covered her arms despite the warm day.

Fishing her keys from her straw bag, May Dean said, "I'd best be getting back. Ev has been fussing over me like a mother hen ever since I told him, and he's liable to call the sheriff for a search party if I'm a minute late." Her voice softened. "I'm due in October." She paused on the step. "We've told each other everything since we were kids. I should have known not to be scared. Love you, and I'll check on you tomorrow."

Rennie blinked back the tears pricking her eyes. "It's wonderful news." She watched May Dean drive away, her blonde hair flying in the breeze.

The bee, still gleaming, flew from the railing and landed on the rocker's arm. She crawled about six inches and turned toward Rennie, vibrating at a frequency Rennie could feel in her soul. The words *Come right away* popped into her head, and with a certainty she didn't understand, she knew she had to go to her uncle Dixon. Still weak from the difficult birth, she struggled to stand, then walked toward her husband with the bee flying alongside her, urging her forward.

Tiny was in the tobacco field, yanking a weed from freshly turned earth.

"I've got to take the truck to check on Uncle Dixon."

Sweat dripped down Tiny's face. "Nope. I gotta go to town."

Rennie's voice was soft but urgent. "It's important. I won't be long."

He squinted down at his wife, a full foot shorter than him. "I didn't hear the phone ring, and I didn't see you get outta that damn rocking chair to call *him*." The bee orbited Tiny's head, buzzing angrily. "Did May Dean tell you to go over there?" His nostrils flared. "She can drive that ridiculous birthday present of hers over to check on him her own self and quit being so pushy for once."

The bee left Rennie's side and landed on Tiny's cheek, glowing like a porch light on a foggy night.

Tiny grabbed his face. "Bastard stung me." He slapped at the bee. "Gotta take an antihistamine and get some ice on this thing before my whole eye swells shut." The bee's motionless body fell to the ground. "Take the damn truck."

The drive to her uncle's house took less than ten minutes, but with each mile, fear ratcheted up in Rennie's stomach. It had only been a month since her last visit with her uncle, but it seemed like a lifetime ago as she sped to his farm. She had been so happy, almost giddy, during their visit as they laughed and talked the afternoon away, neither realizing that tragedy was about to strike.

As a child, Rennie had two working parents, which meant

she had spent most of her summers with her aunt and uncle, and she had developed a deep love for them both. Her aunt and uncle recognized Rennie's interest in nature early on and had delighted in teaching her about the world around them. While her classmates were driving with their parents into Nashville to the roller rink or the movie theater, Rennie was crouched by her uncle, learning about the bioluminescence of foxfire or collecting fronds of fiddlehead ferns with her aunt for a salad. Rennie's favorite pastime, though, was listening, entranced, to their stories, which could be about bumblebees that held hands as they napped in the curve of a tulip poplar blossom, or how a person could tell if the coming winter would be mild or harsh if they knew how to interpret nature's coded signs.

May Dean would sometimes join in the adventures, providing the perfect companion for those long, lazy days. They would play in the bee yard for hours, pretending the scarlet elf cup mushrooms by the spring were goblets, or the delicate Dutchman's breeches blooms were their dolls' laundry hanging on a gossamer green clothesline. Their hickory stick dolls would watch from their pawpaw leaf rafts as the two girls waded in the bend of Flat Rock Creek, peeping under stones for a bashful crawdad or sunfish.

At the thought of the creek, an image came to Rennie of a glowing bee, luminous through the dark water—the same light that had emanated from the bee that had stung Tiny. She grasped at the memory, but it eluded her. She shook the fragmented recollection from her head. What she needed to focus on now was getting to her uncle.

As Rennie bumped along Dixon's gravel driveway, she spied his ancient pickup in its usual spot under an enormous elm. She parked beside it and jumped from the truck, tripping on the root that had caught her foot so many times. After steadying herself, she brushed by the rowan tree her aunt Eugenia had planted to ward off evil from entering their home and ran inside the handsome farmhouse built with her uncle's own hands decades ago. The Kit-Cat clock in the empty kitchen swung its black tail and rolled its eyes in a rhythmic cadence that contrasted with her own racing pulse. She hurried into his bedroom, where a double bed was neatly made with a colorful quilt. "Uncle Dixon!" she called. Nothing. She jerked open the bathroom door and then dashed into the second bedroom. No sign of him. The back porch, where she had listened to dozens of her uncle's stories about the old days, was her next stop. His green wicker rocker sat empty, as did the porch swing. She stopped in her tracks and willed her heart to slow down. *Think, Rennie!*

A breeze carrying the sweet smell of bee balm blew through her hair. Of course. The hives. She bolted off the porch and down the well-worn path, running past trees and then the climbing rose arch. Masses of flowers her aunt had brought as seeds and bulbs from her home in Appalachia as a bride bloomed on either side of the path, while a stone statue of a rabbit peeped out from under an astilbe leaf. She charged through a clearing with a small area of grass and a little ledge reaching out over a bend in Flat Rock Creek, not hearing the spring splashing against the rocks.

She turned a corner, and there it was, the bee yard, so ethereal and magical that as a child Rennie had pretended she was a princess in an enchanted land anytime she visited. Delicate anemones, more of Eugenia's handiwork, bordered the edge of the woods, along with bluebells, coneflowers, woodland phlox, and marsh marigolds. Bees bobbed around the puffball flowers of a witch alder bush. Some distance from the water, shaded by a massive linden tree's heart-shaped leaves, were three little hives, painted white, with shingled, pitched roofs, resting in a thick bed of moss. Each hive looked like several boxes set on top of one another, with bees moving in and out of the small hole at the base of each box. Between the water and the hives, a delicate iron settee was nestled under a maple. About three feet from the first hive, her uncle lay crumpled on the ground.

CHAPTER 2

"UNCLE DIXON!" RENNIE CRIED AS SHE RUSHED TO HIS still frame. Kneeling beside him, she gently touched his face. "What happened?"

The man slowly opened his eyes. "I knew they'd tell you," he whispered.

"Who?" Rennie asked.

"The bees. They know I love you."

He's hit his head and isn't making sense. "I love you too, Uncle Dixon. Are you able to move?"

Pressing his arm against the soft grass, he struggled to sit up. "Do you think you can get me over there?" He nodded to the small iron bench about four feet away, crafted with intertwined vines and flowers. A central medallion that resembled a rose bloomed across the back. "I just need a minute to collect myself."

Rennie slid her arms beneath his body and tried to raise him to a standing position. "I can't," she panted. "I'm too weak."

"Let's both rest here a minute, then I bet we can do it. A few deep breaths will help."

Soft wind brushed their cheeks as they sat in silence. A bed of yellow trout lilies basked in the sun, while in the distance Rennie spied pink coral bells bobbing in a wooded thicket. *So peaceful*, she thought, watching bees buzzing near hives that seemed to pulse with encouragement. *I could stay here forever.*

"I think I'm ready. Are you?" Rennie asked. After he nodded, she was able to lift her uncle to his feet. She had a good grip on his arm, which felt as skinny as a twig in her hand.

He had worked his fifty-acre farm for decades, doing backbreaking work every day. Although he seemed so frail, it was easy for Rennie to remember her uncle being strong and healthy enough to hoe the rows, strip the stalks, lift the bundles of leaves into the barn rafters, and manage the thousand other physical tasks a tobacco farmer had to perform. She could sense a vibrant man was still in there somewhere, just not where you could see with your eyes. If you looked with your heart, though, you could see the dashing man her aunt Eugenia had fallen in love with all those years ago in the foothills of Kentucky.

Gingerly, he lowered his body onto the seat and gently patted the rose medallion, as if greeting an old friend. "Eugenia loved this bench, and so do I." Gesturing for Rennie to sit beside him, he said, "I came down here to tell the bees something and lost my balance when I raised my hand to knock on their roof." He looked at his niece. "I should prolly tell you too." He paused to observe bees resting on the landing board at the base of one of the hives. "A while back, I had a stroke."

Rennie gasped. "What? I had no idea. When?"

His voice was soft. "You were in the hospital with Gabriel."

Rennie flinched at the memory of the day that she both birthed and lost her only child.

"I was sitting on the porch with my new neighbor, Ambrose Beckett, and he noticed I was slurring my words and looked kinda funny." He chuckled. "More funny than usual, I mean. He got me to the hospital in Nashville, and the doctors did a buncha tests, kept me there too long for my liking, then sent me home. Said the stroke was mild, that I should be mostly okay."

"I wish you had told me. I could have helped you."

"You had your own life to deal with." He patted her hand. "And Ambrose's been coming by to see about me. Yesterday afternoon I asked him to take care of the bees, and he said he would."

Hearing Ambrose Beckett's name for the second time that day gave her pause. Both May Dean and her uncle thought a lot of the newcomer, but she made a mental note to learn more about this man. Her uncle had managed on his own for years, but now the independence she had always admired had shifted to vulnerability, and she needed to make sure this Ambrose Beckett could be trusted to be a part of her uncle's life, caring for what he held most dear, his bees.

Her uncle added, "I can still look after myself. Just need to get a little stronger." He studied her face. "Something we can work on together as you go on without your Gabriel." After a moment, he said, "I hope you know how much he loved you and cherished being your son."

Her uncle had a well-deserved reputation for telling the truth no matter the topic. She had cried for so many things since her son's passing, and hearing from him that

Gabriel was aware she was his mother and felt their bond, however brief, was a balm to her soul.

Rennie lifted her face toward the sky, relishing the warmth caressing her skin before a cloud crossed the sun, instantly chilling her. "I'll never understand why I was given what I desired most in the world only to have him taken from me so quickly." She bowed her head and added, "Tiny says it was my fault, that I must have done something wrong to go into labor so early."

"There's a lot in this world we aren't meant to understand, at least not yet." His voice took on a flinty edge. "But let me tell you one thing I *do* know. You were not responsible for your baby coming too early. Tiny is wrong to blame you and cruel to tell you so." He patted her hand. "You know what I'm grateful for? All Gabriel ever knew was love. Think about how you both lived in those few hours. That perfection was something you needed to see. The bees and I agreed on that." He wrung his hands. "It's so important that I tell them my news."

She turned her focus on her uncle. A head injury was serious. Tiny had once recounted a story to her about how he had hit a fastball that had struck the pitcher in the head with enough force that the man was out for the rest of the season. "He didn't know up from down for a solid month," Tiny had gleefully reported.

She frowned. Did her uncle have a concussion? "Can you tell me again why you needed to come to the hives today?"

"I must tell them something. Our survival depends on it."

Growing up, she made a game of talking to the bees, and they had answered her in her head, like when she spoke for her dolls. "*A vivid imagination*" is what her mother said about her, using a tone that indicated this attribute was not a blessing. She had listened to her uncle speaking to his bees hundreds of times, but now he was saying the conversations were life and death. This had to be a concussion or maybe even another stroke. She needed to call Doc Grisham.

"Let's head up to the house. You'll be more comfortable there."

"No." He pointed with a shaky finger toward the beehives. "They've got to know. I'm already late in telling them." He looked at Rennie and then back toward the three hives bustling with activity. "When someone dies or there's a big change in the family, you need to tell your bees right away. If you don't keep them up to date with all the goings-on, they get sickly and die. Then your crops are poor, you got no honey, and everything goes sour. Listen to the buzz. That might as well be our heartbeat. The bees and us, we're connected." He shifted on the bench. "I've told them three times about you—the day you was born, when you married Luther and then left that same night for him to be a baseball player up north, and then losing your boy."

Her uncle had regaled her with tales her whole life—stories about the doings of the kestrels and vireos that flew over Cooke County, how trees communicated with each other through their roots and leaves, or why the star-nosed moles and swamp rabbits around the farm were such good friends. And of course there were lots of bee stories, like the way they would push any bee from the hive who had gotten drunk on fermented fruit, or how they could warn each other of danger from a predator. One of her favorites was a story about how a brave little bee had saved her whole hive from one of its worst enemies, yellow jackets. But this wasn't one of his lighthearted yarns that had anywhere from a dash to a full helping of truth. What he was telling her made no sense. "Wouldn't you feel better lying down in your bedroom? I could let Doc Grisham know about your fall."

"No, this needs to get done." His voice shook a bit as he spoke. "Eugenia taught me the rules. Tell them everything, whether joy or sorrow. Say the truth the best way you know how." Squaring his shoulders, he continued. "It about killed me to come down here and tell them about her passing, but I had to do it."

Uncle Dixon's eyes filled with tears. "The day Eugenia died, I brought down three little pieces of black fabric and tacked one to each roof to let them mourn like any other member of the family." His hand wobbled as he pointed. "Step over there and feel of that first roof on the left."

Rennie rose and stood before the hive, running her hand along the roof until she brushed a little nail surrounded by a tattered scrap of cloth, bleached out from fifteen years in the sun. Her heart twisted at the thought of her uncle coming down here with his black fabric, hammer, and nails.

"Would you knock three times on each roof for me?"

After doing as he asked, she nodded to her uncle. He cleared his throat and in a thready voice said, "Okay, bees. Here's some news. I've had a stroke, which means I'm not strong enough to care for you. A good man named Ambrose Beckett'll be taking over for me. He was raised up around bees and knows the old ways. He's got hives of his own, brought to Spark when he moved here from Kentucky." His voice shook. "You'll be well tended to."

Dixon rubbed his hands along his thighs. "It's best to tell

them before the sun has set and risen, but as long as they've been told as soon as I could get to them, it should be okay." He looked over the bee yard. "This way everything will go along as it should. You know a lot about bees, and I would have asked you to tend to them, but you're still healing from Gabriel. I hope you understand about me askin' Ambrose and not you to care for 'em."

Rennie nodded. "I can still check on them, right?"

"Absolutely." A look Rennie could not recognize crossed his face. "They know you love them, and they know you love me. I think they'd be hurt if you didn't look in on 'em." He nodded to the closest hive. "See how they're on the landing board?" Rennie glanced at the slanted piece of wood at the hive's entrance, what Rennie always thought of as a kind of welcome mat. "They're taking in the information so they can dance for any of 'em that was away from the hive for the announcement." He peered into her face. "Have I told you why bees dance?"

She'd heard several versions of how bees dance to communicate everything from a warning about a new wasp nest in the area to how a load of nectar had come in and everybody needed to get to work, but she never missed a chance to hear her uncle's latest spin on one of her favorite tales. "Tell me about it."

"Bees know what helps one bee also benefits the whole hive. When a bee finds good flowers, like a big patch of asters or yarrow, she dances out a map. The other bees watch and learn how far they need to fly, which direction to go, and about any dangers, like hornets, from the information that bee is dancing out to them."

"That's a lot to get out in a dance."

"And no bee ever wants to sting you. If she does, she'll die. A bee has to believe it's worth giving up her life to harm you."

Rennie's mind flashed back to the bee that was so insistent about getting her attention, the one that stung Tiny when he said she couldn't take the truck to check on her uncle. The bee had fallen to the ground, dead.

"Bees are some of God's best work, and a bee in June is best of all. A swarm of bees in June is worth a silver spoon, like the poem says." His eyes studied the hives nestled under the trees. "Watch a bee and she'll show you what's right and how we should go. Treasure every bee you see, Rennie."

"I will."

He looked up and pointed to the maple. "It's fixin' to rain. We'd best get on back."

Rennie scanned the clear sky. "How do you know that?"

Uncle Dixon nodded to the branches of a tree. "The maple's showing her petticoats. When the wind blows so you can see the underside of the leaves, you know rain's coming."

As she rose from the bench, Rennie asked, "Have you eaten lunch yet?" When Dixon shook his head, she added, "I'll call the doctor, then fix you something." She helped him to his feet, and together they slowly made their way from the ring of trees surrounding the hives, through the arch brimming with New Dawn roses, and up to the simple farmhouse that held some of Rennie's happiest memories.

A gray cat rubbed against Rennie's legs as she began dialing her uncle's phone. "Looks like Lewis Carroll is glad to see me." After talking briefly with the receptionist at Doc Grisham's office, Rennie hung up the receiver. "The doctor's coming by to check on you in about an hour. His nurse said you can carry on like normal if you feel up to it."

"I'm fine. You don't need to fuss over me, Rennie."

"I know, but I'll feel better knowing the doctor's seen you."

She glanced at Lewis Carroll's bowls and topped off his water dish. Opening the fridge, she looked over the possibilities. *Hmmm, not much here.* "How about a grilled cheese and tomato sandwich?" she asked. "And some iced tea?"

He nodded gratefully and sat at the small oak table. Rennie fixed his lunch and took a mental inventory of his fridge and pantry, planning a stop at the BuyMore grocery store before her next visit. A closer look around the always pin-straight home revealed a thin layer of dust. Maybe that next visit needed to come sooner than she thought.

After finishing his sandwich, which he proclaimed delicious, he pulled a cigarette out of his shirt pocket. "Will you help me with this?"

She took the cigarette from him with a disapproving frown. "You shouldn't smoke anymore. It could bring on another stroke, or you could fall asleep and start a fire." Even as she fussed, she struck a match.

"No man is perfect. There are so few things left in this world for me to enjoy, and my Lucky Strikes is one of them." A little of the old sparkle came back to his eyes. "I'll take it out on the porch."

"I'll clear up these dishes and then sit with you while we wait for the doctor."

A light breeze greeted her as she stepped onto the oak planks of the porch a few minutes later. Uncle Dixon was in his favorite chair, a willow rocker with a faded green cushion. Rennie settled beside him in her spot, a wooden swing hanging from two chains. She pushed her toe against the floor, causing the swing to move and the chains to squeak softly. Lewis Carroll appeared and hopped onto Uncle Dixon's lap. Looking over his backyard, her uncle stroked the cat's soft fur.

"I feel more peaceful now that I've told the bees about Ambrose."

"You sure love your bees."

"I do, and they love me back." He rocked gently in his chair. "They love you too, you know. The bees even saved your life when you was little."

Rennie sat up. "What?"

"That time you fell into the creek and sank clear to the bottom. The bees saved you from drowning."

No family story had ever been told about her nearly drowning, and although her mother never talked about anything that could be perceived as complaining, surely *someone* would have mentioned it to her if it had really happened. Hadn't it been an hour already? Rennie glanced anxiously at her watch and then at her uncle. He was still confused, a sure sign of a concussion. She rose from the swing. "I'll call the doctor ag—"

A black sedan was rumbling up the driveway. "Thank goodness. I'll go fill him in." She hurried off the porch and toward the car. After a moment, Rennie brought Dr. Grisham to her uncle's side. He shone a light in Uncle Dixon's eyes and examined his head, then asked several questions about any blacking out, confusion, or dizziness. The doctor turned to Rennie as he helped her uncle inside.

"I want to do a more thorough exam. I'll come get you when I'm through."

About twenty minutes later, the doctor stepped back onto the porch. "He's had a nasty fall, but no concussion and no sign of another stroke. He's in his bed and needs to rest, but he'll be fine."

Rennie frowned. "But what about it being life and death he tell the bees something and how they saved me from drowning?"

The doctor tucked his stethoscope back into his bag. "Older people sometimes get mixed up. It's nothing out of the ordinary." He picked up his bag. "I'll check back on him in a few days if that'll make you feel better." He paused. "And call my office if you see anything that worries you."

After the doctor left, Rennie tiptoed into the bedroom. Seeing her uncle still awake, she pulled a quilt over his thin body. Touching one of the double wedding rings fashioned from bright bits of cloth, she said, "This is my favorite of your quilts."

"Eugenia's mother made it for us. It was our favorite too. I love being able to use it every day." He patted the soft cloth. "When I'm gone, I want you to use it, not hide it away in some trunk because it has memories." A slight smile crossed his lips. "I hope you'll be as happy living here as I was. It does my heart good to know the farm will be in your hands."

"Please don't talk about dying. You just need to get stronger and you'll be fine." She stepped to the window. "I'll draw the curtains and you get some sleep, okay?"

The man nodded, eyes already heavy.

As she tiptoed from the room, she paused in the doorframe. "Uncle Dixon, you're my bee in June."

His face sagged a little, but maybe that was because of the stroke. "And you're mine, Rennie. Your visits are a tonic for an old man who thought his happiest days were long since gone."

Just as Rennie opened the screen door to head back to the farm, a loud clap of thunder startled her. Uncle Dixon had been right, and so had those petticoats.

CHAPTER 3

HOW COULD SHE THINK OUR CONVERSATIONS WERE *pretend, like playing with dolls?*

Completely understandable, considering the foolish way humans raise their young. Children learn the most important parts of life through fables and stories the adults tell them and then are told by those same adults that none of it is true.

What's the point in explaining to them how the world works if the adults will claim the fairy tales are only stories to amuse little ones?

It has something to do with what they call growing up, rejecting what they embraced in childhood and shouldering the attitudes and responsibilities of adulthood. Dixon and Eugenia understood, but her parents, her teachers, and her friends taught her not to believe what her heart knew was true. And she listened, which is why we lost her.

Humans are supposed to be smart.

Some are, and others are not, like that slubberdegullion she's married to.

She's always been one of the smart ones. She'll remember us.

And that is precisely what will get her through what is ahead.

CHAPTER 4

THE *WHOOSH* OF THE NEWLY INSTALLED AUTOMATIC door of the BuyMore grocery store startled Rennie as she approached. The sign in the window read *Get Your Lunar Party Supplies Here*, with a chalkboard countdown sign—*32 Days Until Landing*. Her shopping list was long, as she was now cooking not only for her and Tiny but also for her uncle. After only two weeks of preparing his meals, she could already see his thin body filling out. They had fallen into an easy pattern, with Rennie bringing her uncle food three days a week and May Dean supplying Sunday dinner. Tiny didn't object, but he made sure Rennie knew his one rule: "If our grocery bill goes up because of him, I'll put a stop to your coddlin'. Make sure he pays you back outta his drawer for anything you spend on him."

Despite May Dean, Ev, and Rennie all asking Uncle Dixon to put his money in a bank, he insisted on keeping all his cash in his home. "I lived through the Depression and watched the bank runs. People lost their life savings. I know Ev is a banker, and I love him, but that doesn't mean I trust his bank with my cash," he had explained.

After dropping off her uncle's meals and groceries, Rennie often found herself lingering at his farm. She and Uncle Dixon would eat lunch together, then visit the hives and talk away the afternoon. And if she dawdled long enough, Tiny might just make himself a sandwich and head across the county line to the Moonshine Lounge in Putney, his place to swap stories and down a few shots of whiskey.

She found herself alone in her kitchen more and more, humming as she rediscovered her love for baking. At first, making the pies and cakes had been only a practical way to get some meat on her uncle's bones, but the more she measured and mixed, the more a glimmer of long-absent happiness began to root in her soul, like one of Aunt Eugenia's tender seedlings, as wispy as a thread, finding purchase in bare soil.

The BuyMore frozen food aisle was her last stop before checking out. As she rounded the corner, she spotted Arden, the Blue Plate Diner's owner, by the dessert section.

"Hi, Arden. How are you?"

Arden jumped. "Oh, Rennie!" She hastily reached into her cart to drag a box of cereal over a frozen pie. "I didn't see you there."

Rennie opened the freezer door and took out a can of orange juice concentrate. "I'm sorry I scared you."

Arden said, "It's just that I had such a vivid dream about you yesterday afternoon. I never nap in the daytime, but one minute I was resting my eyes on the back porch, and the next I was dreaming I was asking you to come work for me while Betty's in Knoxville takin' care of her mama after her surgery." She scanned her cart and pulled a bag of turnip greens over a box of cloverleaf rolls. "And then here you are."

"I didn't know Betty's mama had surgery. I'll add her to my prayers."

"Could you put me on there too? Tryin' to get all the food ready and keep everything runnin', plus not smarting off to the rude customers, is about to kill me. People have mostly been nice about Betty bein' gone, but not all of 'em." She rolled her eyes. "I told one man complaining about his catfish being greasy that if he was going to be so ugly he could go on home and cook his own dinner, but that's not very good for business." She hesitated. "Maybe my dream was my brain trying to solve my problem for me. Would you be interested in helping me out at the diner until Betty comes back? You're the best cook in Spark and I'm really in a jam." She frowned. "But it may be too soon after, well, um, after your loss."

When Rennie was a child, a bowl of batter and a cookie sheet had offered her a way to tune out her parents' bickering. And sharing the cookies made from the recipe on the back of the chocolate chip bag gave a shy girl a way to make friends. As a teen, she realized she preferred the quiet of a kitchen to noisy football games and dances, with only an invitation from the dreamboat Tiny Hendricks to watch him play baseball drawing her away from her mama's antique oven and hand-me-down Pyrex and Corningware. Later she started creating her own dessert recipes, and her reputation as a baker began to spread across Cooke County. Brother Cleave himself would request her chess pies for church socials. When her mama got so sick, Rennie took over all the cooking duties and found solace in the predictability of recipes and measurements, knowing if she just followed instructions, doing exactly as she was told, she would be successful. And when Tiny managed to win *both* her offerings at the Civitan cakewalk the summer after their sophomore year of high school and then asked to escort her home afterward, she knew cooking could change her life.

A doe-eyed Rennie had gazed at Tiny on their stroll home under a full moon. "I didn't realize you had such a sweet tooth."

He had grinned at her. "I hate anything with sugar in it. Desserts have empty calories that add fat, not muscle. I like meat and potatoes, man food."

"But you must've bought so many tickets to win both my cakes. I thought you must crave sugar."

"You are so naive," he said, pulling her closer to him. "It's something else I crave." He tilted her head up with his finger so he could gaze into her eyes. "Even sweeter than sugar." He bent down to kiss her, and Rennie's knees had buckled. She stepped back, shocked. With a soft chuckle, he added, "Let's just say I wasn't leaving the Civitan hall without what I came for." And that had begun their romance. No one could believe Tiny had chosen mousy little Rennie to court, and the only one more stunned than the gaggle of jealous girls in their class was Rennie herself.

When she began to settle into married life with Tiny up north, he objected to the extra expense of dessert ingredients on their grocery bill. "Did you even check the price of a pound of butter before you bought it? And eggs aren't free like at home. We can't keep hens in the middle of the city," he had grumbled. So she had given up her beloved baking, focusing instead on menu items that supported the needs of a star athlete, like meat loaf and pot roast. She found some pleasure in preparing the savory food, but she missed the challenge of a delicate angel food cake or a decadent Mississippi mud pie.

Arden's hopeful face studied Rennie. "I'll pay you well, the same I do Betty. It's not a fortune, but it's above minimum wage. You could take Dixon anything he wants from the menu and pack up meals for you and Tiny too. I'm closed Sundays and Mondays, and Tuesdays are pretty slow, but I would love you to come Wednesday through Saturday." She bit her knuckle. "Rennie, I'd be so grateful. A couple of days ago a customer sent back his chicken-fried steak. Said it was as tough as shoe leather, and the truth is, it *was*. I let it go too long in the pan 'cause I was remaking the biscuits 'cause they were as hard as doorstops." Pushing the turnip greens and cereal aside in her cart, she pointed to the frozen chocolate silk pie and added, "I'm not fooling anybody with this store-bought stuff."

"What kind of hours would there be?"

"I'd need you from opening until the lunch rush is over, around two o'clock. I can manage the supper crowd on my own since I'd have some of your food to serve. If they could eat your turnip greens and pork chops, or a scoop of that chocolate cobbler you dreamed up, my customers would be happy and I would too."

"Can I let you know tomorrow?" She had learned the hard way never to make a decision on the spot. "I need to sleep on it."

"Of course. I'll be at the diner, praying over the fried chicken you'll say yes." She shook her head. "I'm so thankful I ran into you today. I never take naps and never forget anything on my grocery list, but I did both yesterday, and I sure am glad I did. Otherwise, I wouldn't have thought of hiring you and then run into you today." She looked heavenward. "It was meant to be, I guess." Arden pushed her cart to the checkout line, turning to give Rennie a hopeful smile before she stepped to the register.

On the drive home, Rennie mulled over Arden's offer. Ever since she'd been spending time at the hives with her uncle, she'd been feeling more like her old self. Her physical strength was returning, and she found herself facing the days with less dread and more of what felt like not joy but peacefulness. Her husband, though, was more volatile than ever, snapping at her about any little thing not to his liking.

She sighed. *Tiny*. He'd been so excited to move up north with his new bride, on his fresh-faced way to becoming a phenom like Joe DiMaggio or Babe Ruth. The first weekend in their new city, the pair had gone to a cheap matinee of *Breakfast at Tiffany's*. When Audrey Hepburn had sung "Moon River," Tiny had kissed Rennie so tenderly and whispered, "This'll be our song." She had left the theater starry-eyed and more in love than ever, with Tiny reporting for training the next week and Rennie perusing the local college's auditing options.

After the first day of practice, Tiny had come home elated. "I've made it, baby. As soon as I get us a big nest egg laid by, we'll go to that Tiffany's store and you can pick out whatever you want, something way better than that Cracker Jack ring in the movie." He had squeezed Rennie's arm. "I'm in the big time, just like Joe was. Baseball's a lot safer than football, so my career will last way longer than my brother's. That'll teach Pa to favor him over me. Joe barely lasted three years before that tackle took him out." He had puffed up his chest. "*I'll* be the family breadwinner now, takin' care of you, my parents, and maybe even throw a little money Joe's way now that he's had to retire from football."

About a month after they arrived in their new town, his new teammates had invited Tiny for a night out. When he'd finally returned home around midnight, he had snatched Rennie from their bed and spun her around like a Tilt-A-Whirl, knocking her copy of *To Kill a Mockingbird* off their cardboard box nightstand. "I'm in," he had shouted. "Some of the guys have a bar they're opening downtown called All Stars, and they're letting me go in with them. I'm investing my signing bonus, so I'll get rich twice—once playing ball and then again when my fans watch the game at my bar, eating and drinking away their paychecks."

The ink was barely dry on their apartment's one-year lease renewal when Tiny came boiling through the front door, slamming it so hard the windows rattled. His face was mottled and his voice shook.

"Got released." A lamp Rennie was so proud of buying for a quarter at a thrift shop crashed to the floor with the impact of the baseball cap Tiny threw across the room. "They cut me because of one little slump." He pounded his fist on their kitchen counter. "What the hell am I gonna do now?"

Tiny tried in vain to get signed with another club. A fellow ballplayer had sent him to talk with his buddy who managed a team, and Tiny was sure this was his big break. "Brett says this guy needs a good fielder and doesn't care my hitting's been a little off," he'd said. "They've got a trainer who can get me back on top in no time." When he didn't come back to their efficiency apartment until after two in the morning, Rennie had moved from *he's out celebrating* to *something's wrong*. She hadn't even finished asking what had happened before Tiny launched into the story. His so-called pals had set him up, Tiny claimed, just so they could all have a laugh at his expense.

Rennie winced as she recalled his meaty hand on her delicate wrist, stopping her from leaving the apartment to let him cool off. She had warily dozed on the sofa that night, not daring to be within striking distance of his still-balled fist. Without consulting her, he had called his father the next day and asked if he and Rennie could live in his grandparents' old house and run their tobacco farm. She'd only heard one side of the conversation as she listened in the bedroom, but it had been enough.

"I *tried*, Pa. They don't want me anymore."

After a moment, she heard, "Could you not bring up Joe for once in my life? You've compared me to him since the day I was born, and I haven't measured up yet." Another pause. "Charging rent to your own son seems pretty low. Meemaw wouldn't've done that."

The sharp tone of her father-in-law's deep voice crept under the closed door as their argument escalated. She heard bits and pieces, like "counting on you," "embarrassing," and worst of all, "such a disappointment."

Tiny's father's identity had always been so tied to both his sons' success. When Big Joe started playing pro football, Wayne was as happy as a pig in mud, and when Joe's NFL checks started clearing, a fancy truck and tractor had both landed in Wayne's driveway faster than you could say, "Charge it to my son." He bragged all around Spark that he had one boy in the big time and was fixing to have another.

Wayne had doled out cigars like a proud new father when word got out that a scout was coming to Spark all the way from New York to see this new phenom who could hit a ball like Hank Aaron. He had clapped friends on the back and boasted that he'd paid for everything for the first eighteen years of his son's life, and it was now Tiny's turn to earn Joe's kind of money. "We got smarter after Big Joe's injury and switched to baseball."

Tiny's voice was booming. "The end of *your* dreams? What about mine?"

A longer pause.

"That seems like a lot for a run-down farmhouse, but I don't really have a choice, do I? Fine. We'll be home next week."

Rennie had been relieved, as she would be going back home to May Dean and Uncle Dixon, but she also had a sense of foreboding thinking about Tiny slinking back into town with his tail between his legs.

The whole bus ride back to Tennessee, Tiny had talked about how this detour in his career was temporary, saying that the scouts would be swarming to Spark once they heard he was available and that he'd be back to playing ball in no time.

Those scouts never showed up, though, and Tiny had to get serious about learning to grow tobacco. The residents of Spark were kind enough about welcoming back the young couple, although Rennie was keenly aware of how often a conversation would suddenly stop when she walked into the Wishee-Washee with a load of laundry or joined a long checkout line at the BuyMore. Only Wasp Fentress had dared to ask Tiny about his change of career, making a joke about being out in a field instead of an outfield, and was rewarded with a punch that broke his nose in two places.

Tiny wasn't cut out for farming, which was obvious to anyone who watched him wrestle with his grandparents' outdated equipment or hack at the heavy clay soil. He spent his days struggling with the land that had yet to yield a good crop, and his nights listening to baseball games, huddled next to his grandparents' old transistor radio.

As she dug the last quarter from her change purse to pay for her groceries, she thought about how the money she'd make at the Blue Plate could help stave off an eviction. And then there was the food. If she could bring home meals, she wouldn't have to buy so much, which would let them put more toward the rent. She about had her mind made up to take the job but was adhering to her rule of sleeping on any big decision. If she felt the same way in the morning, she'd tell Tiny over breakfast and then call Arden.

Dusk was falling as Tiny shambled through the kitchen door. Rennie was at the stove, preparing country-fried steak and mashed potatoes. "Grady Neal says he's lookin' to hire some extra help at the Emporium. I told him you'd take the job." He stretched his muscled arms over his head. "It's minimum wage, but that extra income'll help out."

"I don't have any background in selling housewares and knickknacks. What if a customer asks me a question I can't answer?"

"How hard can it be to sell birdseed and pot holders?"

Rennie nervously stirred the potatoes. "You know I don't like to be around a lot of people, especially ones I don't know well."

"I don't see you comin' up with anything better."

She broke her own rule. "I got offered a job this morning. I'm gonna take it."

Tiny's eyebrows shot up. "Where at?"

"The Blue Plate. Arden's cook is gone for a few weeks, and Arden asked me to fill in until she gets back." She wiped her hands on her apron. "I understand cooking. I'll be good at it."

"What's your pay?"

"Arden said she'd pay me—" A spark caught her eye, and she glanced toward its source, the window. She was expecting a lightning bug, but it was a bee buzzing against the screen. Bees didn't fly at night. What was going on? The sound, reminiscent of a rattlesnake shaking its tail in warning, chilled her heart. Was her uncle in trouble again? The bee flew off in a flash of light.

Tiny interrupted her thoughts. "What were you saying about your pay?"

She glanced at the screen, but the bee had vanished. She chose her words carefully, forcing out the first lie she'd ever told her husband. "Minimum wage, the same as at the Emporium." She risked a small smile. "But I'll have a great benefit working at the diner. Arden will let me bring home food for you and me plus Uncle Dixon. Our grocery bills will go way down."

Tiny scooped her into his arms and spun her around the room. "That's my girl. I'm proud of you, Rennie." He kissed her deeply and then set her back in front of the stove. "I'll tell Everett down at the bank you're allowed to deposit your paycheck into my account, but bring it home first so I can look it over."

"The bank's right on Market Street. Wouldn't it be easier for me just to walk my check over there when I get it?"

He paused, and the lines on his forehead deepened. "I want to make sure nobody's cheating you. You're very trusting, which I love about you, but not everybody has your best interest at heart like me." He rubbed his hands together. "This will help our money problems a lot."

Tiny's rare good mood gave her the courage to ask a question she'd been wanting to ask for months. "What about money from the All Stars bar? Shouldn't you be getting some returns on your investment by now?"

Tiny's smile vanished and his deep voice was suddenly too big for the small room. "We've been over this. That's not for day-to-day expenses. It's for the future, our nest egg." Without waiting for an answer, he grabbed his bottle of Early Times from the counter and strode onto the porch.

Rennie went to bed and fell asleep immediately but woke up about an hour later. She paced to a window of the little farmhouse she had called home the last four years and peered through the glass. The yellow bulb of the moth light glowed enough for her to make out the form of her husband hunched over the radio listening to a fast-talking announcer excitedly describing a baseball game. The tip of Tiny's cigarette glowed in the night, so different from the bee's vibrant light that had stopped her from telling Tiny about Arden's offer to pay her well.

CHAPTER 5

THE FORGOTTEN ITEMS ON HER LIST SEEM REASONABLE, but using a dream was a bit cliché, perhaps?

It was the only resource that would be effective when involving someone so sublunary. Human logic is less of an impediment during sleep.

Did the council or the queen approve of such an unconventional liberty?

Yes, as our girl was only a few hours away from being hired at the dime store.

If that had happened, though, she would have accomplished what she set out to do, find a job and make money.

Her goal was simple. Our objective is more complex, and part of it requires her to be in the presence of the woman who runs the diner.

Is this not interference rather than guidance?

The rules change when an unnatural death is imminent.

CHAPTER 6

THE BLUE PLATE HAD BEEN A FIXTURE IN SPARK FROM the moment Arden had cut that blue plaid ribbon across the front door twenty years ago. Arden Gatewood had shown up in town one day, and the next thing anyone knew, the *For Rent* sign was gone from the old Dine-In Diner window and the tantalizing scent of good country cooking began wafting down Market Street. Ever since opening day, Arden had a steady stream of hungry customers, and things hadn't really slowed down since. People had tried to puzzle out who Arden was—who her people were—but no one had succeeded. She wore a wedding ring, but she never mentioned a Mr. Gatewood, either alive or dead, and any questions about him went unanswered. "Why do you want to know?" she'd ask, looking down her nose through cat-eye glasses at any questioner. And no one had ever come up with a good enough answer to elicit a response, so Arden's past remained as unknown as the secret ingredient in her irresistible brisket.

From the day Arden had driven into town from Mississippi, she had been quickly accepted into the Spark pack. She served familiar fare, like fried chicken and banana pudding.

She chatted about things they understood, like the merits of Bradley tomatoes versus Cherokee Purples. Even if her background was mysterious, they could all get behind someone whose motto was "Food is love."

A few detractors did voice their disapproval, though, as Arden always steered clear of the gossip that swirled through town like eddies in Flat Rock Creek. An illicit affair, a husband who drank too much, or even the sensation of the whole Posey Jarvis mess was endlessly interesting to most of the ladies and a few of the men in Spark, but Arden never participated. One brave soul had tried to draw Arden into a lively conversation at the Curly Q beauty shop about a dress someone had worn to a recent wedding. With curlers in her hair, the woman had leaned over to Arden, who was reading a *Life* magazine in the chair next to hers. "You know what they say about wearing red to a wedding—it means you did the deed with the groom." Raising one eyebrow, she added, "She'd need a closet full of red dresses from what I hear."

When asked to comment on the offender, Arden had responded, "All I know is she always speaks so kindly of you," instantly shutting down the discussion.

The diner's name was common enough—every meat and three had a blue plate special on the menu—but Rennie had always suspected there was a hidden story behind the Blue Plate's name, just as she sensed there was more to Arden than the bare-bones account she had told about coming to Spark because she needed a change of scenery from the bayous and flatwoods of her native state.

As she waited for Arden to finish up a phone call, Rennie studied the cerulean plate with a wide white rim decorated with gold-painted braid that hung next to the cash register. Clearly a piece of fine china, it was affixed to the wall with a brass hanger, whose prongs always reminded Rennie of tiny hands clinging to a life ring.

Rennie had a seat at one of the tables and looked around the diner, curious about one of Market Street's mainstays. She and Tiny had never eaten there, even though most of Spark stopped by for steak tips and gravy or pulled pork at least once a week. Tiny told anyone who assumed he was familiar with the diner's offerings that he ate at home because his wife's cooking was so much better, but Rennie knew Tiny's concern was his wallet, not his taste buds.

The floor was worn from decades of steady foot traffic, highlighting pathways to the booths that sat around the perimeter of the simple wooden building. Formica-topped tables were arranged in orderly rows on either side of the center aisle, each with matching chrome chairs upholstered in the diner's signature blue vinyl. Cheerful checked curtains hung from the sparkling clean windows, while the swinging doors leading to the kitchen, usually flapping like flags in a windstorm, stood motionless. The diner wouldn't open for another thirty minutes, and she and Arden were alone.

"Sorry to make you wait, hon." Arden approached Rennie with two glasses. As she placed the water in front of Rennie, she added, "I hope you have good news for me."

"I've decided to accept the job, so I hope that counts as good news." Rennie took a grateful sip of water to soothe her parched throat. Why was she nervous when Arden had already offered her the position? "You said I'd be able to take food for Tiny and my uncle, right? If I'm here cooking,

I wouldn't have time to get their meals fixed." She glanced up at Arden, waiting for a nod. "Uncle Dixon barely eats enough to keep a bird alive, but Tiny wolfs down food like he hasn't eaten in a week. Are you sure it's okay to pack up two dinners every afternoon?"

Arden frowned. "Shouldn't that be three dinners? You can take whatever and how much you want." Arden took a long sip from her glass. "Let's talk about your pay. You'll get a check every Friday showing you've earned minimum wage, which is $1.30 an hour. You will also get a cash payment of five dollars over that in a separate envelope for the difference between your real earnings and what the government thinks you make. It will be your business who you tell and what you do with that cash. The only thing I ask is that you don't spread it around town how I do my payroll. There's a coupla husbands and a banker I know who might object to my system." Arden set down her glass. "Being a woman, and especially being a wife, is hard work. The men have it set up so that everything falls in their favor. That's not right, and I know firsthand how uneven it all is. This is just my way of offering, well, options. Is that okay with you?"

Rennie's thoughts turned to the bee that stopped her before she revealed anything to Tiny about being paid well. "I've only worked on my husband's farm, so I've never earned money before. Tiny will be expecting a check for the full amount."

Arden snorted. "I bet he will." Her expression darkened. "There's nothing worse than advice you didn't ask for, but I'm gonna say this anyway. Once a man has an expectation about *anything* from his wife, things go badly when she doesn't meet that expectation. If Tiny is under the impression that you make, oh, let's say 10 percent less than you actually do, then he'll be upset with *me* for paying you less than he thinks I should. If he ever gets the idea that you're holding money back, then *you're* the one he'll be mad at." She looked over her glasses. "And I've seen Tiny mad." She leaned in toward Rennie. "A safety net is always a good idea, especially for a married woman. I'd think long and hard before I gave up the chance at a little umbrella for a rainy day." She picked up her glass and touched the beads of condensation forming from the already warm morning. "Everybody gets rained on sometime, Rennie."

"I think I understand." Rennie rubbed her wrist, remembering the day Tiny grabbed it hard enough to leave a bruise. "I accept the job. Thank you."

"I'm not doin' you a favor, so there's no need to be thanking me. We'll be helpin' each other." Arden glanced at the clock on the wall. "Customers'll be wantin' their breakfast pretty soon." She stood. "When can you start?"

Rennie grinned. "How about now?"

After a quick tour of the kitchen, Rennie began preparing the breakfast menu. She had been worried about being able to manage in another woman's domain, but the layout made sense to her. The pots and pans rested on shelves to the right of the stove, exactly where Rennie would have put them. The spice bottles were lined up alphabetically, and even the refrigerator was arranged in a way that allowed Rennie to find what she was looking for without searching. The only mishap was not realizing the jar labeled *Biscuit Flour* was self-rising instead of all-purpose, but other than the one casualty of that first pan of biscuits, the morning went well.

As Rennie started her third skillet of fried chicken, she heard a familiar voice on the other side of the swinging doors. "I know she's busy, Arden, but I just want to congratulate her." The door opened, and Darlene, her neighbor who had a habit of both learning and then broadcasting everybody's business, stepped into the kitchen, a wide grin on her face. "Rennie Hendricks! Look at Arden trying to hide you back here. The minute I took a bite of chicken, I said to Dewey, 'This isn't Arden's chicken, and Betty's not back either. This chicken reminds me of what Rennie fixes for the Founders Day picnic. I'll bet you a dollar Arden's hired Rennie.' Dewey owes me a dollar, and I just wanted to hug your neck and tell you how glad I am to see you out after your tragedy, and how happy all of Spark will be once they find out they can get some of your good cookin' any day they come to the Blue Plate." After she gave Rennie an embrace, she added, "Aren't we lucky!" She held Rennie at arm's length and said, "We are all just so sorry for your terrible loss, but you're young and can have other children. I guess God needed another angel in heaven." Darlene frowned as she dusted a bit of flour from her dress. "God works in mysterious ways. Anyway, I'll let you get back to work. Love you bunches."

Rennie sagged against the kitchen counter, then stumbled for a stool. The loss of her Gabriel was never out of her thoughts, but Darlene's comments brought everything back to her. People had good intentions, but to attribute Gabriel's death to God's failure to have an adequate number of angels on hand was cruel. What about Rennie's need to have her son safe in her arms instead of in a cold grave?

Arden put a hand on Rennie's shoulder. "Hon, you okay?"

Rennie wiped her eyes with the corner of her apron. "I'm, I'm a little tired, that's all."

"I can finish the lunch rush if this is too much for you."

Rennie stood. "No, I'm okay."

At the end of her busy shift, Rennie packed up three dinners. She lingered by a dirty pan, but Arden shooed her out of the kitchen. "It's two o'clock. I can manage the dishes on my own, and I don't like my ladies working past when I said they'd be through. Go see your uncle and get some rest, because we'll do it all again tomorrow."

CHAPTER 7

AFTER SLIDING THREE BLUE PLATE DINNERS INTO THE fridge, Rennie peered out the kitchen window to confirm Tiny was in the fields. He was standing by his grandparents' tractor with a wrench in his hands. He'd likely be out there the rest of the day, cursing and banging around under the hood. *Good.* She didn't need another argument about the price of butter, but she was on a mission, and she couldn't accomplish her goal with margarine.

She flipped on the oven and assembled ingredients for the dessert she was using as an excuse to check out Ambrose Beckett. Choosing which pie to bring had been a hard decision. Classic chess or maybe decadent chocolate? Which flavor would get her all the answers she needed? Her uncle had mentioned Ambrose a few times and spoke of him in a way that made it seem they had been friends for years, not weeks. Was this man as upstanding as he sounded, or did he have ulterior motives? Her uncle owned one of the largest farms in the county, situated on a scenic bluff overlooking a bend in Flat Rock Creek, and more than one farmer had hinted they'd give a lot to own it.

She settled on cherry, hoping to invoke the "cannot tell a lie" spirit of George Washington. Crimping the crust, she formed her first question. Where, exactly, was he from? As she transferred the fragrant filling into the shell, the second question came to mind. Why did he choose to move to Spark? As she wove an intricate lattice to grace the top, she added one more question to the list: What did he hope to gain by befriending her uncle? She opened the window wider to allow the telltale smell to drift from the kitchen, and she rehearsed her questions again as she slid the pie into the oven.

⌒

She set her uncle's Blue Plate dinner on the floorboard next to a bag of coffee she'd bought for him at the BuyMore, while a wicker basket lined with a vibrant red-and-white cloth sat on the passenger seat. Inside was her excuse to meet this newcomer. As she made the turn off Creekside Road and bumped down the dirt driveway, nerves tapped her spine. She was too naive and always had been. Believing the best of everyone had been an admirable trait, she had thought, until she had gotten swept up in Tiny's golden vision of life in the big leagues. After the last speech had been made in the gym at their high school graduation, Tiny had grabbed the microphone from the principal. With a flourish, he had pulled a letter from his pocket and read aloud the notice that he had been signed to the major league farm team and was expected to report to training camp immediately. As their classmates clapped and whistled, Tiny had said, "Only one thing could make this day any better." He had pulled Rennie from the alphabetical lineup and gotten on one knee. "Rennie King, marry me tomorrow. Then we'll leave for Boston together as man and wife." Shocked and thrilled, she had nodded. The whole auditorium had erupted in cheers, momentarily drowning out the thunderstorm raging outside.

Somewhere between their apartment's anemic radiator and the constant honking from the busy street below, Rennie had realized life in the big city was not the Shangri-La her husband had promised. She had always been shy and awkward, and trying to make friends with the other players' wives took a social ease that Rennie did not possess. She had learned her lesson, and not one taught at the university Tiny had said she could attend before he found out how expensive even auditing a class was. People take care of themselves and their kind, and it was wise to peek under any initially friendly facade for the underlying motive.

Pulling up to the Sawyers' old white clapboard house, she grabbed the basket and slid from the worn bench seat. The wringer washing machine that had nested for decades in an overgrown patch of kudzu was gone, and the porch had been swept clean of the leaves that had gathered in its corners. A Mason jar filled with water sat on the porch railing, bringing to mind her aunt's tradition of collecting moon water. Every full moon, her aunt would set a jar of water outside and use the contents the next morning to wipe the doorways to ensure only good energy could enter the house.

An orange pearl crescent butterfly flitted to a large pot of geraniums at the base of the stairs leading to the door, and a bright American flag snapped smartly in the afternoon breeze. Twisting up a wooden lattice was a vigorous climbing rose bursting with pale pink roses. She had just leaned in to smell their rich fragrance when the screen door swung open. A man appearing to be in his late twenties, tall with broad shoulders, stepped out. He smiled. "Hey there."

Rennie jumped like she'd been caught doing something wrong. "My aunt grew roses just like these called New Dawn. I just wanted to smell them."

The man smiled. "Help yourself. New Dawn roses are the best, so much better than the soulless hybrids they raise for flower shops. Bees love 'em. They're as tough as nails and as beautiful as a summer sunrise, all while smelling as sweet as the kiss of an angel." He touched a blossom. "As soon as I saw these New Dawns, I knew this would be my home."

"The scent brings back such lovely memories."

He nodded. "Roses are good at that. They remind me that the world is still beautiful, even when you don't think so. Like they say, we can complain that rosebushes have thorns, or we can rejoice that thornbushes have roses."

Pushing aside the anxiety that made her awkwardness shine like a searchlight piercing a foggy night, she stepped forward. She had a job to do, and no amount of discomfort could keep her from it. "I'm Rennie King Hendricks. Welcome to Spark." Holding out her basket, she added, "I made you a cherry pie."

He descended the porch steps and, reaching for the basket, said, "Thank you, Rennie King Hendricks. I'm Ambrose Beckett. So am I lucky enough to have you as a neighbor?" His eyes were as green as the petticoat side of a maple leaf.

In the rehearsals of this moment in her head, she had been direct and no-nonsense as she drilled down to this stranger's true intentions, not blushing like a schoolgirl. "Yes, that's right. I live, that is, my husband and I live on Beasley Court, just past the Baptist church on Creekside Road."

He gestured toward his house. "Come on in." The sun glinted off his curls, as black as Poe's wings.

Rennie followed, trying not to admire his broad shoulders. "Am I keeping you from anything?"

His smile was easy and open. "Not at all. I was just filling the birdfeeders on my back deck."

As she climbed the steps, she gestured to the Mason jar. "Taking advantage of last night's full moon? My aunt used to collect moon water. I didn't realize other people did it too."

Ambrose grabbed the jar and chugged the water in one gulp. "Oh, I was just using the jar as a glass." He gestured to the yard. "I've been pulling weeds and got thirsty."

"My uncle Dixon says you're from Kentucky." Good, back on track with the first question from her list.

"Yep, from a little town back in the Appalachian foothills called Travers."

He set the basket on the kitchen counter. "How 'bout we get to know each other over a slice of this gorgeous pie?" After Rennie nodded, he opened a drawer and extracted a knife. "Care for some coffee to go with it?"

"No, thanks. Just one of my many oddball qualities is that I'm a tea drinker." Heat warmed her cheeks. Would she ever learn to handle a difficult social situation without embarrassing herself?

Ambrose grinned. "Me too." He filled a kettle on the stove with water. "I only offered coffee because that's what most people drink. Picked it up from my grandparents, who were Scottish." He lifted a canister from the counter. "Darjeeling okay?" Rennie nodded again. He scooped loose tea leaves into the teapot. "Do you have children?"

The first time in her life the answer could be both yes and no. "No."

"And do you work? What occupies your time?"

How to answer that? She, what? Mourned the loss of her son? Tried to take care of Tiny, who seemed to think his Early Times whiskey was the answer to any problem? Fed her crow pumpkin seeds and peanuts in exchange not for the shiny bits of metal he brought her as payment, but as a way to see up close the freedom of a magnificent, unfettered soul, so different from her own, which was tethered to a small grave in Cedar Hill cemetery? "I've just started filling in for the cook at the Blue Plate Diner while she's out."

This was *her* fact-finding mission, not his. Time for question two. "What brings you to Spark?" She waved her hand. "It's not exactly well-known."

Ambrose busied himself with the teapot as he spoke, avoiding her gaze. "My granny told me stories about her best friend who moved to Spark. They wrote letters back and forth until her friend died. So I'd always heard about Spark, and when I decided to leave Kentucky and buy my own tobacco farm, I came for a visit." He handed Rennie a mug, grabbed a bottle of milk from the fridge, and gestured to the sugar bowl. "I liked what I saw—the town square, the shops, and lots of good farmland. People seemed friendly here, and when I found this place, I bought it." He nodded to the front yard. "And those New Dawn roses seemed like a sign I was in the right place."

"Must have been hard to leave all your family behind."

Ambrose shrugged. "It was just my daddy and me, and he died right after I graduated from college. I had a good offer on our farm, so I took it."

"The Sawyer place has been abandoned for at least a decade. It's going to need a lot of work."

"That means I can put my own mark on it." He pointed to a pile of lumber visible from the large kitchen window. "My first project is adding on to the deck. I'm an amateur astronomer, and I'd like a clearer view of the heavens, away from the trees." Placing a wedge of pie in front of Rennie, he asked, "What about you? Have you always lived here?"

"I was born in Spark and grew up about a mile from here, in a house next door to the Baptist church off Creekside. I lived up north for a year because of my husband's job, but we came back about four years ago." It was honest enough to be true but vague enough to avoid questions.

Ambrose took a bite of pie, and his eyebrows shot up. "Wow! Is everything you make this good?"

Oh, Lord. More blushing. "I'm happiest in a kitchen, measuring and stirring. I can escape without having to go anywhere." She cringed, fearing he would ask what she was escaping *from*. Mercifully, he did not.

"Is Rennie a family name?"

"It's from my parents, Robert and Irene. They started off

calling me Roberta, but my cousin May Dean shortened it to Rennie, and it stuck."

"I'm guessing your uncle is my neighbor, Dixon King."

"That's right." Ambrose had opened the door, and she could just sail on through it with question three. "It sounds like you all have been spending quite a bit of time together." She looked at Ambrose expectantly.

"He came by to introduce himself, and it didn't take us too long to figure out my granny's friend from Travers was his wife, Eugenia."

"So you never had a chance to meet my aunt?"

He studied the scar on his hand when he answered. "I never had the pleasure." He looked back up and added, "Before I was born, your aunt saved my granny's life when she was so sick with whooping cough. Dixon hadn't heard that story, and his face beamed when I told him how her poultice was what saved my granny, that the doctor had already said she wouldn't survive. And we talked about bees, of course. Come out to the deck and I'll show you my hives."

Rennie followed Ambrose, stepping over a few crumbled bricks from the fireplace onto a modest wooden platform that offered an expansive view of Flat Rock Creek in the distance. "You'll have plenty of time to get your fireplace repaired before cold weather hits."

His expression darkened. "No fires. I'm having it torn down."

"You'll freeze."

"I'm putting in central heat. I don't like fires."

"You're a tobacco farmer, right?" When he nodded, she added, "What about the fires to cure the leaves?"

"I'll grow burley tobacco. It's air-dried." Gently taking her arm, he led her to the edge of the deck. "The view's the reason I bought this farm. I'm going to expand the deck out another twenty feet."

Rennie pointed to the telescope. "This is for that hobby you mentioned?"

He nodded. "I enjoy skywatching. If you want to get your troubles into perspective, spend five minutes looking into the galaxy and then see how you feel." Ambrose gestured to his left. In a clearing of oaks, Rennie could make out two hives similar to the ones her uncle had. "Dixon feels the same way about bees as I do, and that's getting increasingly rare as the world gets so commercialized. He likes the old ways, same as me. It was an honor for him to ask me to care for his bees. A big responsibility, but an honor."

"Thank you for taking him to the hospital when he had his stroke. I'm grateful you were with him." She set her mug down on the deck's railing. "I really should be going. I need to drop by my uncle's with his dinner."

Ambrose smiled at her. "I hope we can visit again soon." He grinned and then asked, "So what do you think?"

Rennie started. "About what?"

"About whether or not my motives are pure in befriending Dixon." His voice softened. "That's why you came, right? To check me out. Your uncle is feeble and owns the most desirable farmland in Cooke County. A stranger shows up and they're instantly good friends. Seems suspicious to me too."

She stuttered, "I-I just wanted to . . ."

Ambrose laughed as they moved through the house.

"You just wanted to ask some questions to make sure I was all right." He raised his hands. "I don't blame you a bit. I'd have done the same thing in your shoes." He held the screen door open for her and then walked beside her to the truck. "I'm glad. That means you love Dixon and watch out for him." He reached for the handle of the dented truck door. "Assuming I passed inspection, or if I didn't and you have more questions before you make up your mind"—he flashed a dimple deep enough to reach all the way to Travers, Kentucky—"come by anytime, Rennie King Hendricks."

CHAPTER 8

HE SHOULD NOT HAVE BEGUN THEIR FRIENDSHIP WITH a lie.

Do you blame him, though, when the truth is so unbelievable?

We need to focus on the overarching objective. They have met, and for that we are grateful.

Why did he not say that Eugenia saved his own life as well? That would have endeared him to her.

He is not ready yet. The truth will unspool a bit at a time until it is all told. Give him time.

Time is something we do not have much of.

CHAPTER 9

ON THE WAY TO HER UNCLE'S HOUSE, RENNIE MULLED over Arden's advice. *"I'd think long and hard before I gave up the chance at a little umbrella for a rainy day."* Money was tight, and every bit would help with their expenses, but having a little cash tucked away somewhere seemed smart. Arden's words echoed in her mind. *"Everybody gets rained on sometime, Rennie."*

Tiny had never been good with money, and his investment in the All Stars bar had yet to produce a dime in the almost five years since he had handed over his sizable signing bonus. Every time she mentioned it, Tiny about bit her head off, claiming she didn't understand business or long-term investments. Which, she acknowledged, she didn't. But it seemed wrong to deceive her husband, and getting an extra five dollars he didn't know about made her uneasy.

If she did decide to keep the cash a secret, where could she hide money so that Tiny wouldn't find it? Her mind flicked over their home, too small for any secrets to be kept for long, before settling on the plastic bag the hospital had given her containing her mother's effects—clothes, eyeglasses, and a small black purse. She had pushed the bag to the back of their coat closet the day her mother died and hadn't touched it since. *Maybe.*

How did Arden know how bleak her marriage was or how often Tiny used his size to make his point? She cocked her head. And how did the bee know to stop her from revealing that Arden would pay her above minimum wage? As she drove, she thought back to the glowing bee that had caused her to check on her uncle. Arden's help was understandable, but did she also have bees watching over her?

She pulled up to her uncle's home and grabbed his food and the bag of coffee. Opening the unlocked door, she softly called, "Uncle Dixon? I've brought your Folgers from the BuyMore."

"In here," he answered. "Be sure to pay yourself back outta the drawer."

Sliding open the wooden drawer, she took out some money. "I'll leave your receipt on the counter." After popping the Blue Plate food into the refrigerator, she walked into his bedroom, where her uncle was dusting his walnut dresser.

"Guess what, Uncle Dixon? I got a job filling in for the cook at the Blue Plate while she's tending to her mama. I can bring you food on the days I work. There's some in your fridge for tonight."

"You'll need to get more money to pay for the diner food."

"It's a benefit of my job." She smiled. "No charge." She held out her hand for the rag. "Let me do that for you."

Dixon shook his head. "Just finishing up." He patted his

belly. "That's very kind of Arden to let you bring food home. Good for you for getting a job." He frowned and added, "I hope it was your idea and not your husband's."

How was it that everyone could guess her situation? Maybe she wasn't as good at hiding things as she thought. "Are you sure I can't do that dusting for you?"

"I've been getting my strength back, and being able to take care of my things brings me joy." He stroked the dresser with his hand. "Especially something this special." In a soft voice, he said, "This was Eugenia's dresser, brought with us from Kentucky. Would you like to hear its story?"

"I'd like nothing better. Want to go out to the porch?"

He chuckled. "You know me pretty good, Rennie girl."

Once settled into his chair, he began to talk, a wistful look on his face. "When Eugenia was a child, a handsome walnut tree grew right outside her bedroom window. She loved that tree like an old friend. She climbed the branches and played with her dolls under its shade. Her daddy put up a tractor tire on a rope, and she used to while away the afternoons swinging and listening to the wind blow through the leaves." He looked at Rennie. "She loved to be outside, just like you. When Eugenia was about fifteen, there came up a terrible storm one summer night. The wind howled and thunder crashed as loud as God's own voice. A lightning bolt slashed right through that walnut tree, knocking it clear to the ground."

"She must've been heartbroken."

"She was. Her pap knew how sad she was, so he took the walnut wood and made her this dresser. He told her, 'Now you can have your friend forever, and it can watch over you still.'" Uncle Dixon wiped his eyes. "When we married, Eugenia and I brought the dresser with us to Spark. It's filled with happy memories of our life together." His voice got softer as he continued. "That dresser and I both witnessed her pass on. My hope is for it to see me die too and finally be on my way to Eugenia." His voice trembled. "I miss her, but I am so grateful she was a part of my life. Heaven is a better place because she's there."

Rennie's voice was barely above a whisper. "Do you think it's God's will that she died? Someone said that to me about Gabriel."

Dixon was silent for a moment before he answered. "What do you think?"

"I think I don't know much about how this world works."

"Are you supposed to?"

Rennie shrugged. "I don't know that either."

"God gave us a beautiful world and filled it with all manner of things for our delight. But if everything stayed the same, if we never lost anything or anyone we loved, we'd stop being thankful for what we've been given. So no, I don't think Eugenia or Gabriel dying was God's will, but I *do* think that loss is a part of love and serves to remind us of how precious our gifts are."

Rennie pushed her foot along the porch floor, causing the swing to move gently. "That helps. Thank you." She stood and pecked her uncle on the cheek. "I need to get on home. Remember, your supper is in the fridge. It just needs to be warmed up in the oven." She walked toward the edge of the porch and hesitated. "The bees, Uncle Dixon. Remind me how you got them again."

He smiled. "Your aunt found them when she was just a wee thing, no more'n five or six, then her parents gave us the hives as a wedding gift." He chuckled. "So in a way, they were just givin' 'em back to her."

She nodded. "Good night, Uncle Dixon."

She walked toward the truck, her shoulders tensing as she anticipated seeing Tiny. As she drove, she puzzled over the bees that seemed to be communicating with her, and she thought of her mother's purse in the back of that closet.

CHAPTER 10

Eugenia

April 23, 1912

EUGENIA DRAGGED A CHAIR TO THE COUNTER SO she could reach the sugar water. Using both hands, she picked up the Mason jar and turned to her father. "Daddy, can I come with you to go beelining?" A weak ray of April sunshine illuminated her eyes, green as a newly sprouted spearmint leaf.

Tom McDonald stroked his daughter's blonde hair. "Huntin' for bees is hard work, Eugenia. Wouldn't you rather play with your dolls in the garden?"

"I'd like to come with you today."

Her father shook his head. "You'd get worn out in a coupla hours. Why don't you stay here and help your mama with the washin'?"

Her voice was soft and steady. "I need to go to the bees."

He turned to his wife. "Can you spare Eugenia today? I never can say no to her."

"It's a long day for a six-year-old, but if you can keep an eye on her while you're tracking the bees, it'll be all right with me." She wiped her hands on her apron. "But she'll need a sweater. It's a little chilly out."

Eugenia's father scooped her out of the chair and grabbed the jar, then pocketed a small bag of flour. "Come on, little queen. Let's get you a sweater, then go find us some bees."

A man was hoisting a yellow table onto his shoulder as the Ford bounced across a field. After they parked, the man spoke. "Morning. Got us a good day. Cloudy sky and no wind." He took off his hat and scratched his forehead when he spotted Eugenia. "I'm here to work, Tom, not babysit. Beelining's not for children."

Eugenia spoke confidently. "I'll be no trouble, Mr. Arlo."

Tom put his hand on his daughter's shoulder. "If she gets in the way, she can take a nap in the truck."

Arlo glanced doubtfully between Tom and Eugenia. "Fine, but if she's a minute of trouble . . ."

Eugenia stepped forward. "I won't be."

She watched carefully as Arlo took the table and a small box with three compartments from the truck and walked to a patch of wild columbine. "Got the flour and sugar water?" he asked. Tom handed him both.

Arlo set the box on the table, then soaked a sponge in the sugar water and dropped it into the first compartment. He sprinkled flour in the center compartment and then pulled a compass from his pocket.

Eugenia watched closely. "How does your trap work, Mr. Arlo?"

"The bees fly into this first part, drawn in by the sugar water, and then I close the door behind 'em. After they've drunk their fill, I lift up the middle divider so's they'll get flour on 'em. When I open the last door, they'll fly to their hive, marked with the flour so we can see them better." He gestured to the bright table. "They'll think this yella table is the biggest flower they've ever seen and fly right back to it. Then I move the table and trap closer to where I think their hive is and do it all over again until I find the colony."

"Instead of all that, couldn't you just ask them where they live?"

"Now why didn't I think of that? I've been beelinin' for nearly thirty years, and in all that time, it never occurred to me to just ask." He leaned down to address a bee resting on a columbine blossom. "Pardon me, miss, instead of me tracking you for hours, could you tell me where your hive is?" He guffawed as he tipped his hat toward Eugenia. "This little lady says it'd be easier."

With a look somewhere between disappointment and pity, Eugenia surveyed the man's face for a moment and then wandered over to some spring beauties to inspect their striped petals.

The next hour passed as Arlo moved the trap through the field and wrote notes on a grimy legal pad. "Twelve minutes to get to the hive and back, this time with four others." He glanced at his compass. "Due east." He picked up his box and walked eastward. "We're getting closer. Should have 'em in another hour or two."

"Their home is this way." Eugenia pointed west. "We should go over toward that hill."

Arlo glanced at Eugenia's father and then at Eugenia. "'Bout time for that nap."

Eugenia's father lifted her into his arms and carried her to the truck. As he settled her into the seat, he said, "We appreciate the advice, but Mr. Arlo's the best beeliner in Kentucky. You have a little rest while he finishes his work." He gently closed the door. "We won't be too long."

As soon as her father was out of view, Eugenia slid from the truck and headed west toward the hill. After about half a mile, she stepped into a bower lined with trees and dotted with coreopsis, whose yellow blooms swayed in a warm breeze. The air was sweet with the scent of honey, and the sun that had seemed so weak in the field was lighting the scene with a warm golden glow. A chickadee called, *Here we are, here we are.* The climb to the top of the hill had been harder than she had expected, and she dropped onto a tuft of soft grass to rest.

Hello, Eugenia.

"I don't know why they didn't believe me when I told them where you were."

Humans tend to think each is an expert in the area of their choosing, regardless of any actual talents. The man is far removed from earth's wisdom and doesn't know what you will know. What you already know.

Eugenia turned her head. "What I know?"

You will help a great many people, Eugenia, with what you know. We are here to help you understand how to do that. That's why we called you to us, so we can come back to your farm and teach you about your abilities.

"Why would you want to come to our farm with me when you could be wild bees and live here in this beautiful forest?"

We've been waiting for you for six years, since that moon-drenched night in June when you were born. It is time for us to be together.

"Won't you be sad to leave your home?"

You are our home, Eugenia.

Eugenia's father came dashing through the trees, panting

for breath. "There you are!" He grabbed her into his arms and held her close, trembling as he clutched her tiny body. "I've never been so scared in all my life." He dropped to his knees and held his daughter tighter. "Thank the good Lord, you're safe."

"I'm fine, Daddy. I've been talking to the bees. They're ready to come home."

CHAPTER 11

AFTER SHE HAD SET THE LAST PAN ON THE DISH drainer, Rennie wiped her hands, slipped off her shoes, and went outside for her evening check on the peanuts, sunflowers, and pumpkins. The soft grass on her feet always grounded her, no matter how frazzled she felt. She inhaled deeply, drawing into her lungs the air that was full of the promise of summer. Soon enough the heat and humidity would become cloying, but for now she welcomed it like a friend. Her little plot of land shone in the golden-hour light. After resting with her uncle in the bee yard following his fall, she had found the energy to dig the holes for the seeds, with Poe circling his encouragement in the skies above her. She was pleased to have finally put in her garden, feeling like she was slowly syncing back into the rhythm of life.

The tender shoots were about eight inches tall, with the delicate oval leaves of the peanut plants resembling butterfly wings, while the bigger pumpkin leaves looked like green umbrellas protecting the smaller leaves underneath. The sunflowers were leaping skyward, taller than anything else growing. So different in appearance, all the leaves had one thing in common, the primal need to reach skyward, toward the sun.

She looked up at the hackberry where Poe rested, keeping a keen eye on her, and then admired the pale moon, always present in the sky but hidden in plain sight by the searing rays of its celestial companion, the vibrant sun. *A good analogy for my life*, she realized. She could be present but not seen, outshone by the likes of Tiny, May Dean, and virtually any other person. It suited her, though, to be overlooked, for with anonymity came safety. She didn't have to deal with the people she found so perplexing, with their loud voices and constant frenetic energy, and could be left to her own devices, reading or baking or visiting with her uncle.

At present the moon appeared no bigger than the button on her apron string. It was hard to imagine the buildings full of scientists reviewing for the millionth time the calculations to ensure the brave astronauts would land safely on its surface and then return to Earth, victorious. The "Moon Mission Fun Facts" column in the *Gazette* stated that over four hundred thousand men worked on the mission, along with a few women. Rennie had wondered about those women. In a world where they were almost certainly given the choices of being mothers, teachers, or nurses, what had spurred them forward to help conquer outer space? And most puzzling of all, how had they found the courage to say no to society's mandates and follow their own dreams all the way into space?

How did the moon feel about the upcoming *Apollo* mission? Since the dawn of time, she had hovered in the sky, providing poets with inspiration, lovers with muted light, and all living creatures with a respite from incandescent sunlight. Did she welcome the astronauts' visit, or did she perceive it as an invasion, a disturbance to her millennia of solitude, longing to remain unknowable, the stuff of wonder that offered soft comfort to adult and child alike?

In grade school, Rennie had fashioned a science project illustrating the phases of the moon using bolls of cotton from a cousin's farm in West Tennessee. In high school, the light of the moon illuminated a romantic path for her and Tiny as they walked along the banks of Flat Rock Creek during their senior year of high school, Tiny laying out his plans to take the baseball world by storm. "If I can get a scout out here, I'll show 'em what I've got, and they'll sign me with the fattest check I could imagine." He had turned to her with that moonlight bathing her pale face, saying, "Can you imagine being the girlfriend of the biggest baseball star since Mickey Mantle?" and then kissing her.

She said good night to the moon and slowly made her way back inside, her bare soles padding against the tender blades of grass.

CHAPTER 12

BY HER FIRST FRIDAY AT THE BLUE PLATE, RENNIE WAS settling into a routine with her duties, proud to be earning money to help ease some of the financial stress at home. As she headed back to the farmhouse after a particularly busy day, her mind drifted to the extra five dollars she'd gotten and Arden's advice not to let Tiny know of its existence. That first crisp bill stayed in her wallet for now as Rennie wrestled with the idea of deceiving Tiny. The only secret she'd ever kept from her husband was the name she had given their dog—hardly in the same category as hiding money.

As she opened the truck door, Tiny stormed out of the house and said, "Something got into the chickens last night. We lost three. Spot's getting too old to do her job."

A few weeks after Rennie and Tiny returned to Spark, Rennie had glimpsed a half-starved gray-and-white dog in a ditch beside Creekside Road. She had stopped, luring the mud-caked animal to her with a piece of ham from her sack of groceries. A deep cut ran the circumference of the dog's scrawny neck, likely caused by a too-tight rope. She had scooped the dog into her arms and put her in the truck. Once back home, she had carried the trembling animal into the barn, where she hosed off the worst of the mud. The dog lapped frantically at the water, and Rennie cupped her hands into a makeshift bowl as the dog drank. Rennie slipped off her sweatshirt and used it to carefully dry the dog, murmuring to her gently as she worked.

She ran to the house and returned with two bowls, one filled with chicken casserole left over from dinner the night before, along with a few ham slices from the grocery bag. The other bowl she filled with water. As the dog ate, Rennie thought over what to do next. She and Tiny had lots of plans for his grandparents' farm, including getting chickens and a dog to guard them, both of which cost money they didn't have. That would be her in.

After closing the barn door, she walked to the field where Tiny was working. "You know how we want to get a guard dog, and you said the Archers wanted too much for even a pup?"

Tiny nodded. "Highway robbery, what they're asking, but we can't get chickens till we have a dog to keep the foxes out."

Rennie offered a smile. "Good news! I've found us one, and she's free."

"What are you talkin' about?"

"I was driving home from the BuyMore and spotted her. She's underweight now, but I can see she'll be the same size as your parents' old dog, Sarge. Come to the barn and see for yourself."

Tiny strode to the barn and threw open the door. The dog scrambled to her feet, studying the intruder, then began to growl. As Tiny approached, the dog lunged forward and changed her growl to a full-on snarl. She then ran to Rennie and faced Tiny, biting and snapping at the air as if tearing a plug out of Tiny's leg.

"Now that's what we need," Tiny said, nodding. "She's protecting you, which means she'll do the same for the chickens. Maybe she's not too smart, but brave just the same. She can stay." Tiny faced his wife. "Good job, honey. I wish she was a male 'cause they're tougher, but beggars can't be choosers. She's got a gray spot on her head, so her name is Spot."

Rennie had pulled a tin of her uncle's bee salve from the medicine cabinet and began massaging the ointment into the dog's neck every morning and night. The salve was just one of the medicines her uncle made from the propolis, or bee glue, he gathered from the hives every year. The bees used propolis, a mixture of tree resin, pollen, and beeswax, to fill holes and cracks in their hives, but her uncle used bee glue for everything from medicinal tea to throat lozenges. A scraped hand, a burn, or an upset stomach was always better after a dose of propolis.

She rubbed in the salve that next night, whispering to ensure Tiny couldn't hear her, and said, "You've had such a hard life, one you didn't deserve, but those days are over for you. I promise I'll do my best to take care of you always and keep you safe. This is just between you and me, but can your real name be Jane Austen? Whenever anyone's around, I'll call you Spot, but we'll both know the truth." The dog turned her head and gazed at her with soulful brown eyes. With a lick to Rennie's hand, the deal was sealed.

When Rennie was a child, her uncle Dixon had asked

her to name his farm animals and the strays that always seemed to find their way to him. He had wanted May Dean to participate, but after only a moment or two around anything with fur, May Dean's eyes swelled and watered, so the naming duties fell to Rennie. At first she chose names like Fuzzy and Cluckie, but as she began reading books, the names changed to authors. E. B. White was a kitten the color of a summer full moon, while Carolyn Keene was a tamed squirrel who had a knack for being in everybody's business. The last animal she named for her uncle was Lewis Carroll, a fog-gray cat who appeared on his front porch over a decade ago. He had a habit of disappearing for a day or two but would always return to his food bowl and warm bed.

Tiny pointed to the now-grizzled dog, napping in the afternoon sunshine. "Spot didn't so much as bark. That's the second time this spring we've lost chickens. Time to be thinking about getting a new dog. I'll speak to Archer about buyin' one of his pups, a male."

Rennie said, "I guess Spot's earned her retirement. She can teach the new dog."

"Nope. Don't need her showing a guard dog how to ignore predators and sneak naps on our bed when nobody's looking."

Fear dashed across Rennie's heart. What did he mean by that?

On the following Friday, Rennie chalked the day's special on the Blue Plate blackboard in her prettiest handwriting—

Poppyseed Chicken Casserole, Scalloped Potatoes, and Tomato and Cucumber Salad. She smiled as she added Lunar Lemon Pie. The whole town was transfixed by the mission to the moon, now only a few weeks away, and every business in town had found a way to participate. The BuyMore had a shelf of space-themed foods—Moon Pies, Space Food Sticks, and Tang drink mix—while Strickland's Drugstore had a table featuring all of Revlon's Moon Drops product line. Dewey's "Moon Mission Fun Facts" column in the weekly *Gazette* was wildly popular, must-read material for all Spark residents fascinated by the almost-impossible mission President Kennedy had first committed to eight years earlier.

May Dean and Ev were squabbling at a booth when Rennie brought them their lunch. "It says it right here, hon," Ev read from the *Gazette*. "The moon is 238,855 miles away from Earth."

May Dean shook her head. "How do they *know*? Was somebody out there in space with a measuring tape? Did someone drive up there and then check their mileage?"

Ev took his plate from Rennie. "What do you think, Rennie? Can somebody calculate how far away the moon is?"

She set May Dean's lunch special in front of her. "I'll add that to the very long list of things I don't know. I *do* know I love Dewey's column, though. Did you see where he said the astronauts will have a piece of the Wright brothers' plane onboard with them?"

May Dean nodded. "I did see that. Any chance you'd be interested in going to Nashville with me next week to do a little shopping? I need to get some maternity clothes, and I'd love some company. I thought we could go to 100 Oaks

Mall." She fiddled with her silverware. "If it's too upsetting, I understand."

"I don't need anything, but maybe an outing would do me good. I'm off Mondays and Tuesdays. Would either of those days work?"

Ev chuckled. "Could you go Saturday afternoon? She's about the size of the moon herself and needs new clothes right away. She's had to wear the same dress two weeks in a row to church 'cause it's the only one that fits, and I'm not sure what would happen if she had to wear it for a third Sunday."

May Dean playfully punched her husband's arm. "Another remark like that and *you'll* be the one in orbit." She looked at Rennie. "Monday will be great. I'll pick you up around nine? And hey, any chance you've got any of the Moon Is Made of Cheesecake back there? It is absolutely divine. Otherwise, I'll have a slice of your Lunar Lemon Pie."

Rennie smiled. "I'll go see what I've got."

CHAPTER 13

THE CONVERTIBLE'S TOP WAS DOWN AND MAY DEAN was grinning. "Hop in. We've got some shopping to do."

Rennie climbed in the passenger seat. "You look great, May Dean."

"You're a liar, but I love you for it. I had no idea I'd already be as big as that picture of the moon Dewey had on the front page of the *Gazette*. Did you see that little arrow marked 'Likely Landing Spot'? How in the world can they know where they'll touch down? Even in an empty parking lot, it's wait and see where I'll end up. I can't be too close to the buggy corral 'cause I'll scrape the side when I pull out. If I'm by any big car takin' up too much space, I won't be able to open my door. It could be raining, so I'd want to be near the store entrance, but it's usually too crowded by the front. It takes me at least two tries to get parked, and let's just say I've been known to tap a bumper or two maneuvering for a spot." She shrugged. "And that's here on earth. Imagine trying to figure all that out on the moon."

Rennie bit back her smile. "I doubt there will be any other vehicles up there for them to deal with." She watched out the window as farm after farm flew by. "So what kinds of clothes are you looking for?"

May Dean tilted her head. "I need dresses for church and something for the Millers' party in a couple of weeks." She merged onto the highway. "That reminds me—the next time you see Ambrose, tell him Sue and Bob Miller's annual bonfire and weenie roast is next Friday night, and he's invited."

After an hour's drive, May Dean turned into the 100 Oaks Mall parking lot. Since its grand opening two years ago, it was the destination of any serious Nashville shopper intent on finding cute clothes, record albums, or even a blacklight poster. Rennie had heard of the mall but had never set foot inside. She followed May Dean, gaping at the storefronts and signs. A directory was situated beside the escalator, and Rennie marveled at the long list of shops. They checked the directory for Modern Mama Boutique.

A woman greeted them at the door. "What can I help you with today?"

"I'm expecting a baby this fall and need some new clothes. We just want to look around for now if that's okay." After the saleslady nodded, May Dean began flicking through the racks. She paused at a yellow dress with black striped sleeves. "How about this one?" she giggled to Rennie. "I can look like one of Uncle Dixon's bees." She put the dress back. "A huge, puffy bee."

With her arms overflowing with options, May Dean made her way to the dressing room. She modeled each outfit for Rennie, who tried hard not to recall her own three Goodwill sacks she wore on rotation when carrying Gabriel.

After buying at least half a dozen dresses and just as many pants and tops, Rennie and May Dean left the store. Rennie glanced in the large window of The Cotton Patch and stood transfixed, mesmerized by a black blouse on display. May Dean followed Rennie's gaze. "Try it on, Rennie. You'd look so pretty in that."

"I'm more tobacco patch than Cotton Patch." She shrugged. "And it's too expensive."

"You don't even know the price yet. It can't be *that* much."

"I had a black shirt once, but Tiny made me get rid of it. He said black made me look washed out, and he told me never to wear anything that color again."

"I wish you wouldn't believe everything Tiny says. When will you figure out the secret to a good marriage is lookin' like you're listening to your husband telling you what to do and then goin' ahead with exactly what you were fixin' to do before he butted in? Turn your smile on and your ears off, and everybody's happy. Besides, your birthday is tomorrow, and the blouse is much better than what I picked out for you. Ev and I would love to give it to you as a present. If you're worried about Tiny's reaction, which, by the way, you definitely should *not* be, you can wear it when he's not around." When Rennie hesitated, May Dean took her hand and led her inside the store. "Just try it on."

The blouse was enchanting. Soft and flowy, it tied at the neck with a little ribbon. The sleeves fluttered at her elbows, and delicate embroidered flowers graced the hem.

"You look like a movie star," gushed May Dean. "It makes your chestnut eyes shine."

Rennie made a face. "We see things so differently. I know what you mean, but remember, Godzilla was a movie star." She shook her head. "And my eyes are mud brown."

May Dean's voice was sharp. "Did Tiny tell you that too? They're Uncle Dixon's eyes, so lucky you."

"I don't think I look right in something so frilly and feminine." She retraced her steps to the dressing room and returned with the blouse back on the hanger.

"You looked lovely, and the blouse fit you like a dream. How did it make you feel?"

"Remember when we would play fairy princesses down by Uncle Dixon's hives? Aunt Eugenia would braid beautyberries into our hair and serve us tea under the linden tree, calling each of us an enchanted princess. That's how I felt—like royalty from a magical story." Rennie sighed and glanced down at the blouse. "Tiny would be so upset for going against his instructions, though."

"Him sayin' that was an opinion, not a commandment, and it would do you a world of good to realize the difference." May Dean pursed her lips and took the blouse from Rennie's hands. "I *do* remember playing fairy princesses with you, and how special we felt. If this blouse reminds you of those happy days, then we're getting it." As Rennie protested, May Dean opened her wallet. "Ev gave me his credit card this morning and said to have fun, and buying you something that makes you feel like a princess is *fun*." She handed the blouse to the saleslady and turned to Rennie. "Happy birthday."

As the sunrise was announcing the dawn of another beautiful morning, Rennie steeped her morning tea and thought about her childhood birthdays. Her mother and father had always managed a little celebration for her, consisting of her favorite homemade caramel cake and a practical gift, like a new pair of shoes, waiting for her at her spot at the kitchen table. The blessing her father offered over their meal on birthday night would include gratitude to the Lord for the gift of their daughter, the closest to praise she ever got from her parents.

Her aunt and uncle had taken a more festive approach. When her parents left for work, Rennie walked to the farm on the hill, cutting through the field that bordered their properties. The well-worn path took about ten minutes to navigate and led first to the bee yard and then to their house. Her aunt would be waiting with pancakes topped with a bit of whipped cream and some of the season's first honey harvest. Mild spring honey was her favorite, flavored with nectar from black locust trees. Each year a book was wrapped in brown paper for her, tied with honeysuckle vines, and fresh bishop's-cap or *Heliopsis* serving as the bow. Every June she eagerly looked forward to her birthday present, with a title like *Charlotte's Web* or *Rabbit Hill*, a treasured classic based on the natural world. The best year of all, though, was when her book was *Miss Hickory*, accompanied by a hickory stick doll.

After breakfast she got to plan the day, which could include swinging in the tire hung from a sturdy oak, wading in the creek, playing princess inside the ring of lindens surrounding the hives, or reading her new book.

"Happy birthday, Rennie," she whispered to herself as

she rocked on the back porch. The day promised to be bright and warm, that near-perfect weather when you didn't need a sweater or a breeze to be comfortable. After finishing her cup of tea, she returned to their bedroom. The shower was already running, so she needed to hurry up with Tiny's breakfast. Before returning to the kitchen, though, she opened her bedside drawer, tugged off the top of a small box, and pulled out her hickory stick doll. She held it gently in her hands, remembering how Uncle Dixon had stood in the doorway and beamed as she picked up the hand-carved gift and admired its delicate features. She touched a twig arm, then returned it to the box and went to the kitchen to make his coffee.

Tiny pecked Rennie on the cheek as she stood at the stove, scrambling eggs. "Happy birthday."

The day before, Tiny had come in the house with a puzzled look on his face, holding the mail. "Why would you be getting something from your cousin in Memphis?"

Rennie set aside her copy of *Rebecca*. "Birdie always sends me a birthday card."

"Oh, right," he had said.

So he's forgotten again. On Rennie's first birthday as a married woman, she had woken up to an envelope by her pillow. She had eased her finger under the flap and pulled out a dime store card featuring a bouquet of garish tulips tied with a glitter bow. *For My Wife*, the elegant script read, followed by a sappy poem about how both wives and birthdays were blessings. In Tiny's hen-scratch handwriting, he had scrawled, "I will bring us your favorite takeout tonight and we can celebrate. Love, Luther." He had come home from practice with dinner and a cupcake adorned with neon blue frosting and a single candle. He had sung an off-key rendition of "Happy Birthday" to her, and she had blown out the candle and wished for a happy life. Then, with a flourish, he had given her a small paper bag. She peered inside and smiled as she pulled out a record, "Moon River."

They had made love that night, and afterward Rennie had stood by the window admiring a full moon and thinking she should have wished for something else, as she already had a life happier than she ever could have imagined for herself. The next morning, she had found a pretty box to put the card in, planning to use it to save all the birthday and anniversary cards he gave her. When it was time to pack up and return to Spark, she had brought the box along. It had sat untouched in the bottom drawer of the bureau in their bedroom ever since, waiting for a second card to add to the collection.

Tiny grabbed the card as soon as she opened it. "'I hope your birthday is as fun as you are,'" he read. With a smirk, he said, "Not exactly good wishes, now, is it?"

Rennie took back the card. "She is remembering me on my special day, which is both kind and appreciated." She nodded to the table. "Your coffee's ready."

He sat at the table as she worked. "I'm going into town this morning. Wait till I get back to go take Dixon his food."

"Okay. I'll get everything cooked, then head on over later."

He crossed to her and gave her a tight squeeze, then twirled her around the kitchen, dizzying Rennie. He held her at arm's length and asked, "Are you happy?"

"Knowing I am safe in my home and cared for by my husband is what makes me happy." She hesitated, then said,

"Are we paid up on the rent? Your daddy's so mean about it if we're ever behind."

As he answered, his blue eyes looked as gray as the limestone rocks he kept hauling out of the tobacco fields. "All paid up, birthday girl. Need anything while I'm out?"

As usual, he had no idea what his wife might like as a gift. She had mentioned twice in the last week that she had a hole in her gardening gloves, but she'd need to take the direct approach. "I've been thinking about some new work gloves. Grady took a pair out of the Emporium window last week for me to try on. They were marked 50 percent off. Could you see if they're still there?"

"Sure."

As she prepared a chicken casserole, she considered her birthday. In two more years, she'd turn twenty-five. She thought about what had transpired in the last year. She had been swallowed whole by the grief surrounding Gabriel's death, while her husband had dealt with the loss by becoming even more volatile. He had always been short-tempered, which she first attributed to the pressures of being a rising star with so many people relying on him for their own success, and then the demands of running a farm. After Gabriel's death, though, he began to change. Confidence evolved into arrogance, and seriousness slipped into bitterness. Worst of all was his anger, which had turned into a sullenness that soaked through both their lives, souring even the sweetest moments.

She began peeling potatoes, wondering what her life would look like when she crossed that quarter-century threshold. If only Tiny could make peace with both himself and his lot in life, she could have a more contented husband who could finally coax a profitable tobacco crop from his grandparents' farm and erase the specter of eviction from their lives forever. That was her birthday wish, made on the tears that formed in her eyes instead of on blown-out candles, since the Tiny she lived with now would never think to bring home dinner or a cupcake, or even sing "Happy Birthday" to mark the occasion. The other wish, the one for a baby she could raise instead of bury, lay deep in her heart, too tender to be transferred from her heart to her brain. It was enough to ask for a happy husband, because once Tiny could somehow be at peace, a baby could follow.

With the last washed dish drying on the counter, she shook out of her shoes and stepped outside. On her way to check on the food she was growing for her crow, she caught sight of Jane Austen napping in the sunshine. "Hi, girl," she said, rubbing her gray-and-white ears. "I'm glad you've got a pretty afternoon to rest, but you might want to patrol around the farm when Tiny is around. And if you could run off a raccoon or fox, that would be really good." She kissed the gray spot on her head that had inspired Tiny's name for her. *The Archers' dogs are really expensive, but I wouldn't put it past Tiny to make one of his deals to get us one early.* Rubbing the neck that had needed weeks to heal, she added, "Don't you worry, though. I told you the day you came to live with us that I'd always take care of you and keep you safe, and that includes from Tiny."

As she walked to her garden, she thought about her commitment to Jane Austen. Should she make the same promise to herself? Was withholding the five dollars Arden was paying her in cash the same as lying? The bills collected in her wallet, tucked in a seldom-used slot. Committing to hiding them in her mother's purse seemed like a betrayal to her, but she still hadn't revealed their existence to her husband. Her mother had always taught her a false witness was the worst thing a person could be. *"The Lord hates a lying tongue."* She would be devastated at the thought of Rennie using her purse to facilitate the deception she was considering.

A bee was hovering over the sprouts as she bent down to pull a weed. The glow from its body seemed to reach straight to her soul. Rennie sat on the soft ground as she watched the bee. *What is going on?* A shining bee convinced her to go to her uncle, who desperately needed help, and then another bee stopped her from revealing to Tiny she would be paid above minimum wage. This third bee was also trying to tell her something. Were they her aunt's bees, coming from their hives at her uncle's farm?

Aunt Eugenia was different from the women of Spark. Unbothered by fashion, she mostly kept to herself. She never gossiped but was often the topic of others' whispered conversations. Brought in from too far away to ever be one of them, she was sometimes referred to as a *brung in*. Others called her worse. Her reputation for understanding things she couldn't have any way of knowing and curing sicknesses that baffled the doctor deeply unnerved the churchgoers of Spark.

Even the most devout Spark residents had their limits, though, and if Doc Grisham's medicine couldn't cure someone of their illness, people knew to knock on the Kings' door, preferably with the benefit of darkness shielding them from the view of their neighbors.

"We need Miz King," someone would whisper at the front door.

"Give her a minute and she'll be right along," Dixon would answer.

Day or night, she'd take her worn leather bag full of glass vials and pouches of dried herbs and hurry to the patient. A poultice applied to a throbbing wound or a few bitter drops of a tincture massaged down a raw throat would more times than not pull them from death's tight grasp. She would sometimes murmur as she worked over a feverish patient, using words and sounds no one comprehended. Some people claimed she communed with angels, and others said it was the devil she spoke to. They still found their way to her door, though, no matter their public stance on her methods.

She once told a lady she had just met that the woman was pregnant and would give birth to a boy in exactly eight months, which turned out to be right, down to the day. Not worrying about the devil part, pretty soon women either dreading or hoping for news of a pregnancy came to hear her predictions, and she was always right.

Rennie had figured out early on there was something different about the woman her uncle had married and had defended her aunt in more than one contentious discussion about whether her aunt had beguiled Dixon King into bringing her to live among the regular folk in Spark. Witches were storybook caricatures, warty and evil, flying on brooms and causing mayhem, while her aunt was the kindest, gentlest woman she knew, and it infuriated Rennie that her aunt was a target of people's gossip. Some of Rennie's classmates steered clear of Rennie only because she was awkward and would rather read on the playground than join in any kickball or jump rope games, but others said things that confirmed she was right to keep to herself.

"Your aunt is a witch," one classmate had said. "My mama says it's not Christian to mix up a powder of roots or burn plants to cure somebody."

"No wonder nobody likes you," another would say. "Your family is touched by the devil."

Only once did she retaliate. Bonnie Sue Greer sidled up to her on the way into school one day. "My daddy says your aunt doesn't sleep like a normal human. *He* says she leaves every night to roam, dancin' around a bonfire and puttin' spells on people, and I should have nothing to do with you and your kin."

Rennie had had enough. "Well, tell your daddy to check with your mama about that, 'cause when I was spending the night with my aunt and uncle once, your own mama came to the door asking for her help because you were so sick with the measles. My uncle woke my aunt up, who was *sound asleep in the bed*, by the way. She went to your house and broke your fever. Your daddy would have known that if he was home with his family, so maybe he was the one out roaming where he shouldn't have been."

Rennie eyed the glowing bee that rested on a sunflower leaf. When she put her hand out to the bee, she crawled onto Rennie's finger. Lifting the bee to her face, she whispered, "Are you here to help me?" A yellow jacket, one of bees' worst enemies, flew toward the bee. Rennie murmured, "Save yourself," just as the bee flew away. She had her answer. *Save yourself.*

CHAPTER 14

IT IS A SORRY STATE OF AFFAIRS WHEN SHE MUST USE her birthday wish to ask for such a basic right—stability—when her heart longs for a healthy baby.

Because she is tied to that beef-witted husband of hers, she is using our hive-mind approach to survival. What is good for one benefits all.

A birthday should be for celebrating, not surviving.

True, but without survival she will have no more birthdays to celebrate.

We can be joyful, though, even if she feels she cannot. Our message has been heard.

CHAPTER 15

TINY HAD ARRIVED BACK FROM TOWN WITH A SMALL parcel stuffed into his pocket. Rennie recognized the green ribbon the Emporium used to gift wrap their packages and smiled. *At least he's making an effort.*

"Happy birthday," Tiny said, holding out the parcel.

She opened the gloves and slipped them on. "They're perfect, Tiny. Thank you." She pecked her husband on the cheek and then loaded up the food for her uncle and headed toward his house.

The scent of the dinner she had prepared filled the cab of the truck. Her uncle had been putting weight back on, and he seemed to be getting stronger. "Bees are medicine," he liked to say. They both gravitated to the hives and had gotten in the habit of sitting on Eugenia's bench to while away the warm afternoons.

Rennie had traced her finger along the iron rose medallion the day before. "Why do you call it Eugenia's bench?"

Dixon closed his eyes and began his story. "She brought this bench with her from Kentucky and chose this very spot to put it so she could keep an eye on her hives. She said the sight of the bees working around their home, flying among the four-o'clocks and wild bergamot, was a glimpse of perfection here on earth. And I think the bees wanted to be near her too."

She pulled up to her uncle's house and parked beside his truck. Uncle Dixon was waiting for her on the back porch in his rocker with Lewis Carroll in his lap. "Happy birthday, sweet girl!"

Rennie bent down to peck him on the cheek. "Thank you."

Dixon nodded to a small velvet box. "That's your present. I'm sorry I don't have it wrapped up all pretty like Eugenia used to do."

"You didn't have to get me anything." She touched the box. "You really shouldn't have driven into town to shop. Just wishing me a happy birthday is all the gift I need."

"I didn't drive or shop, either one." He nodded to the box. "This was your aunt Eugenia's. It's been sitting in her dresser, and I thought it was high time someone was wearing it."

Inside lay a delicate necklace, a gold chain with two entwined hearts attached with a tiny loop. Rennie closed the box. "It's too precious for me to have. It should stay with you."

"No, it's yours."

With trembling hands, she clasped the thin chain around her neck. "I will cherish—"

The rumble of an unfamiliar truck interrupted her. "Are you expecting anyone?"

"Yep. Ambrose Beckett."

Ambrose emerged from his truck, carefully holding a bag.

He made his way to the pair on the porch, maneuvering around the protruding root. "Hey, Dixon, and happy birthday, Rennie."

"Thank you. Oh, I've got a message for you. You're invited to the Millers' bonfire party. It's an annual thing in their back field with hot dogs and marshmallows—"

He set down the bag. "I have other plans."

"But I didn't even say when it is."

"I don't like fire."

"I didn't mean to upset you. It's just that I promised May Dean I'd tell you about the party."

"I appreciate the invitation but will have to decline." He reached into the bag and extracted a card. He handed it to Rennie, who was startled to see an exquisitely rendered watercolor of a New Dawn rose. She opened the card and read, "'An old rose for a new friend. Happy birthday from Ambrose.'" Bewildered, she looked at him. "You painted this?"

He smiled shyly. "I did." Was he blushing? "Those New Dawns aren't just *like* your aunt's roses; they *are* your aunt's roses. Or at least grown from her cuttings."

Dixon nodded. "Eugenia loved to share seeds and clippings from her gardens. If anyone so much as commented on a plant or flower, she'd send them home with a way to grow their own. Years ago, our neighbor Annabelle Sawyer was here and admired the rose arch leading to the hives. Eugenia sliced off a branch with my pocketknife and gave it to her, which she must have planted on the trellis against her house."

Ambrose pulled a pan wrapped in foil from the bag. "I'm a little embarrassed to give you this homely thing, but I made a cake." He hastened to add, "It's from a mix. I went to the BuyMore and asked the nice lady at the checkout stand what to get. Did you know Betty Crocker makes something called an Answer Cake that has the mix, frosting, and pan all in a box?" He unwrapped the cake and chuckled. "The only thing not in there was somebody who knows how to bake it. It's got a couple of ruts in it where the cake didn't cook evenly." He smiled ruefully. "I added some sprinkles to help hide my mistakes, but anyway, happy birthday." He carefully lit the single candle.

Rennie hadn't been given a birthday cake since she married Tiny. She looked at Ambrose, catching his eye. "It's beautiful, Ambrose. Thank you." She stood, flustered. "I'll get us some silverware and plates."

When she returned from the kitchen, Ambrose and her uncle sang "Happy Birthday" to her. She forced her heart not to jump when Ambrose sang "dear Rennie." Those tears she had shed while she made supper earlier that day were back. She blew out the candle, wishing the happiness and contentment she felt at that moment could stay with her always.

Lewis Carroll hopped into Ambrose's lap.

"Wow! He never does that with anyone but me or Uncle Dixon."

Ambrose stroked the cat's gray fur. "He reminds me of the black cat I had growing up in Travers. My dog Millie found him as a kitten, half-starved and covered in ticks, and carried him to the house in her mouth. She raised him as her own, and I'm not sure Coal ever knew he wasn't a dog." He scratched under Lewis Carroll's chin. "I miss having an animal around. Maybe I'll get one after I'm a bit more settled."

They visited awhile on the porch, talking about Eugenia's flowers, Ambrose's plans to add on to the back porch, his stargazing, and, of course, the bees. Uncle Dixon told a story about a man from Nashville who tried to buy one of Dixon's hives after Dixon had won his second blue ribbon in a row for his honey at the state fair. "He kept pullin' more money outta his wallet, and I kept saying selling bees was the same as selling your luck, and he shouldn't be tryin' to buy them neither, 'cause it's bad luck he'd be buyin'. He finally put all that cash back in his pocket and called me an old fool."

Rennie picked up her purse and then her birthday card. "I think I'll leave this here so I can see it when I bring supper by." She looked at Ambrose. "It's beautiful, and I like the idea of it being so near Aunt Eugenia's roses. How about I put it in the kitchen window so it can overlook the backyard?"

Ambrose's expression changed. "I hope I didn't offend you by giving you the card. I certainly didn't intend anything improper or mean to suggest—"

Rennie raised her hand. "Painting me that rose was so kind, and I am honored, not offended. It's just, um, my husband might not appreciate another man giving me something so, well, thoughtful."

Ambrose bowed his head. "I understand." He took the card from her hand. "I'll put it in the window for you."

She popped a last bite of cake into her mouth. "Thank you both for such a special birthday. I'll never forget it."

Ambrose grinned at her. "June's the perfect month to have a birthday. The weather's always nice, and no holidays to overlap with. May Dean's little girl will have to get used to being a Halloween baby, same as me."

Uncle Dixon covered a smile with his hand, and Rennie's eyebrows shot up. "How do you know it's a girl and when her birthday will be?"

The happy expression vanished from his face, and he shifted in his chair. "Oh, well, she's carrying high. You know how us Kentucky folk are with our superstitions. And she told me she was due toward the end of October, so I'm just hoping she delivers on my birthday." He stood. "Actually, I need to get on home." He turned to Dixon. "Thank you for including me in Rennie's celebration. I'll be back tomorrow to check on the hives." He looked back at Dixon as he walked toward his truck. "I'm not sure what you said to them about me taking over for a little while, but we're gettin' along just fine."

Rennie eyed her uncle. "Tell me more about these bees." She looked toward the hive. "When I found you after you fell, you said, 'I knew they'd tell you.' At first I thought you hurt your head and were confused, but now I'm thinking it's something else." She looked into his eyes, cloudy with cataracts. "What did you mean?"

"These bees aren't the regular type most people have. They're descendants of the ones Eugenia found." A breeze blew through the lavender blossoms, lifting their scent into the air. "They understand love better than most people do. They know I love you and that you love me. When I fell I needed help, so they flew to get you. Because you love me, you understood and came."

"Why didn't you tell me all this before now?"

"You used to know, Rennie, but you forgot, what with growing up and all."

"Did you ever tell me about keeping the bees up to date on family news? I feel like I would have remembered that."

"I didn't."

"Why not?"

Uncle Dixon answered, "Death, Rennie. To understand about telling the bees, you have to understand that people die, even when you love them, even when you still need them, and even when you think it's too soon for them to go. I didn't want to bring all that up to a young'un, so I skipped that story and just made sure you knew that talking to bees was normal."

Rennie looked toward the hives. "Do they know I love them?"

He grinned. "What do you think?"

As she walked to the truck, she glanced at her watch and was startled to see it was already past five o'clock. *Oh Lord, Tiny gets so cranky when his supper is late. Gotta hurry or I'll never hear the end of it.* When she slipped into the driver's seat, she noticed several bees gathered on the windshield, blocking her view. "Hey, friends, I need to get going." The dozen or so bees remained on the glass, even when she got out and shooed them away with her hand. "Please fly back to the hive," she begged. "You don't want to get me in trouble, do you?" More bees joined the ones already on the glass. Was this a swarm forming? It was too late in the year for swarming, but that had to be what was going on. "I'm sorry, but I have to go. Tiny'll kill me for being late." She hopped back in the truck and accelerated, and one by one, the bees blew off the windshield.

Once home, she went to Tiny to show him her uncle's

gift. Touching the dainty necklace, she said, "I remember my aunt Eugenia wearing it."

Instead of admiring the necklace, he reached over to her chin and wiped off a small smudge of sprinkles and frosting. "Where did the cake come from? Your uncle can barely walk, so don't give me some bullshit story about how he made it for you or drove to the Blue Plate to get it."

She froze, unable to think of a cover story. "I . . . I . . ." She took a breath and told her husband the second lie of their marriage. "May Dean came by Uncle Dixon's and brought it."

Tiny's eyes narrowed. "May Dean brought a cake by here about thirty minutes ago to wish you a happy birthday, so you can stop lying to me. Someone *else* made you that cake, the same one who gave you that necklace." He grabbed the delicate chain and ripped it from her neck, throwing Rennie off balance. "You are my wife and belong to *me*. Cheating with another man and using your crazy old uncle as a cover is pretty low." He flung the necklace with the speed and force that had so impressed the baseball scout back in the Spark High School bleachers. "No one makes a fool of me!"

Jane Austen rushed to Rennie's side, hackles raised, and snapped at Tiny. As Rennie fell to the hard earth, the dog's teeth sank into Tiny's calf. He yelled out in pain, then grabbed the dog's neck and pulled her from his leg. Slinging her across the yard, he yelled, "Damn dog," before turning his attention to his wife. "Humiliate me again and I'll kill you."

CHAPTER 16

HIS VIOLENCE IS ESCALATING. THE FATHER FOUND HIS son at that tavern in Putney last night and demanded the rent. Embarrassment in front of one's peers, mixed with the fuzzle of alcohol, is a recipe for opening old wounds. The two men had quite a fight. If it were not for the steady patronage of the younger one, the barkeep would have alerted the sheriff to the altercation.

The father was wrong to impose his own dreams on his son. He compounded his error by lashing out when those dreams went unfulfilled. The son was equally wrong to accuse the father of sabotaging his life. He did that all on his own.

Why do humans insist on burdening others with their own shortcomings?

Because it is easier to blame someone else for one's failure than to be the one doing the failing.

Amid all this pain, we have one bright spot of happiness. She's beginning to remember.

It will make what's ahead easier for her.

We don't have time for the memories to work themselves out

on their own, like some deep-buried splinter. She needs that strength now.

Can we forfend the trouble until she is better able to manage?

We were unable to stop her from going home to the dispiteous husband. We are powerless to override her free will.

But we can help her, yes?

Yes. We swear by every flower in the field that we will.

CHAPTER 17

RENNIE PULLED INTO THE PARKING LOT OF STRICKland's Drugstore and picked up the wool scarf she had dug out from among the winter gloves and hats in a bottom drawer. She wound it around her neck and anxiously checked the rearview mirror before stepping out of the truck.

Shorty Strickland looked up from a ledger from behind the register. "Good morning, Rennie. You're out early today."

"Yes, sir." She approached the Moon Drops makeup display and began scrutinizing the unfamiliar bottles. She chose a likely shade of foundation and approached the counter, nervously pulling the scarf tighter around her neck.

"Is the weatherman callin' for snow today?" Mr. Strickland laughed at his own joke.

"No, sir." Rennie kept her eyes downcast as she paid for her purchase and hurried back to her truck. She drove to the Blue Plate's parking lot, thinking about what had transpired the night before. After Tiny had ripped the necklace from her neck, she had stood back up, using the splintered handrail of the porch steps to help steady herself. She had then gone to check on Jane Austen, who was warily watching Tiny from the corner of the yard. After determining that Jane Austen was shaken but not physically injured, she returned to the house to wash the blood and dust from her neck. The wound gaped open and likely would leave a scar, but she dared not seek medical help, as intrusive questions would be asked.

After cleaning the wound, she'd coated the raw skin with the same bee salve she had used for her dog's neck. She stood before the mirror, wincing as she massaged more thick ointment into the wound. Water gushed from the faucet as she rinsed her hands, and when she caught sight of her pale skin and bloody gash, she was struck by the contrast in colors. Staring at herself, she hardly recognized the woman who had only an hour before been at her impromptu birthday party, laughing and smiling.

About an hour later, Tiny had walked into the room with a stem of goatsbeard in his hand, picked from their fence line.

Rennie had drawn back her shoulders and in an even voice said, "Ambrose Beckett brought that cake over. Uncle Dixon and Aunt Eugenia always had a little celebration for me when I was growing up. Uncle Dixon was trying to re-create those old days, so he asked Ambrose to bring a cake. I didn't want to upset you about another man being there, so I panicked and said May Dean brought the cake."

His voice was low. "Will you forgive me?" He walked to their record player and dropped the needle on the 45 of "Moon River," then enfolded her into his massive arms. Swaying around the kitchen, he nuzzled her neck, tender from where he had torn off her necklace, and placed delicate kisses along the injury. "I'm so sorry I hurt you, my sweet precious Rennie." He held her at arm's length and looked into her eyes. "I'll never do it again, I promise." He kissed her deeply, leaving her short of breath, then left her standing in the kitchen as the needle of the record player rhythmically bumped against the end of the recording. A moment later, she heard his truck's engine.

After stepping to the window to ensure he had left, she purposefully walked to the closet. She moved a manila envelope marked "All Stars Contract" and extracted her mother's purse from the hospital bag. The latch, unused for almost ten years, caught a little before it yielded. Inside was a handkerchief, half a roll of mints, and three pennies. She carried the bag to her sewing basket and dug under a torn shirt and a pair of ripped pants for her scissors. With a single slice, she cut the lining of the purse. The resulting slit created the perfect hiding place for the five-dollar bills from Arden. Tiny would never forget she had lied to him. She was going to need that money.

⁓

Rennie shook from her head the memory of what had transpired the day before and focused her thoughts on the task at hand, one that wouldn't be easy—fooling Arden. She opened the back door of the Blue Plate and slipped inside, grateful not to see anyone, and entered the bathroom. After taking off the scarf, she dabbed at the gash with the Moon Drops. She bit her lip. If anything, her neck looked worse with the makeup, which mixed with the dried blood to create a garish orange color. Maybe she could tie her apron strings in a way that would conceal the wound.

Arden was coming around a corner as Rennie exited the bathroom. "Good morning, Ren—" Arden stopped in her tracks. "Honey, what happened?"

"I, uh, a necklace got caught on something and I jerked away. It cut my neck."

Arden peered over her glasses. "Don't do that."

Rennie's voice shook. "I'm sorry?"

"Don't tell me something that's not true. And don't be sorry either." Arden sat at a table and pointed to an empty chair beside her. "Sit." After Rennie had lowered herself into the chair, Arden asked, "Was it Tiny?"

Rennie's voice was barely audible above the whir of the air conditioner unit blowing cold air into the room. "Yes, but it was all my fault."

"This was *not* your fault."

"But I lied to him."

"So what? You think every word he says to you is the gospel truth?"

Rennie's eyes filled with tears. She was well aware of how easily a lie sprang to Tiny's lips, especially if his judgment was being questioned. "I don't want to talk about this."

Arden sighed and walked to the counter. She opened a drawer, pulled out a blue silk scarf, and returned to Rennie. As she tied the scarf gently around her neck, she said, "It'll cover the wound so you won't get any nosy questions." She hugged Rennie close and whispered in her ear. "It's not your fault."

Word had gotten out about Rennie being the new cook at the Blue Plate, and she was busy from the minute the restaurant opened until 2:00 p.m. when she finished work. As she packed up three dinners for her family, she fretted that her uncle would ask about the scarf. His eyesight was failing, but he always picked up on whatever was different. She had managed to lie to Tiny twice, but she could never be untruthful to her uncle.

She untied her apron and hung it on a hook. Arden was busy peeling Granny Smiths for the next day's fried apples, but she looked up as Rennie was collecting her things. "Thank you for your hard work today. Your paycheck's on the counter next to your envelope." Rennie paused, keys in hand, waiting to hear her parting words about Tiny, or about hiding the extra five dollars, but Arden turned back to her apples without additional comment.

As Rennie drove, she scanned the sky. Dark clouds were rolling in from the west, and it was about to storm.

CHAPTER 18

SHE SLIPPED INTO HER UNCLE'S HOUSE AND WALKED quietly to the kitchen. As she tucked the container of roast beef, mashed potatoes, and green beans into the fridge, she heard his voice call out from his room.

"That you, Rennie?"

She poked her head through the bedroom door, barely able to make out her uncle in the dark room, lying on his bed. "How are you feeling today?"

He nodded toward the porch. "Will you help me onto the porch? I love the smell of the wind right before a rain."

"Sure thing." As they walked, her uncle eyed the scarf. "How are you, Rennie?"

"I, uh, had a busy day at the diner."

As he settled into his chair, he asked, "Anything you want to tell me?"

Her voice was quiet. "No, sir."

She could feel her cheeks warm as he studied her. "Wait here a minute." He rose from his chair and went inside, returning with a set of keys. "Been meaning to give you the truck. The gas gauge is broken, so don't let it get too low on fuel, but otherwise it's good as new. My driving days are over, and between you working and taking care of me, you need your own transportation." His brown eyes darkened to almost black as he handed her the keys. "Best not to rely on Tiny."

"Are you sure?" Rennie stared at the keys.

"If I do something, it's because I mean it." He nodded across a field. "Maybe we could get Ambrose to drive it to your house, and then you could run him home. He's comin'—"

"No! I mean, uh, I'd hate to impose. Tiny can drive me over here later, and then I'll drive your truck back to our house." She looked down at the worn leather fob with two keys on the ring. "What's the second key for?"

He chuckled. "The front door, I think. Been so long since I locked it that I'm not rightly sure."

"I'll take good care of the truck."

"Focus on yourself first, then worry about the truck." Uncle Dixon turned toward the house. "I think I'll head in for that nap." With his hand on the screen door, he added, "I'm givin' it to you, not Tiny. He's not to sell it. Make sure he knows I said that."

"I will. While you're resting, may I go down and sit with the bees for a little while?"

"Anytime. You never have to ask."

The fragrant air soothed her nerves as she made her way down the path to the bee yard, thinking about her uncle's gift. Why had he given it to her now and not on her birthday? She frowned and touched the scarf. He had a way of knowing things, the same way her aunt had. The truck had been a gift but also a message. *Best not to rely on Tiny.*

She sank gratefully onto the bench. *Everything seems so nice here, so safe.* The soft hum from the hives reverberated into her soul. The rich scent of the mountain mint and verbena, the water splashing against the stones of Flat Rock Creek, and the stir of the breeze through the leaves all lulled Rennie into a sense of well-being she hadn't felt for a long time. She reached to her neck and untied the scarf, welcoming the warm wind on her wound.

A bee dipped into a thick patch of quaker-ladies, then landed on one of its delicate flowers. "You're lucky, having this magical place as your home. I wish I could." The bee moved to a different bloom. "I'm not sure I could live with a whole hive of other bees, though. Just one husband is too much for me." She sighed. "Do bees ever get upset with each other? Or is it like having thousands of good friends around you all the time?" She watched a bee fly in an arc over a clump of wild ginger, then duck into one of its bell-shaped blossoms. "I wish I had someone to talk to. There's May Dean, of course. But she begged me not to marry Tiny. She'd just say, "I told you so." And she's so happy with Ev that I don't think she could understand just how bad a marriage can be." Her voice shook. "I could use a best friend about now. I feel so alone."

Look up.

Rennie's eyes darted around the bee yard. Was someone nearby?

She spotted Ambrose approaching. She quickly retied the scarf. Had he heard her talking to the bees? And had they just warned her to stop talking so he wouldn't think she was crazy?

"Hi there. I came to check on the hives before the rain." He looked around. "Are you alone?"

She blushed. He *had* heard her. "Hey. Just me and the bees."

"I, um, forgot something I left in the truck. See you later." With a quick wave, he strode back to the house.

Rennie slipped off the bench and walked to the hives. "Thank you for telling me to look up. It's rare I stop *before* I embarrass myself." She looked toward the path. "I wonder why he hurried off so fast."

A clouded sulphur butterfly soared by her head, and she followed it to the creek. As its yellow wings flashed through the leaves of a river birch leaning over the water, a memory of another yellow flash crossed her brain. She stared at the rocks scattered across the creek bed as she grasped for a memory.

"My uncle said I nearly drowned right here, but I've never heard about it." She turned to the house. He'd been right about the bees telling her to come find him the day he fell. Had he been right about the drowning too? Time to find out.

She stepped onto the back porch, where she was surprised to see her uncle in his rocking chair. "I thought you were taking a nap."

He shook his head. "Couldn't sleep." Looking at her scarf, he added, "Got a lot on my mind." He ran his hands along his thighs. "I'm gonna ask you something, Rennie, and I'd like an honest answer. Are you okay over there with Tiny?"

She froze. She had never lied to her uncle and wasn't

going to start. "Mostly." She shrugged. "He has a temper, but I'm managin' all right."

Uncle Dixon rocked for a moment, then said, "You know I love you and want only the best for you. Promise me you'll take care of your sweet self."

Tears clouded her eyes as she nodded. "I will."

"That truck can go plenty fast and pretty far if it needs to." He looked directly into her eyes. "You hear me, Rennie?"

She nodded. "Yes, sir." She paused for a moment and then said, "And now I want to ask you something. That day you fell, you said the bees saved me from drowning. I've never heard anything about that, though. Did it really happen?"

Dixon nodded. "Sure did. Your mama made Eugenia and me swear we wouldn't tell a soul as long as she was alive, so we didn't."

"Would you tell me now?"

He nodded. "Have a seat. This could take a minute."

CHAPTER 19

Eugenia

July 1, 1948

EUGENIA STOOD AT THE KITCHEN TABLE OF THE FARM-house Dixon had built for them as newlyweds. Almost twenty years old, the house was as tight and level as the day he first carried her over its threshold. Groupings of damp star grass, jewelweed, and mullein lay in neat piles on tea towels, waiting to be placed on screens to dry in the sun.

"Yoo-hoo, anybody home?" Irene King walked into the kitchen with a sleeping three-year-old Rennie in her arms. I was hopin' I could gather some watercress from your creek for our dinner tonight."

Eugenia's face beamed at the sight of her niece, who resembled a newly born rabbit nestled against her mother's body. "Of course." Rennie awoke, twisted in her mother's tight grasp, then reached toward her aunt. Eugenia held out her arms for the child. "May I keep Rennie with me while you work?"

Irene pulled her daughter's arms back and turned away from Eugenia. Nodding toward the plants on the table, she said, "No. She's liable to get into *your* work and make a mess."

Eugenia pretended not to hear the disdain in her sister-in-law's voice, so like the voices of the townsfolk. Trying to hide her disappointment, she busied herself by refolding an already folded tea towel. "All right, then." She smoothed the towel with her hand and asked, "How's Bobby getting along today?" Irene's husband had gone off to war in the spring of 1942 an ordinary enough man and was sent home the summer of 1945 a different man altogether, angry and volatile. His leg was badly injured, but it was his heart that would never be the same. The only bright spot in his life was his daughter, born nine months after he returned from the front.

"He's fine," Irene answered in a flat tone. "Everybody's fine." After shifting Rennie on her hip, she opened the kitchen door and headed in the direction of the creek that bordered Dixon and Eugenia's property.

Twenty minutes later, Eugenia was kneeling by a patch of sweet flag when a bee rushed to her side.

The baby is at the bottom of the creek, near the river birch.

Eugenia ran with every ounce of strength in her body, racing past Irene as she dipped her hand into the icy water for another strand of watercress. Kicking off her shoes, Eugenia dashed into the creek, swollen from recent rain. She dove to the bottom, opening her eyes to search for Rennie. Nothing. She rose to the surface, gasped for air, and dove again. This time she spotted Rennie's still body, curled up like a tiny hummingbird egg in a nest of pebbles on the creek bed. She grabbed the motionless girl and rushed her to the bank of Flat Rock Creek.

Irene stood with her mouth agape as Eugenia pumped her hands on Rennie's chest. After a terrifying minute when the crickets stopped chirping and the birds stilled their songs, Rennie spluttered, then vomited up creek water. As Rennie began to cry, Eugenia grasped her tiny body and began soothing the child. "I see the moon, the moon sees me," she sang softly. "The moon watches over us all—"

"My baby," Irene cried. She snatched Rennie from Eugenia's arms and sank to the ground, rocking back and forth. "I thought she was right beside me." She looked up. "Thank the good Lord you saw her." She smoothed Rennie's wet hair and said, "You can't breathe a word about this, not until I'm dead and buried."

Eugenia shook her head. "Dixon and I have no secrets, but I will tell no one else."

Irene gathered up her bag of watercress, and the women walked to the farmhouse. "I need to get Rennie cleaned up before Bobby gets back from town." She gripped Rennie's hand tightly and cast down her eyes. "I'm beholden to you," she said.

Eugenia watched Irene hurry to their rusted Oldsmobile, half dragging little Rennie as she tried to keep up with her mother's quick pace. As the pair drove away, Eugenia stepped into her garden and sank onto the ground, her wet clothes clinging to her small frame. Tears stood in her eyes as she considered how close they had come to losing Rennie. Despite her daily ritual of red clover tea and chasteberry tonics, Eugenia's womb had remained empty. As a way to assuage her sorrow, she had come to consider Rennie, in a way, as hers. "Thank you," she whispered to the bees crawling on the starry blooms of borage. "She is so precious to me."

The answer was swirling in the summer breeze. *And also to us.*

CHAPTER 20

ARDEN HAD WARNED RENNIE AS SHE WAS LEAVING work one Wednesday that Friday would be particularly busy. "I forgot to tell you the ROMEOs are coming for lunch. We've got forty-eight hours to prepare for the invasion."

Rennie cocked her head. "Who?"

"Really Old Men Eating Out. On the last Friday of the month, every male over the age of forty will be here, plus I swear they drag in a few more from surrounding counties. They think they're hilarious, calling theirselves ROMEOs. I'd go ahead and make a double batch of biscuits, maybe even triple." She opened the fridge and peered inside. "What dessert should we have? I've been so happy letting you handle all the sweets that I haven't even given it a thought. I really should have remembered to warn you ahead of time, and now I've put you in a pickle."

"I have an idea, Arden. Just make sure we have plenty of vanilla ice cream, and I'll take it from there." She picked up four empty water pitchers. "I'll bring these back in the morning." She grabbed her purse and the bag of leftovers. "See you tomorrow."

After the short drive to her uncle's house, she found him reading on the porch. "Hey, Rennie. What you got there?"

"I was hoping I could pick some blackberries down by the hives. I'd like to make a cobbler for the diner." She smiled. "I'll save you some, of course."

"Sure thing. Help yourself." He looked at her clothes. "Why don't you slip on one of Eugenia's long-sleeved shirts and grab my hat out of the closet? Blackberry thorns can be nasty." He pointed toward the house. "Her things are in the trunk at the foot of our bed." He smiled. "She won't mind at all."

"I'm sorry, what?"

"Eugenia is glad to loan you her shirt. If it's worrying you, though, I can tell her when she gets back from town that you've taken it."

"Uh, no. There's no need to mention it to her."

Rennie walked to the bedroom and opened her aunt's cedar chest, frowning over her uncle's confusion. A few articles of clothing were folded neatly in two stacks. She smiled at an apron she had seen her aunt wear dozens of times, then lifted a familiar cardigan to her nose. It smelled of lavender and roses, bringing memories of her aunt rushing back to her. She chose a worn chambray shirt, buttoned it, and gently closed the lid.

Her uncle's closet was neatly organized, with a half dozen identical blue plaid shirts on their hangers next to three pairs of faded overalls. A tan wool sweater and brown flannel jacket waited for cold days, while the hat she was borrowing rested on a nail. She slipped out the door and headed toward the bee yard and the blackberry bushes beyond.

She set three of the pitchers on the bench and carried the fourth one over to the masses of thorny bushes along the fence line, adjusting the hat as she walked. Bees darted in and out of the wispy broom sedge, seeming to keep a watch over Rennie as she picked the plump berries. One bee landed on her sleeve. "Have you mistaken me for a flower?" she asked gently. The bee's front legs kneaded the fabric and her antennae quivered. "Do you recognize the shirt? It was Aunt Eugenia's." The bee moved to Rennie's elbow, where a fold in the fabric covered its body like a blanket. "Can you smell her?" The bee stood motionless. "How lovely to be enveloped in her memory. Kind of like when I opened the chest." Was the bee nodding? "I miss her too."

"Hey, Rennie. I didn't know you were down here," Ambrose called from the path.

"I was just picking some blackberries. I'm making cobbler tomorrow for the Blue Plate."

He held up a second pitcher. "Need a little help?"

"That'd be great." They worked in silence, choosing the plumpest berries to add to the pitchers. After a few minutes, she eyed her full pitcher. "I've got this one done. How about yours?"

Ambrose reached for her pitcher. "I'll set these on the bench and bring the other two." She tracked his movements as he strode to the bench, but quickly dropped her gaze when he turned and caught her watching him. He walked back to Rennie holding the other pitchers. "Here you go," he said, extending his arm.

Fat berries plunked into the pitcher as she picked. "Are you feeling settled in Spark yet?"

"Mostly."

"Making friends?"

He shrugged. "I imagine *you* have a big social circle, what with you being such a good cook and your husband being a big sports star."

Rennie's eyebrows rose, and he grinned. "People love to tell me about Spark and especially about the people who live here. I've heard all about you." He frowned. "You haven't mentioned any friends, but surely you have them."

"I'm not really interested in having friends. When I was in school, kids teased me a lot, claiming my aunt Eugenia was a witch. That was such a mean thing to say, and I tried to explain she just understood the way nature can heal someone, but they wouldn't ever let it go. I asked her once if she was a witch, and of course she said no. I'm embarrassed I ever brought it up to her, and even suggesting such a thing to her is something I'll always regret." She shook her head. "She was a lovely, kind, gentle woman, not some cauldron-stirring crone, casting spells and putting curses on people." She gave a wry smile. "Although I know a couple of people who could have benefited from a curse or two."

Ambrose wiped sweat from his brow but didn't respond.

"Just because I'm an introvert, though, doesn't mean I'm against friendships for other people. Maybe *you'd* like to meet new people. How about getting involved in the church?"

"God and I aren't exactly on speaking terms right now." Ambrose looked away. "And I'm not really interested in having friends either. You trust someone, and then they find the most vicious ways to break that trust. I'm better off on my own." He dropped a few more berries into the pitcher.

"There's no pain quite like a friend who turns against you." He waved his hand. "Sorry. Just me being melodramatic."

And this is why I don't have friends. I can't even make small talk without making things awkward. "I didn't mean to pry."

"You weren't." He held up the pitcher. "Filled this up pretty quick. Do you think you have enough?"

She eyed her pitcher. "With those other two, probably. Can I get you some lemonade as a thank-you? It doesn't seem right to have you work and then not offer you anything."

He smiled. "That'd be nice."

"Great. I'll meet you at the bench."

When she returned with two glasses of lemonade, Ambrose was crouched beside one of the hives. While she knew he couldn't see her, she took a moment to admire his broad back and the way his dark curls shone in the sun. What was he doing? She watched as he nodded, then patted the side of the hive and stood. When he spotted Rennie, he walked over to her with an expression that was a mix of happiness and confusion. He grinned as he walked toward her, his green eyes shining in the afternoon sun. "I have an idea, Roberta Irene King. What if you and I were friends?"

She dipped her head but then looked up with a shy smile. "I'd like that."

"Excellent," he said. "And now that we're officially friends, you let me know if I can ever help you." His dimple was deep as a crater on the moon. "That's what friends are for."

As Rennie parked the truck back on Beasley Court, she heard her husband's booming voice drifting through the open window. "I'll just tell her what I did about Rex, that it's a dog's instinct to go off on their own to die." A pause. "She bought it once, why not again?" Another pause. "Archer doesn't have any available yet, but that dog bit me, so she's lost the right to live. She's been eating my food and napping in the sun like she owns the place, all while she lets foxes get my chickens. She'll see who's boss around here. Turn on me and you pay with your life."

Rennie was lightheaded, and she sank to the ground.

"I've been wantin' to try my pawpaw's old shotgun. I can get some shells when I go into Putney Saturday afternoon to pick up some Early Times and cigarettes, then do it Sunday." His chuckle chilled Rennie's blood. "Seems fitting to send her to heaven on the Lord's day." He snorted at whatever was being said on the other end of the phone. "Naw, she believes whatever I tell her. One of the reasons I married her. No gumption means no questions. And no questions means I can do as I damn well please."

Rennie had been frozen to the ground, but as soon as she realized Tiny was hanging up the phone, she rose, quietly backed up to the truck, and gingerly opened its door. With shaking legs, she climbed back into the cab. Rex was his parents' German shepherd that had disappeared during their senior year of high school. Rennie had wanted to search for him, but Tiny and his father had both told her Rex was gone, that a dog recognized when it was dying and separated itself from the pack. Her stomach clenched as she realized the truth. Rex *hadn't* gone off to die. They had killed him. And now Tiny was talking about doing the same to Jane Austen. He had been irritated about her not protecting the chickens, but with that bite to his calf, she had sealed her fate.

Rennie leaned her head against the steering wheel as she frantically searched for a way to save her dog. She needed an idea fast and didn't know what she was going to do yet, but the one thing she *did* know was that getting her uncle's truck was the start of her plan. She tapped on the horn to get Tiny's attention, hopped out of the truck, and loudly slammed the door. "Tiny, I'm home," she called. "Get in. We're going to my uncle's to pick up my truck."

That night as Tiny snored, Rennie slipped out of bed and padded to the kitchen. She poured herself a glass of water and headed for the back porch. The night air was warm as Rennie rocked, Jane Austen at her feet. The cicadas whirred, mimicking her own agitated brain as she puzzled out her plan. Jane Austen had to vanish. Taking her to her uncle's or May Dean's was too risky. If Tiny caught sight of the dog, there would be hell to pay for deceiving him. She needed somewhere Tiny would never go but a place she could visit. After several tense minutes of rocking and pondering, she had formulated a plan. "It might work," she whispered. "It all depends on Ambrose."

CHAPTER 21

HE HEARD HER ASKING THE BEES FOR A FRIEND, SOMEthing he also needs desperately for himself. He wanted to suggest a friendship but panicked, rushing back to his truck like a scared rabbit. The plan will never work if he cannot befriend her.

Taking the opportunity to speak with him while she was fetching the refreshments was wise. It begins with a friendship, so he must allow his heart to have a friend. Such a simple task on its surface but so difficult for him to do. Our reminder of Eugenia's words to him all those years ago brought a smile to his face that was lovely to see. He was able to broach the topic of a friendship, and she has accepted. A happy day indeed.

There are sparks between them as bright as our own. It has begun.

Do not become too enraptured with a love story when we have a life story to work out first.

CHAPTER 22

Rennie untied her apron and hung it on the hook by the refrigerator. "Arden, would it be all right if I took one of my homemade moon pies?"

"Sure, hon."

When she pulled up to Ambrose's house, he was tending the roses growing on the trellis. A few bees floated in and out of the blooms, and their presence instantly eased her anxiety. Ambrose put down his pruning shears as she got out of the truck.

He gave her a smile, and Rennie tried hard not to fall into that dimple. "Hey there. Is everything okay with Dixon?"

"Um, yes, as far as I know. I'm headed there next, but I was hoping I could talk to you first."

"Sure thing." He wiped his hands on his pants. "What's up?"

"You said we were friends now and to let you know if I needed anything."

He nodded. "That's right. Why don't we go inside and we can talk about it."

"It didn't take me long to need something." She handed him the moon pie. "Here's a bribe."

"I don't need to be bought off to help you, but that does look delicious." He held the screen door open and led her to the back deck. "Let me get us some lemonade. We can share this gorgeous treat, and then you can tell me what's so important."

After he handed Rennie a glass, she took a long sip and began her story. "When we first moved back to Spark, I found a dog. Tiny calls her Spot, but her real name is Jane Austen."

"Lewis Carroll, Jane Austen." He nodded solemnly. "I'm sensing a pattern here."

"I was reading *Alice in Wonderland* when Lewis Carroll showed up. And my favorite writer is Jane Austen. Her books are so lovely and elegant, so far from the life that sweet dog had endured. I was hoping I could make her world beautiful again, so I gave her a head start with her name." She took a bite of moon pie. "I wasn't kidding about always reading instead of being with other kids."

She continued with her story, skimming over why Jane Austen had bitten Tiny, but the way Ambrose's face changed told Rennie he'd figured it out. "So after that bite, he called the Archers and arranged to buy one of their pups." Her voice shook. "He's going to shoot Jane Austen on Sunday." She gulped. "I can't let that happen. I have to hide her." She debated telling this next part, but saving Jane Austen was worth the embarrassment. "On Saturday nights, if there's a baseball game on the radio, Tiny sits on the back porch and listens while he drinks whiskey till he's blackout drunk, which means he'd never hear my truck start up. The Braves are playing, so he'll be glued to the radio. I know this is short notice and a lot to ask, but can I bring her here Saturday night after Tiny's gone to bed, to hide her until I can find her a permanent home?

"No."

Rennie bowed her head. "I understand."

"No, you don't. Bring Jane Austen to me, Rennie, but not to hide her. To bring her to her new home. My farm is so far off the road, Tiny will never spot her."

"You'll take her?" Her voice caught in her throat. "Oh, thank you."

"There's no need to thank me. As of yesterday, we're officially friends, Rennie, and I'll always do my best to help you. Tell me what you've got so far, and let's see if we can figure out the rest."

Ambrose listened, nodding thoughtfully as she explained. After she outlined her plan, he said, "We need to minimize the amount of time you're away from your house. I'll meet you at the Baptist church at midnight. That's the closest building to your house with a parking lot. Pull around to the back so no one driving by can see you. Don't bring her food or her blanket or anything else. It's going to have to look like Jane Austen has simply vanished. Listen, Rennie, this is going to work. You've saved her."

"Not yet." She choked back tears. "I am so grateful for the chance, though."

"Hey, I'm just helping out a friend." His voice was as soft as the sunlight that surrounded them.

She opened her arms to hug him but then froze. What would he think of something so forward? She changed her arm movement to point awkwardly toward the driveway. "I'm going to check on Uncle Dixon, then I'll get the plan started."

Ambrose followed her out to the truck. She was about to drive away when he put his hand on her arm through the open window.

"Wait," he said.

The warmth of his touch seared her skin, and she could feel her cheeks redden.

"The dome light." He pointed inside the truck. "Unscrew it so it won't come on when you open the door. It could catch his attention."

"Good thinking," she said, trying to will her heart to stop beating so fast. As she drove away, she could still feel the warmth of his hand on her arm.

༝

Arden surveyed the counter brimming with food. "I think we've got enough chicken for all the ROMEOs, and you've made plenty of blackberry cobbler. The turnip greens and mashed potatoes are done, and the tea is ready, so we just need the biscuits. Why don't you get started on those, and Dixie and I'll get the tables ready." She paused. "I've been excited to tell you this since yesterday. A man who owns a restaurant in Nashville came for dinner to try your food after his brother kept raving about it. He said to tell you your corn bread was divine, and he fell *out* over your banana pudding."

"That's quite a compliment." Arms full of buttermilk bottles, she shut the refrigerator door with her hip. "All the way from Nashville," she said, setting the bottles on the counter.

"He left me his card. It's in the drawer by the register."

Rennie pulled out the card and read:

Alan's
Southern Food at Its Finest
Since 1953

All the way from Nashville, Rennie mused as she returned the card to its place in the drawer.

Sheriff Ricketts was the first ROMEO to arrive. "Hey, Arden," he said. "Lookin' forward to Rennie's good cooking." He grinned. "Don't go tellin' Barb I said so, but Rennie's is the best I've ever had." He took his customary seat where he could see both the front door and out onto Market Street. "When you figure Betty's comin' back?"

"Her mama's healing up pretty well. She should be back soon, but I'll hate losing Rennie."

The door opened, and several more ROMEOs came inside. The next thirty minutes were a flurry of activity as Arden and Dixie waited on the forty or so men in the Blue Plate. Dixie stepped into the kitchen. "Hey, Rennie, one of the fellas dumped over a whole pitcher of tea. I need to mop it up, and table two is askin' for more biscuits. Would you mind takin' them over there when they're ready?"

"Sure, no problem," Rennie said.

When the biscuits were out of the oven, Rennie transferred them to a platter and walked into the dining room. As she approached a table, she saw a group of six men engrossed in conversation. She slipped into a narrow hallway leading to the storage area when she realized her husband was their topic.

"He bragged he was talkin' with a scout for another ball team, but that was almost a year ago."

Another man chugged his tea, then said, "When we was over at the Moonshine Lounge drinking, he told me he only has one more season of tobacco farming left since he's doin' so well with his investment in that bar. Of course, he was sloshin' full of his Early Times."

A third man chimed in. "We've all heard his get-rich-quick schemes, but I think he's finally got hisself a solid plan."

The first man asked, "And what's that?"

"The only things you can count on are death and taxes. And nobody's ever gotten rich offa taxes."

"What are you talkin' about, Hal?"

"Mr. Big Shot's missus is the niece of that crazy old man, the one that was married to the witch. Tiny's wife is all teed up to inherit his farm, and Tiny'll turn right around and sell it. He figures the old goat'll be gone in six months, tops."

Another voice chimed in. "Y'all are listening to the wrong Hendricks. Wayne told me he's fixin' to evict his son and daughter-in-law for not payin' him the rent. He's got somebody interested in buying the place and is gonna sell. You know how the Hendricks men are, tighter'n ticks with their money. Tiny begged off when the baby was coming, but, well, things are different now, and the old man said Tiny's gotta pay up or pack up. Blood is thicker'n water, but I guess a thick wad of cash beats it all."

"I heard his wife gotta job right here in the diner. She's probably in the back, cooking all our food. Shouldn't that help?"

"Not enough, I guess."

Rennie was rooted to the floor.

Arden approached with a worried look across her face. "Why are you in the hallway? Those biscuits are gettin' cold." When Rennie didn't move, Arden took them from her hands. "Why don't you get on back in the kitchen? The cobbler smells like it's done."

Rennie numbly finished cooking for the ROMEOs, but her mind was spinning. After that incident with his father coming to the house to demand money, Tiny had sworn he had gotten current on the rent, but that was obviously a lie. She picked up her paycheck and her envelope with the five-dollar bill in it and tucked them in her purse. She had first resisted hiding that extra money, but now she was grateful for it. As she walked to her truck, she wondered just how soon she'd need it.

CHAPTER 23

RENNIE PARKED IN HER UNCLE'S DRIVEWAY AND LET herself inside. "Uncle Dixon," she called.

"In here," he answered in a weak voice.

She went into his bedroom, a look of concern on her face. "Are you okay? Can I bring you some water?"

"I'm all right," he said, though his pale face told a different story. "Just thinkin' about my Eugenia. Today is our anniversary, June 27th." He struggled to sit up. "Would you like to hear how we met?"

"I'd love that." She stepped toward the bed and asked, "Could I bring the maple rocker you made in here? The one in my old bedroom? It reminds me of rocking with Aunt Eugenia, and I'd love to use it when I sit in here with you."

"Of course. I just wish I was strong enough to carry it for you."

"I've got it, don't worry."

After she returned with the rocker, he resumed his story. "It was springtime and a buddy of mine in Kentucky had asked me to come up there to help build a house for him and his new missus, so I went. I was a bachelor and had pretty much given up on ever finding a bride."

"I couldn't imagine you ever giving up on anything."

"The good Lord had someone chosen for me, I was sure of it, but I could not for the life of me figure out where she was at. I reckoned she'd have to be the one to find me 'cause I'd run out of places to look, although I still asked the Lord every night to send me my wife. He let my prayer go unanswered for a long time. Until the day of the church homecoming."

Uncle Dixon paused, and the sweetest smile crept across his lips when he resumed his story. "Everybody who'd ever attended that church was invited to a special sermon and then dinner on the grounds. My buddy asked me to join him for the celebration. I had no sooner finished my prayer about showing me my bride when something amazing happened."

"What was it?" Rennie sat forward.

"You know how the air changes right before a summer thunderstorm? When it stops feeling thick and heavy, and gets all full of energy instead?"

"Yes."

"I was in that pew and my skin kind of lifted up, the air in the church got electric, and I knew my life was going to change. I could feel her, Rennie. Before I ever set my eyes on her, I could feel her presence. God was telling me, 'Well, you've sure been patient, Dixon. Turn around and meet your wife.'"

"You knew she was there without seeing her?" Rennie asked.

Uncle Dixon nodded. "I twisted around to look behind

me, and there she was, smiling, like she was saying, 'Yep, it's me.' She was sitting beside one of the men helping out with the house we were building, George McDonald, but she was a stranger to me. Well, that's not exactly true. I didn't recognize her face, but I knew her heart. I understood right then that she was my wife but that we just hadn't met yet."

"I've heard of love at first sight but never love *before* first sight."

Uncle Dixon chuckled. "She put out her hand and said, 'My name is Eugenia McDonald.' What's the proper way to greet your wife for the first time? I finally said, 'I'm Dixon King. I'm glad to finally meet you.' Which I realize was silly, because she didn't know I'd been waiting on her all those years. But it turns out she did know." Tears sparkled in his eyes. "Are you sure this isn't boring you?"

"This may be the best story I have ever heard in my life. Please tell me what happened next, if you're not too tired."

"Right after the service was the picnic. Eugenia told me she needed to fetch her chess pies, and that she hoped we could talk at the dinner."

"And did you?"

"By the time she got to the picnic area with her basket, a group of fellas three deep was clustered around her, like bees drawn to the sweetest flower in the garden. I figured I'd have to wait my turn to even get to speak to her. But then she looked up and met my eyes."

"What happened next?"

"She excused herself from all those fellas and headed straight for me. 'Why, there you are, Dixon. I've been waiting for you.' I said, 'And I've been waiting for you.' She never asked what in the world did I mean. It's like she knew same as me that we had finally found each other."

"How soon were you engaged?"

"It was a few weeks until I asked her to marry me. We went for a stroll one night, when the biggest, fullest moon you ever saw was shining almost as bright as the sun. We rested from our walk on the garden bench that you and I have been sitting on out by the hives."

Rennie's hand flew to her chest. "That's so romantic."

Uncle Dixon's eyes misted. "I said, 'Eugenia, I never thought I would be blessed with a companion I could love and cherish the rest of my life. I had given up, figuring the good Lord had other plans for me. And then he sent me to that church because you were there.' Her face looked like an angel's as I confessed what was on my heart."

His voice grew huskier as he continued. "Then I took both her hands in mine. 'Eugenia, that day was called a homecoming, and I *did* come home that day. Home to you. You would make me the happiest man in the world if I could spend the rest of my life coming home to you. Will you do me the honor of becoming my wife?'"

"And she said yes?"

He nodded. "She did, and I kissed her right on the lips there in the moonlight. I'll never forget the day we went into Knoxville and picked out her wedding band. I was the proudest man in the world, buying the ring that would show the world this perfect woman was my wife. And when I slipped it on her finger, I'm not ashamed to admit I was crying." Dixon dabbed his eyes. "It never left her finger the whole time we were married, and it's my most cherished possession. It's in her dresser, in the top drawer. I aim for you to have it after I'm gone."

"What a treasure." Her uncle looked drawn and paler than she liked. "Can I get you anything? Something to eat or drink?"

"Not a thing, sweet girl. You're clucking over me just like Eugenia used to do. Have I ever shown you her photograph?"

She froze. She had never seen any pictures of her aunt, who had died when she was seven, and the memories of her appearance had faded. "You have a picture of her?"

"I do. Open the top right drawer of Eugenia's dresser. There's a Bible in there on the left-hand side." Under some letters, she found the black leather book with the name Eugenia McDonald stamped in gold on the cover.

"Turn to Proverbs 3, verses 5 and 6."

Rennie's hand was shaking as she thumbed through the tissue-thin pages of the Bible. There between the pages was a faded sepia photograph.

Looking down at the photo, she studied the young woman peering back at her. She had a sweet face, the kind you want to describe as angelic. Her hair was light, loosely woven into a long braid. Her simple dress was modest but did not hide her beautiful figure. Her head barely reached her husband's shoulders.

"Her eyes," Rennie said. "They're so kind. I can't remember, were they blue?"

"No, green. The color of a bells of Ireland blossom. That's why I have them planted by the porch, so I can feel like she's looking over me when I sit out there."

Rennie returned her gaze to the photo. Uncle Dixon stood proudly beside his wife, strong and full of life. His face was so familiar yet new to her at the same time. He looked younger, healthier than she ever remembered seeing him. He wore one of his signature plaid shirts, which made her smile. His shirts hung off his too-small frame these days, but in the photo the shirt fit him well.

"A few days after we were married, we attended the county fair. A photographer had a booth set up, and we decided to get our picture made. It was a pretty big deal back then, and we was poor as church mice, but we were so in love and wanted a memento of that day. I am so thankful we decided to spend the money. That's the only picture I have of her. It seems the older I get, the more I feel her absence." A tear rolled down his wrinkled cheek. "The picture reminded me of how much I missed her, so I put it away. I tucked it in Eugenia's Bible, by the only verse that helped me through her death. 'Trust in the Lord with all thine heart; and lean not unto thine own understanding. In all thy ways acknowledge him, and he shall direct thy paths.' That verse tells me it's okay I don't understand. I'm not supposed to."

"I need to remember that. There's so much I don't understand."

Her uncle nodded. "We thought we had our whole lives ahead of us, but we managed to fit a lifetime of happiness into the years we were given."

She studied the photograph, feeling the love emanating from the young couple. "Why don't we keep this out? I could put it in a frame for you so you could look at it all the time."

"Put it in the Bible and back in the drawer, please. I don't need the picture anymore. I get to see the real Eugenia now. She visits me to tell me we'll be together soon."

Rennie's eyes shot toward her uncle's weathered face. She'd heard of deathbed visits from deceased loved ones, but she couldn't bear the thought of losing her uncle. *This isn't about me. Don't be selfish.* "I'm glad she comes to see you. That must make your heart happy."

"It does. More than you know." He yawned. "I think I'll have a little nap."

She touched her own hastily chosen wedding ring, the cheapest one in the Sears display case. "I'd better get on home to Tiny." As she walked to the truck, she thought of how deeply her uncle loved his farm, and, thanks to the ROMEOs, how eager she knew her husband was to sell it.

CHAPTER 24

A GOOD LOVE STORY IS A BALM FOR THE SOUL.

So few mortals understand the concept of eternal love, but those two do.

We were right to tell her to attend that homecoming.

Matchmaking is technically not our purpose, but when viewed through the lens of facilitating a human's rightful path, our involvement becomes more understandable.

Did she ever tell him we sent her to the homecoming?

She said to him on their wedding day: "My heart told me to come to the church that day, Dixon King, and I will spend the rest of my life grateful that I listened."

So she did not mention the bees?

Are we not her heart?

CHAPTER 25

SATURDAY MORNINGS WERE ALWAYS BUSY IN SPARK. Ladies were doing their weekly shopping on Market Street, picking up their groceries at the BuyMore, or filling a prescription at Strickland's. Anyone in need of housewares could likely find something suitable at what used to be called Jarvis Emporium, but once Grady Neal became the owner, was simply known as the Emporium. The Wishee-Washee was filled with neighbors who washed, dried, and folded the day away as their children wrested orange Nehis from the metal drink machine with coins cajoled from their mothers. Command central, though, would always be the Curly Q, where any Spark lady could get her hair shampooed and set plus be brought up to speed on gossip all in one appointment.

The day was hot and sultry with the kind of humidity that could make you tired just thinking about going outside. As she drove to the diner, Rennie rubbed her stiff neck, confident the aspirin she had swallowed with her tea wouldn't dull her headache. She reminded herself that her whole day had to be normal, with no deviation from her typical activities, if she was to be successful with her plan to save Jane Austen. She must strictly adhere to her routine, ensuring Tiny wouldn't suspect a thing.

When Rennie opened the door to the diner, the blast of icy air was a blessed relief, and she took a moment to stand in front of the window unit as it churned out frigid air. She was sweating, and not just from the hot day.

Arden was taping space-themed posters to the front window, entries in the contest she was sponsoring for Spark Elementary third graders. First prize was a free dinner for the winner's family, and the competition was fierce. Customers placed their vote in a fishbowl after they paid for a meal. The leading candidate depicted the *Apollo 11* liftoff, with children from all over the globe clasping hands around the rocket. Close behind was a poster of a grinning Neil Armstrong standing on the surface of the moon, shaking hands with an alien.

Despite staying busy cooking for hungry diners all morning, the day dragged. Rennie had been up most of the night worrying about Jane Austen, reviewing the details a dozen times in her head. She felt the plan to save her dog was both flawless and doomed. Wasn't that how every crime drama on TV turned out? The criminal's downfall was always a seemingly insignificant but crucial overlooked detail.

She had burned a pan full of sausage and dropped a carton of eggs on the linoleum floor, breaking all twelve. When an unhappy customer sent his pot roast back, Arden came into the kitchen.

"What's goin' on, sweetie? Is it Tiny?"

Rennie looked up from a tray of flat biscuits. "I-I didn't

sleep well last night. That's all." She pointed to the plate of food in Arden's hands. "I'll remake that."

"I'll do it. Why don't you go home early today?"

"No!" *No deviation from the norm.* Panic filled her throat. "I mean, no thanks. Let me redo that plate, and I'll make another batch of biscuits."

Arden studied her face with a frown. "Tell you what. Let's do it together."

———

As Rennie was clearing the dishes from the supper she had served Tiny, which she had placed on the table at exactly six o'clock, he opened a cabinet and grabbed a glass and a fresh bottle of whiskey. He pushed the cabinet closed with his elbow. "So I was thinking, why don't you go to your uncle's and make him a big Sunday breakfast. I bet he'd love some of your waffles and bacon for a change."

So it's true. Tiny was well-known for being more talk than action, but he was going through with his plan to kill Jane Austen the next morning. She cranked on the kitchen faucet to drown out what had to be the audible sound of her heart beating out of her chest. With as even a tone as she could muster, she answered carefully. "That's a great idea. I'll call him right after I finish the dishes."

"All right, then." Tiny stepped onto the porch, letting a blast of still-hot air into the room. He flipped on the radio and settled in for a long night of alcohol and baseball.

Rennie was scrubbing the kitchen sink when the sound of country music wafted through the window. Her shoulders stiffened. *What happened to his game?*

He opened the screen door. "Forgot my cigarettes."

She tried to keep her voice light. "I thought I heard music. Is your game not on?"

"It's a damn rain delay. No tellin' when they'll have the game back on."

Ambrose was expecting her to be in that parking lot at midnight. How could she alert him to the change? Beads of sweat dotted her upper lip. Calling Ambrose and claiming she was phoning her uncle was too risky. So was asking her uncle to get a message to Ambrose. She rubbed her tight shoulders. Would Ambrose wait for her or give up and go back home, thinking the plan was off? After Tiny fell asleep, she could drive to Ambrose's house, but that would add to the time she was gone, giving Tiny more of an opportunity to wake up and realize she was missing. Her stomach twisted. Jane Austen's life depended on her.

Her uncle answered on the third ring. "Hey, it's Rennie. I thought you might enjoy a home-cooked breakfast tomorrow morning. How about I come by to make you waffles and bacon?"

"You don't have to do that."

"I know, but I'd love to cook breakfast for you. Is nine o'clock okay?"

"Sounds perfect. You're sweet to take care of me so well."

She spoke the next words slowly and deliberately, silently wishing she could ask her uncle to pass along the message to Ambrose. "Oh, I might be late. Tiny's game has a rain delay, so our schedule is a little off. I'll still be there, though, I promise." As she hung up the receiver, she hoped that if Ambrose called her uncle, he would recount their conversation.

At 11:00 p.m., Tiny was still on the porch, yelling at the radio. *At least the rain delay is over.* Rennie lay in bed and watched the clock hands tick to midnight as Tiny continued to shout. Ambrose was looking for her behind the church, and she was a no-show. *Please wait, Ambrose.*

At around 1:30 a.m., Tiny finally fell into bed. He was snoring shortly afterward, but she was afraid to move too soon. After what seemed like an eternity, his snoring became steady. It was time. She slipped from the bed and tiptoed out of the room, then held her breath as she gingerly opened the porch door, glancing behind her for any sign of her husband. Stepping onto the back porch, she changed into the clothes she had stashed behind a chair when Tiny went to check on the chickens. As she zipped her pants, she checked behind her again. Nothing. She slowly opened both doors of the truck, silently thanking Ambrose for thinking of the dome light, and then went to the doghouse next to the hens' enclosure.

Jane Austen was asleep on her blanket. "Wake up, girl," Rennie whispered. Jane Austen raised her head and squinted at Rennie. "Come on, sweetie," Rennie cajoled. As the half-asleep Jane Austen struggled out of the doghouse, Rennie scooped her in her arms and placed her in the truck.

The engine had never sounded so robust, and Rennie nervously looked toward the farmhouse. No telltale light to indicate Tiny was up. Once safely on Beasley Court, she sped toward the church and Ambrose. She reached over and stroked her dog's head as she drove. "Do you remember when I told you I would take care of you and always keep you safe?" She rubbed Jane Austen's velvety ears as she drove. "You're going to live with Ambrose Beckett, but

I'll visit you all the time. He's a nice man—" Her cheeks flushed as she remembered the feel of his hand on her arm. "He's a nice man who's helping me keep that promise to you. It's not safe for you to be around Tiny." As she drove, she pondered how those last words applied to her too. She wasn't safe either.

She pulled into the church parking lot, cutting her lights as she drove around to the back. Tears pricked her eyes when she spotted Ambrose pacing outside his truck. *He waited.* Relief flooded his face when he saw her. As soon as Rennie turned off the engine, Ambrose opened the passenger door. "I was so worried. Did Tiny see you?"

"I don't think so. There was a rain delay, and I couldn't call, and I was so afr—"

He lifted his hand. "Shhh. It's okay. I told you I'd be here." His voice was low, and his smile looked a little lopsided in the moonlight. "I was going to wait all night if I had to." He gently moved Jane Austen from Rennie's truck to his own. "I went into town yesterday and bought dog food, then got her a dog bed and bowls at the Emporium." He glanced at his watch. "You need to get back." Shutting the door with his hip, he added, "I didn't sleep at all last night, worrying how this was going to go." Ambrose ran his hands through his dark curls. "Here's the thing. I know we said we wouldn't deviate from the plan, but I've got to know if you make it home safe. I came up with a signal. Is your porch light usually on or off?"

"Off, unless we're sitting out there or expecting someone."

"When you get home, if Tiny's still asleep, turn the porch light on. I'll drive by there ten minutes after you leave this parking lot. If the light's on, I'll keep driving, but if it's off, I'm comin' in."

"Tiny would kill you if you showed up at our house."

"And he'd kill *you* if he's found out what we're up to. Light on, everything's fine. Light off, I'm comin' in."

"Thank you, Ambrose."

Tears slipped down her cheeks as she drove home. She had saved Jane Austen and would never have to worry about her safety again. Her troubles weren't over, though. There was a chance the truck engine had woken Tiny, and he could be on the back porch right now, waiting for her to return. She chewed her lip. No plausible story had come to her to account for her outing, and just hoping Tiny hadn't noticed her absence didn't seem like much of a plan. That was all she had, though. She shuddered. A fight between Ambrose and Tiny would be a nightmare.

As she crested the hill of Beasley Court, she cut the motor and glided into her driveway. The porch light was off, a good sign. After gently closing the truck door, she crept back inside the house. Tiny's rhythmic snores were audible from the doorway. She flipped on the porch light and watched moths dart around the yellow bulb as she changed back into her nightgown, then slipped into bed beside her sleeping husband.

The next morning, Rennie was buttoning her blouse when Tiny came into their bedroom, frowning. "Have you seen Spot?"

She painted a worried look on her face. "She wasn't in her doghouse?"

"No, and she's not in the yard either. Maybe we should go look for her."

"Oh, gosh. I hope she's not hurt." Rennie made sure to add a little panic to her voice. "Could she have gotten trapped in the barn?"

"Already checked there."

The pair circled the farm, calling for Spot. They walked the fence line and checked under the porch. No Spot.

Tiny dropped into his rocking chair. "It's not like her to wander."

Rennie nodded. "I need to get to Uncle Dixon's to fix his breakfast, but when I get back, we'll search again." She opened the screen door, picked up her purse, and stared at her husband. "I just had a terrible thought. Maybe she's gone off to die, like with your parents' dog, Rex. Remember, you told me it was a dog's instinct to separate themselves from the others when it was their time. I have a feeling our sweet Spot is gone." She conjured a weak sob. "I bet she'll never come back."

"Could be right," Tiny grumbled as he headed to the field.

CHAPTER 26

A JOYFUL DAY! SHE HAS REMOVED HER ANIMAL FROM harm's way and taught herself she can defy the varlet.
  One success will beget another.
  Courage to her as she proceeds. She will need it.

CHAPTER 27

RENNIE STEPPED BAREFOOT ONTO THE SOFT GRASS and walked to her little garden growing pumpkins, sunflowers, and peanuts. The plants were flourishing, despite their late start. Glancing in the hackberry tree, she spotted Poe, who seemed to be watching her. *He's very interested in making sure his food is coming along.* She knelt and touched the light green leaves, marveling at their softness. Out of habit, she glanced toward Jane Austen's kennel when she started toward the house. The cedar house remained empty, even as Tiny talked about Jane Austen's replacement, "one that will protect our chickens, not some reject from the side of the road." The thought of Jane Austen safe and likely snoozing on Ambrose's sofa brought a smile to her lips. *I set a goal and accomplished it.*

She ambled back to the porch, relishing the warm morning, and shook seeds from the coffee can onto the rusted enamelware plate. A slight breeze blew through the roses, scenting the air as she searched the skies for Poe, who had left the hackberry tree. A rare sense of well-being enveloped her. With help from her talks with her uncle down at the hives, she had transitioned from an immobilizing numbness over Gabriel's death into a type of mourning that allowed her to be grateful for his life, even as she still cried over his loss. She felt her body healing as she breathed in the air fanned by thousands of bee wings and hoped she would be well enough to conceive again, giving her another chance at the child she wanted so desperately.

Over two weeks had passed since Ambrose had taken in Jane Austen, who was thriving under his care. Her only worry was her uncle, who was fading before her eyes. His moments of confusion had advanced from momentary slips to daily occurrences, as his appetite dwindled from eating regularly to rarely being interested in food. The week prior, she had found a bottle of milk on the pantry shelf and a pair of socks in the oven. Mercifully, it wasn't on, but the chance of a fire was a real concern. Once, Rennie had let herself in and heard his thready voice coming from his bedroom. She had assumed he had a visitor, although the driveway was empty when she pulled up.

"Won't that be glorious, Eugenia? To be with you again will be my greatest joy."

She recognized she was intruding on an intimate moment, so she slipped his dinner into the fridge and quietly got back in her truck and returned to the farmhouse on Beasley Court.

A sharp *caw* from the hackberry tree alerted her to Poe's presence. He swooped from a branch, something shiny in his beak. Rennie squinted. A metal button. Poe's eyes met Rennie's as he dropped the disk onto the plate, then scooped up a few seeds. As he flew off, Rennie put the button in the mug with her other treasures.

Ev and May Dean had invited her and Tiny to dinner that night, and not wanting to arrive empty-handed, she decided to bring a dessert. Although Tiny had groused about May Dean's inedible cooking, he had agreed to go. "We'll eat on their dime, not ours."

During her most recent visit with Uncle Dixon, she had talked about her job cooking for the Blue Plate and mentioned how making the desserts was her favorite task. "I've done cobblers, pies, and enough banana pudding to fill the entire Spark reservoir. I'd love to come up with something new, something my customers aren't expecting."

Dixon had nodded to a long row of honey jars on his kitchen counter. "Why don't you take those and see what you can dream up? I asked Ambrose to get them down from the shelves. I'd rather people enjoy them than have them just gather dust." He pointed out the window. "And that doesn't even count what I have stored in the barn."

The jars in the BuyMore bag her uncle had given her rattled all the way home, and she fretted one would break. She breathed a sigh of relief when she unloaded them from the bag and saw they were all intact.

As she stood in the kitchen trying to decide what to bake, she pulled salt, flour, and baking powder from the shelf. A shaft of sunlight shone through the window, illuminating the glass jars of honey on the counter. She picked up one of the containers and lifted it into the sun. The glow from the amber liquid reminded her of something—what was it? Of course. The light. The honey radiated the same luminosity she had seen being emitted from the bees. It had taken a while, but she had finally realized they were shepherding her, and she was grateful. She turned back to her baking with renewed energy. The honey would be the star of the cake, honoring the bees.

Reaching inside her cabinet, she pulled out the rest of her baking supplies. It had been so long since she'd had the desire to prepare something for herself rather than the Blue Plate, and handling the wooden spoon and measuring cups reminded her why she chose baking as her way to be happy. Without really thinking about it, she began measuring and stirring, sifting and folding. Eggs from her hens, with their rich golden yolks, turned the batter a warm yellow. Holding the jar of honey in her hands, she poured it into the batter, letting her heart tell her when to stop. She buttered and floured her mother's old cake pans, poured in the rich batter, and set them in the oven.

As the baking cakes filled the kitchen with a welcoming scent of honey and vanilla, she began the frosting. Unsalted butter, confectioner's sugar, and a splash of cream went into a bowl, followed by another generous pour of honey. As she mixed the ingredients, a shiny, silky concoction began to form, perfect for the fluffy cakes rising in the oven.

The screen door banged closed as Tiny entered the kitchen. He watched Rennie drizzling honey across the white frosting. "A whole cake for four people? Seems like a waste."

"It's my way of saying thank you for them having us to dinner."

"What time are we supposed to be there?"

"Six o'clock." She nestled the cake inside a Tupperware carrier. "So we need to leave in about twenty minutes."

Ev and May Dean's white brick house on Redbud Lane was small but charming, anchored on either end by enormous boxwoods planted by Ev's grandfather, with a bay window, gabled roof, and circular drive. Confederate jasmine twisted up the old mailbox, while white Annabelle hydrangeas lined the herringbone brick walkway. Neat stacks of lumber and bricks sat by the partially built addition they were putting on for the new baby.

Rennie looked down at her shapeless blue shift when May Dean opened the door wearing a billowy white dress. Her cousin had a way of eternally appearing like the subject of a photo shoot, while Rennie looked ready to pull cutworms off tobacco stalks. She thought of the elegant black blouse hidden under the bed as she stepped inside with Tiny following behind her.

May Dean eyed the Tupperware carrier. "What have you brought us, Rennie? Something divine, I'm sure."

"A cake. I made up the recipe this afternoon."

"What are you calling it?" she asked as she took the cake from her cousin. "Your cute names are just so darling."

She hadn't thought to name the cake, but it seemed appropriate. With one glance at the fluffy white frosting, it came to her immediately. "It's called a Honey Moon Cake."

"Perfect. I just love how everything is space-themed these days. Did you see the latest 'Moon Mission Fun Facts' column in the *Gazette*?" She picked up the paper from the kitchen counter and read:

Great Gertie's Girdle!

The company famous for Playtex bras and girdles is in charge of creating the astronauts' space suits. Seems all the big manufacturing companies were lacking one essential ingredient when it came time to construct the space suits—a woman's touch. After a nationwide search, NASA realized something ladies have known for years: nothing is more indestructible than a Playtex garment. A special team of seamstresses put the lingerie aside and handmade the 21-layer suits, designed to survive any conditions.

She looked up. "It seems a little scandalous to be discussing ladies' unmentionables in the paper, but it's interesting that out of all those big companies competing to make the space suits, NASA chose ladies who make bras and girdles all day to sew the most important garments ever worn." She set the paper back on the counter. "Not counting Jesus' robes, or any for the apostles, of course." She paused. "And Mother Mary's dresses, and whatever John the Baptist had on, and . . . Well, anyway, the space suits are important."

May Dean dropped ice cubes into four glasses. "I made lemonade."

Tiny frowned. "Don't you have any whiskey?"

Rennie noticed the look Ev and May Dean exchanged. May Dean turned to her husband. "Darlene brought us a little bottle when you had that bad cough last year. Why don't you pour Tiny a glass, Ev?" She pointed to the countdown calendar on their refrigerator. "Can you believe it's only two days till liftoff? And then just four days after that those men land on the moon. Brother Cleave has us praying every night for a safe trip." She turned to Rennie. "We'd love for you all to join us one Sunday. The sermons have been inspiring, all about hope and the power of believing in what is possible. Brother Cleave is devoting the whole service to the astronauts on the 20th. Maybe you could come to that one. I think the astronauts picked a Sunday to land because they know every church in the country will be praying—"

Tiny interrupted. "I don't need a lecture, May Dean. You know I don't believe in church any more than I believe in this so-called moon landing." He downed his drink. After the ice hit his teeth, he added, "They're both fake, dreamed up by the government to fool people."

May Dean's shoulders stiffened, but she didn't answer Tiny. Instead, she turned to Rennie. "Would you like to see how the builders are comin' along? Ev's sister in Atlanta is going to stay with us when her husband gets sent to Vietnam, so she'll be here when the baby comes. Honestly, I'm thankful she'll be here to help me with the baby. I have no idea what I'm doing. The doctor keeps giving me pamphlets, but I don't think they're going to help. We're building a nursery so everybody will have their own room. I hate the idea of anybody having to sleep on the sofa. It's just so *messy* having a suitcase out in the middle of the floor, and with us up at all hours making bottles, she couldn't get any rest. Come on, I'm *dying* to show you." Her voice was a little too cheerful, and when she slipped her hand into Rennie's and practically dragged her from the room, Rennie followed. Once they were away from the men, May Dean whispered, "What in the world is wrong with Tiny? I mean, we're all used to him being a Grumpy Gus, but, my stars, this is bad even for him."

With a shrug, Rennie answered, "Spot's missing, and he's upset about that." Thanks to the ROMEOs, she knew the real answer, but she couldn't bring herself to articulate the words, even though May Dean had listened to and then kept every whispered childhood secret Rennie had ever confessed. But this news, that Tiny was failing at the only thing he had left—keeping a roof over their head—was too much to share.

May Dean's life was charmed—the homecoming queen engaged to the quarterback who effortlessly stepped into his family's banking business, and then was carried across the threshold of Spark's most adorable house as an eighteen-year-old bride. Indulgent, doting parents, a large circle of friends, head-turning good looks—it was all so easy for her cousin. May Dean had expected her life to turn out like a fairy tale, so it did. Rennie's reality of a no-nonsense upbringing, homely looks, relentless bullies, and a lack of confidence was a sharp contrast to May Dean's experience, and when Rennie chose a man who made her feel important, only to discover he was worse than any of her childhood tormentors, she became all too aware of the gulf between her and May Dean's worldviews. As much as she longed for a confidant, someone to tell the whole sordid tale to, she kept her lips firmly closed.

Ev called out to his wife. "Us menfolk are getting pretty hungry, hon. The timer went off, so I think the roast is ready."

Around the Queen Anne dining table, the conversation turned to Ev's work at the bank. "Being a vice president is a lot of pressure, but I love helping people with their money. When customers come in with questions about a home loan or advice on an investment, it makes me feel good to know the answer." After a bite of roast, he turned to Tiny. "How's your investment going? So many places fail, but I heard yours is going great guns."

"Yeah, that's right." Rennie's head swiveled in his direction, but she didn't say anything.

Ev stretched his arms. "Like I tell my customers, the whole key to anything like that is the terms of your contract. Understand what you're getting into before you get into it is what I always say."

May Dean picked up a bowl of mashed potatoes and handed it to Tiny. "Wouldn't it be fun for us to go up there and visit your bar? We could be VIPs." She gave a sweet smile and said, "I could tell everybody I know the owner. I bet they'd put one of those fancy cherries *and* a little umbrella in my Shirley Temple."

"Let's plan that." He glared at May Dean and spat out his words. "I'm sure Everett would love to fly us all up there first class. The stewardesses could bring us umbrella drinks with cherries the whole way."

May Dean didn't miss a beat, but Rennie noticed her face redden. "Let's have Rennie's dessert." She left the table and returned with the cake, resplendent with swirls of honey across its silky frosting. As she cut slices, she commented, "What I can't understand is why they're not waiting till a full moon to land. The *Gazette* says the moon will be—what was it, Ev? A waxing crescent? The picture showed something no wider'n Granny Bradford's lower dentures. Shouldn't they go when it's full, to give them a better chance?"

Ev's voice was soft. "I think they'll be okay. With all those prayers and all those scientists, they're bound to land safely, no matter how small the sliver." He pointed to his dessert plate. "Speaking of slivers, I already know I'll need another piece. This is fantastic."

May Dean nodded. "It's the best thing you've ever made, Rennie, and that is saying somethin'." She turned to Tiny.

"Ev and I are coming to the Blue Plate's launch breakfast. We think it'll be fun to watch it in a crowd. Are you coming?"

"Nope."

As Rennie and Tiny prepared to leave, May Dean began packing up the cake. Rennie said, "Please keep the rest of it. It's my thank-you for havin' us to dinner."

"I can't. My doctor says I'm gaining too much weight already, and even if we keep it for Ev, I know I'll eat it if it's in the house." She rubbed her protruding belly. "It's all that good food you're fixin' at the Blue Plate. Maybe Ev could take it with him to the bank tomorrow."

Ev nodded. "I'll set it out on the counter in the lobby with the coffee urn." He chuckled. "I'll be as big a hero as those astronauts. That cake is out of this world."

On the way home, Rennie debated broaching the topic of the All Stars contract. Tiny put Rennie off whenever she brought it up, but every time there was a knock on the door, Rennie expected to see her father-in-law, with Sheriff Ricketts holding eviction papers right behind him. Long-term investments were useless in the midst of a short-term financial crisis. She looked at Tiny's clenched jaw and decided to keep her mouth shut.

Once home, Tiny went onto the porch with a bottle and a glass. He flipped on the radio and lit a cigarette, and Rennie knew he was out there for the rest of the night.

She opened the hall closet and grabbed the manila envelope marked *All Stars Contract*. After glancing toward the porch to confirm Tiny was engrossed in his baseball game and drink, she slid the stack of papers out and scanned the first page. Long sentences with minuscule print, with enough *wherebys* and *heretofores* to almost make her return the contract to the closet, but she had to know what her husband had signed and when they would get paid.

She found a section marked *Terms of Investment* and read: "As an investor, Luther Hendricks will be entitled to 20 percent of all profits, paid quarterly."

Rennie kept reading. On the last page was a section marked *Nullification and Forfeiture*: "All parties agree that the terms of this contract will become null and void if the owners of All Stars, LLC are unable to secure the necessary zoning changes needed to construct and operate a bar and grill. In the event the proper zoning cannot be obtained within 180 days from the first zoning request, all parties agree this contract is null and void, and all monies invested will be forfeited."

"Rennie?" Tiny's voice was flinty. "What the hell are you doing?"

She fought to keep her voice calm. "I'm reading your contract. You've never let me look at it, but with what Ev said tonight, I wanted to see for myself."

"Did you notice the part about me getting 20 percent of the profits?" He puffed out his chest. "They wanted to give me 15 percent since I came into the deal late, but I insisted on 20."

Rennie lowed the paper and looked at her husband. "So they got the zoning issues worked out?"

Tiny knit his brows. "Huh?"

Rennie's voice shook. "The zoning, Tiny." When her answer was a blank look, she added, "The whole deal is off if the zoning falls through."

"What are you talking about?"

"They don't have to give your money back if they can't get the city to approve the zoning changes." She sank into a chair. "*This* is what you signed?"

Her husband's face lost its florid color. "Give me the contract." He snatched the papers from her hands. "Where does it say that?"

With a shaky voice, she answered, "Page five, toward the bottom."

Tiny read from page 5 and then stormed from the house, a string of oaths reverberating behind him.

CHAPTER 28

WHY DO HUMANS SPEND SO MUCH TIME MISrepresenting *the truth to one another? Do they not understand that veracity is the bright beacon that guides their way through their aphotic world?*

Our girl has revealed the man's foolish mistake, and he is not likely to take kindly to it.

Did the man not make a fool of himself by signing documents he clearly did not understand? She simply pointed it out.

He would be the last to acknowledge any misdoings even if he comprehended that he made mistakes. Humans' most tenacious lies are the ones they tell themselves.

CHAPTER 29

THE BLUE PLATE WAS OPENING EARLY WEDNESDAY morning for the special launch breakfast. Arden had taken out an ad in the *Gazette*.

> Launch breakfast at the Blue Plate
> Wednesday, July 16, 7:45 a.m. sharp
> Join us for a buffet breakfast of eggs, pancakes, hash browns, and bacon as we watch the *Apollo 11* launch on TV.
> See Arden for reservations.
> We'll be watching Walter Cronkite on CBS.
> Don't ask me to change the channel.

A drenching rain was soaking Spark, and Rennie shook her umbrella as she slipped in the Blue Plate's back door. "I'm glad the astronauts have better weather than we do." She pulled out the frying pan and retrieved a slab of bacon from the fridge while Arden poured pancake batter onto the griddle.

As she flipped a few pancakes, Arden said, "I wish we coulda done a launch lunch, but NASA forgot to check with me when they scheduled liftoff for 8:30 in the morning." She transferred the pancakes to a cookie sheet and popped them in a warm oven. "Did I tell you Dewey'll be here to take pictures for the *Gazette*?"

"It's great publicity. You were smart to think of setting up a TV and taking reservations. And sponsoring the poster contest was brilliant."

"Part of running a business is thinkin' of clever ways to market yourself."

"I guess you're a natural-born entrepreneur."

Arden snorted. "Far from it. I learned to run this diner because I had to." Rennie, like the rest of the town, had always been curious about Arden's history and how she came to be in Spark, but Rennie was loath to intrude on her privacy, so she kept her follow-up question to herself.

Arden glanced at the clock as a crash of thunder shook the diner windows. "Land sakes! I need to get the door open."

The crowd in the dining room was animated as they speculated on the launch, only moments away. Fear, exhilaration, and pride swirled through the roomful of excited spectators.

Rennie's neighbor Darlene was first in the buffet line. As she piled pancakes onto her plate, she chatted with Queenie, the owner of the Curly Q beauty shop. "I got chill bumps when I heard President Kennedy say, 'We choose to go to the moon not because it is easy but because it is hard.' Dewey made it the *Gazette* headline." Darlene made a bacon raft on top of her pancakes. "We both thought he was a little bit crazy, but here we are." After dousing her breakfast with syrup, she said to Queenie, "Come sit with Dewey 'n' me. We're over by the window."

At 8:20 a.m. Arden tapped a water glass with a knife. "It's starting!" Everyone crowded around the television, whose black-and-white images showed an enormous rocket pointed skyward.

Rennie turned to Arden. "I remember when President Kennedy was killed and Mr. Cronkite was crying as he announced it. Now here he is, not even six years later, narrating Kennedy's greatest dream coming true." Rennie thought for a moment about her own dreams. Security and happiness didn't *seem* like they'd be unattainable, but she had more faith in a bunch of scientists guessing how to send a spindly rocket careening through space and victoriously landing on a chunk of unknown material thousands of miles away than she did in feeling safe and loved.

Walter Cronkite had informed the country of every national event for the last seven years on the *CBS Evening News*, but on this day he was making a morning appearance. "The horsepower is equal to 543 jet fighter planes," he noted.

Rennie's heart pounded in her chest. What had given the astronauts the courage to climb into that rocket, strap into their seats, and wait to be catapulted to the moon? The next few minutes would be either exhilarating or catastrophic, with no chance for anything in between. Did they truly believe they could they be launched safely into the stratosphere, experiencing in actuality what had until that moment been only a theory scribbled on paper and blackboards, or were they secretly expecting that smoke billowing from the engines would turn to flames and consume them?

"They have 5,662,000 pounds of fuel on board, equal to ninety-eight railroad tankers," Cronkite said.

May Dean turned to Ev. "I hope that's enough. It's not like they can pull into a filling station. I'd have asked for at least a hundred railroad tankers' worth, just to be sure."

"At liftoff the noise will reach 120 decibels and has been compared to 8 million hi-fi sets playing at once."

The man giving the countdown from mission control announced, "T-minus three minutes."

May Dean squinted at the screen. "There's so much smoke. How can they see to drive?"

Rennie was startled to see a bird fly by the rocket. Had it come to observe this hulking mass of metal attempt to leave the earth? Did the bird recognize another flyer eager to experience the vastness of the sky, or was it simply a loud intrusion into the bird's usual habitat, generated by humans who had a penchant for disturbing the natural world? Would the sound of 8 million hi-fi sets playing at once thrill the bird or deafen it?

"T-minus sixty seconds."

The Blue Plate's diners' chatter stopped, and the tension in the room rose as everyone stared at the screen. "Lord, be with them," someone whispered.

"T-minus fifteen seconds."

"Twelve, eleven, ten, nine, eight."

Rennie offered up a prayer for the men and thought of their wives, parents, and children. Were they sobbing or cheering?

"Three, two, one, zero. We have liftoff."

The rocket rose. While the Blue Plate diners clapped and whistled, the spaceship hurtled toward outer space, no longer tethered to Earth. As it faded from view, men clapped each other on the back and ladies hugged. Spouses kissed and children cheered. Several waved the little American flags Arden had put on each table.

As the event turned into more of a party than a breakfast, Rennie retreated into the kitchen, busying herself with another skillet of bacon as she thought over what those astronauts must be feeling at that very moment. Her musings were interrupted by the phone. Arden answered and immediately looked at Rennie as she listened. When Arden hung up, she came to Rennie's side. "That was Betty, my cook. She's comin' back tomorrow."

Tiny stared at Rennie, who stood dripping wet in the doorway. "She can't just tell you the regular cook's comin' back so you don't have a job anymore."

"It wasn't like that. I knew when I started that it was temporary." She looked at him. "And so did you." She slipped off her rain jacket and hung it on a peg by the door.

"And so what's your plan now, Miss It's Not Like That?"

Rennie hung her head. Her response, "I don't have one," was drowned out by a crash of thunder.

"Damn it, Rennie. You should have insisted on knowing when that cook was due back or at least started looking for another job as soon as you hired on at the Blue Plate."

"I would have felt disloyal. What if I found another job and they wanted me to start right away? Arden would have been left in a lurch."

Tiny's face was flushed with rage. "Why the hell are you so loyal to everybody but me? Arden, your lunatic uncle, and that dim bulb cousin of yours, May Dean—they all have your full devotion. What about your husband?" He glowered at her. "Or are you too busy with whoever *really* gave you that necklace to think about me?"

Her chin shot up. "My uncle gave me that necklace." She wanted to shout that she knew about the rent, that they were on the verge of eviction, and a real husband would have ensured his family always had a roof over their heads, the same as he would have read a contract and realized he was being swindled before handing over their nest egg. She knew better, though.

A flash of light from a jagged streak of lightning filled their room, illuminating the defeated look that crossed his face.

"I called up one of the guys from the All Stars deal, and you know what? He *laughed* at me when I asked for my money back. Said I could read the fine print about as well as I could hit a curveball, which was not at all, and that my money was long gone." Rain pummeled their roof, providing a theatrical emphasis to his next words. "No one is loyal to me."

She said in an almost whisper, "I am."

He grabbed her bare arm, squeezing it until she winced. "I thought you would be, but I was wrong. You were a weird little nobody when I started dating you. After people saw us together, they treated you different. I thought you'd be grateful, devoted to me no matter what. That's why I married you, Rennie. I thought you'd always be my number one fan, cheering me on."

"This is real life, Tiny, not baseball."

He shoved her hard enough to send her flying backward. Her head slammed against the corner of the table, slicing a gash across her face. Something in her knee made a sickening pop, and a stream of blood filled her eye.

"Real life *is* baseball!" He charged out of the house, oblivious to the raging storm, slamming the screen door behind him.

CHAPTER 30

HE HURT HER.

Yes. But he did something else too.

Broke her spirit?

Her spirit was shattered long ago. What she saw today is the depth of his anger.

She will leave now?

Sometimes humans cling to their chains, and she is as shackled as the dog she calls Jane Austen was before we sent her to that roadside to be found by the girl. But now she knows all the maybes have turned to whens, and for that we are grateful. Her heart is returning to our wavelength, which will serve her well when it is imperative that she hear us.

Like the humans with their goal of reaching the moon, we, too, are so close to what seems impossible. Let us press forward.

CHAPTER 31

THE NEXT MORNING, MAY DEAN YOO-HOO'D INTO THE house from the back porch. "Rennie, are you home? Tiny? Anyone here?"

Rennie hid in the bathroom, willing her cousin to go away.

"Rennie," May Dean called louder. "I see your truck out there. I'm comin' in."

She gasped when Rennie limped from the bathroom. "Dear Lord, what happened to you?"

"I-I tripped on that root at Uncle Dixon's that sticks up. I was in a hurry and wasn't paying attention. I cut my face and twisted my knee pretty good. Totally my fault."

May Dean eyed her suspiciously. "That's a pretty bad cut. Did you call the doctor?" As Rennie shook her head, May Dean set the cake carrier on the counter. "I wanted to return this and ask you about planning a Landing Day party at Uncle Dixon's Sunday night. Ev and I had so much fun at the diner's launch event and wanted Uncle Dixon to experience that excitement. Ev's bought a portable TV so we can all watch it together." She looked around the kitchen.

"I went to the Blue Plate and Arden told me about Betty turning up, so I figure you're free."

Rennie made a face. "I'm definitely free. Let's think up a really special menu." As she reached for a tablet of paper, her sleeve rode up her arm.

May Dean grabbed her hand. "What is that?" she asked sharply.

A bruise in the shape of Tiny's fingers bloomed across her arm. "I told you. I tripped over that root."

"So the root has fingers the same size as—"

Rennie's head pivoted toward the porch. Tiny was opening the screen door.

May Dean squeezed Rennie's hand. "Well, hi there, Tiny. I hope you don't need your bride today, because I *do*. Ev can't come to my doctor's appointment in Nashville, and he doesn't want me going up there all alone. I'm such a *dim bulb* that I can't be trusted to remember everything they say to me, so I need her to help me listen and tell Ev everything the doctor said when we get home. Rennie said she couldn't go, that she needed to get your lunch ready, but I told *her* I thought a grown man as clever and smart as you could manage to make a *sandwich* all on his own." She pulled Rennie toward the door. "I knew you'd understand. Tootles."

Rennie hopped down the porch steps, unable to put any weight on her left knee. May Dean offered her arm, and Rennie grasped it as she struggled to the car.

Without a word, May Dean pulled out of Rennie's driveway. When they turned onto Redbud Lane, Rennie realized they were going to May Dean's house, not Nashville. May Dean parked in the empty bay of her garage and pushed the button to lower the door. "Let's sit out back on the terrace. Are you able to walk that far if I help you?"

Rennie winced as she put weight on her leg. "I think so."

After they were settled onto the wrought iron chairs on the brick terrace, May Dean spoke. "The next words out of your mouth will be the absolute truth, Roberta Irene King."

Some people saw truth as coming in lots of versions, like a spinning pinwheel that could appear pink or orange or gold all at the same time. Others saw the truth as a solid block of information, as unmalleable as a cornerstone of a church. Rennie had always thought the truth was an easy thing to access. Either you lied or you didn't. Now faced with the choice of how to interpret May Dean's admonition, she hesitated.

"Ev went by your house last night. Everybody went crazy over your Honey Moon Cake when he put it out in the lobby. People thought it was from some fancy bakery in Nashville and begged to know where he got it from. Ev said you made it, and it was a gift, not something you could go buy, but three people tried to place orders anyway, and he was so excited to tell you that he went to your house right after dinner even though it was pouring rain. He was on the porch ready to knock on your door, but he stopped when he heard the fight." May Dean took Rennie's hands. "Tiny said horrible things to you. After he threw in that bit about me being a dim bulb, Ev left. He was so mad and wanted to go in there and slug Tiny, but he felt like he'd be intruding on what was obviously a private moment." May Dean softened her voice. "I see now he should have stayed. Ev should have scooped you up and brought you over here." May Dean twisted her wedding band. "Things got worse, didn't they?"

Tears welled in Rennie's eyes, and all she could do was nod.

"I'm fixing us two cups of tea, and then we're going to talk it out, just like we used to when we were kids."

May Dean returned, handed Rennie a mug, and sat down. When Rennie remained silent, May Dean said, "You're safe, honey. Tiny thinks I've dragged you off to Nashville, Ev is in meetings all day, and the construction guys aren't coming back until the plumber installs some shutoff thingy tomorrow. My car's hidden in the garage and there's no doctor's appointment." She looked at Rennie. "It's just you and me."

When Rennie was a child, if she began to articulate any problem, from an earache to the relentless teasing of her classmates, her mother had quoted the New Testament. While other mothers offered a warm compress and aspirin or a sympathetic ear and wise counsel, Rennie's mother turned to one of her many favorite passages in the Bible. Her go-to for any hardship was from Romans: "And not only so, but we glory in tribulations also: knowing that tribulation worketh patience; and patience, experience; and experience, hope." *"And we all need a little hope, right, Rennie?"* her mother would say. Solutions like a phone call to the doctor or school principal were eschewed in favor of a reminder that Rennie was missing an opportunity to be more pleasing to God. She had learned early on to be self-reliant, whether it involved figuring out how to manage her first menstrual cycle or understanding that a closed door was better than a closed fist. Books offered her first escape, and a kitchen offered her the second. As she rubbed her aching knee, she realized there was no escape from Tiny without help.

Rennie squared her shoulders and spoke slowly. "You were a couple of years ahead of me, so you didn't see it going on, and I didn't want to tell you, but I got picked on a *lot* at school. And it wasn't just the kids. In second grade a substitute called me *eccentric* when she caught me reading instead of playing Heads Up, 7-Up like everybody else. Then she realized no one understood that word, so she explained that it meant weird and different, which gave the whole class permission to call me that too."

"I always thought it was fun to have a substitute because they didn't care if we did our work or not." May Dean looked down. "I never realized it wasn't that way for you."

Rennie shrugged. "I found it exhausting to deal with people, so I just didn't. My parents had long ago given up on figuring me out and were too busy working to pay me much mind. The reason I always had my nose buried in a book was so I could be transported to wherever those characters were and not in Spark. Wandering the moors of England, shooting the rapids of a treacherous African river, or riding a dog sled in the Yukon—all of it was so much better than even one minute spent living my own life. The only time I was happy was when I was at Uncle Dixon and Aunt Eugenia's."

"This is breaking my heart, Rennie. How could I not have noticed?"

"It's okay. You had your own life to worry about, and I just accepted that everyone was right—I *was* different. I tried to do like Mama said and endure it, but I *did* get upset when they said Aunt Eugenia was a witch. She was just a woman from the mountains who understood how herbs could help people, but of course they didn't listen to me."

May Dean was pale. "Nobody ever said anything like that to me."

"They didn't dare. You were cute and popular and had fun sleepover parties. Your mama bought you the newest records and the cutest clothes, and you had cokes in your fridge and a whole drawer in your kitchen filled with candy. Those girls knew you'd drop them like hot potatoes if you caught wind of what they were saying to me." She looked down. "Mama always told me to bear my trials with an obedient heart, so I did."

"You should have told me. I was two years ahead of you, but I was still in the same school. I'd've marched to your classroom and set those girls straight right quick."

Rennie gave a sad smile. "Exactly. You would have pounded somebody like Bonnie Sue Greer into the ground if you knew, and I didn't want to get you in trouble, so I didn't say anything."

May Dean grimaced. "Bonnie Sue could have used a little comeuppance."

Rennie continued, "So when Tiny Hendricks started paying me attention, I couldn't believe it. At first I thought some of the kids put him up to it, that he would do something like invite me to a dance and then ditch me in front of everyone, but that's not what happened." She sipped her tea. "We talked a lot, mostly about his dream of being a baseball star. By then I had discovered cooking, and I would talk about wanting to become a famous chef. We'd drive into Nashville so he could go to the batting cage, and I'd watch him hit, so proud to call this strong, handsome guy my boyfriend."

She studied a pot of bright flowers on the wrought iron coffee table. Telling the next part would change things, and she wasn't sure if she was ready for that. Maintaining the fiction of her happy marriage for so long had become a habit, and letting that go took more strength than she thought she had within her.

A single bee landed on a zinnia, and she sensed the bee's energy emanating toward her, offering her encouragement. She reached to touch the zinnia's petal, reveling in its softness, so different from the harsh reality she was about to reveal to her cousin.

She turned to face May Dean. "He was controlling even then, but I didn't notice it. He told me what to wear and how to style my hair, but I thought he was helping me fit in." She shook her head at her own foolishness. "And it worked. Once I was with Tiny, people were nicer to me, and I thought he knew better than I did. *'Don't ever cut your hair short again.' 'You look like a clown with makeup on your face.' 'Never wear black.'* He talked and I listened. When his daddy spoke about Tiny's future, how he'd be like his big brother, the pride of Cooke County, I got to feel like a part of that, like I was successful too just by being near him. I felt like I had people who cared about me. Aunt Eugenia and Uncle Dixon did, of course, and your parents, but they *had* to because I was family. And then when Tiny got that baseball contract on graduation day, he was glowing with excitement. He swung me around the gym and said all his dreams were coming true, and I believed that too. When he proposed in front of everybody, I was so caught up in the moment, I said yes, thinking I was the luckiest girl in the world. And I was, for a little while." She bit her lip. "We moved up north and started our new life together. Then he got cut from the team and everything changed."

May Dean spoke softly. "It wasn't your fault he got dropped."

Rennie shook her head. "It *was* my fault. You know how shy I am around new people, and all the other ladies knew each other and were always going to lunch or shopping together. They invited me a couple of times, but I was too nervous to say yes, not to mention we didn't have money to spend, and they finally quit asking. Tiny said I got the reputation of being unfriendly, and while he was building relationships with the team, I was going behind him and tearing them down."

"You realize how wrong he was, don't you?"

"It's the truth, May Dean, and we both know it."

"It is *not* the truth! It's another one of that man's lies, told to keep you from realizing how strong and beautiful and brave you are." May Dean's eyes flashed. "I'm so sorry he said those things to you, and I'm even more sorry you believed them for even a minute."

"When we came back home, he was embarrassed to take his parents' offer to rent his grandparents' farm, but we didn't exactly have a lot of options. We struggled along, with Tiny withdrawing from me more every day. When I found out I was expecting a baby, I thought that would bring us together, and it did for a while. When I first told him, he said, 'That baby's a boy, and there'll be no discussion about it,' like I can just pick what I'm going to have. He was so excited, talking about teaching his son to play baseball. He wanted him to be a pitcher so all eyes would be on him as he struck out batter after batter." Rennie's voice shook. "Then Gabriel came too early. He said that was my fault too. Maybe I picked up a bag of groceries that was too heavy or didn't eat enough to keep the baby healthy."

May Dean's face was pale. "Honey, why didn't you come to me?"

"Remember after he asked me out for a first date, you told me not to get mixed up with him? You said something felt off, that you didn't trust him."

With a shake of her head, May Dean answered, "And that kept you from telling me all this?"

"My mother is probably rolling in her grave, with me complaining about my trouble. She always said it was dishonoring God to complain."

May Dean's voice was firm. "Your mother was so fond of using the Bible to justify her opinions, but it would have done her a world of good to have thought of Galatians 6:2, which says we are supposed to bear one another's burdens, help one another." May Dean squeezed Rennie's hand. "She was always so sour and never seemed to have a happy day, but she should have at least made sure you knew you were loved."

"Was I?" Rennie bit back tears. "I was going to undo all the damage my mama did by loving Gabriel with my whole soul, the way a child should be loved." She gazed at May Dean's rounded belly. "The way you're gonna love your baby."

The bee had settled on one of the bricks, resting at her feet the way Jane Austen did. She looked at the bee and then at May Dean. "There's more. Tiny hasn't been paying the rent and his daddy's going to evict us. I overheard some men at the diner saying Mr. Hendricks already has a buyer for the property. I jump every time the phone rings, thinkin' it's Sheriff Ricketts tellin' us to get out."

"Is that why he was yelling at you last night?"

"No, I haven't told him I know about the eviction. He was yelling because I figured out he lost his investment in the bar." Tears welled in her eyes. "It's gone, May Dean. Every dime of his signing bonus. After Ev talked about reading the fine print whenever you put a deal together, I checked his contract. Those guys fixed it so he took on all the risk. The money's been gone for ages. We just didn't know it." She took another sip of tea. "And then I told him Betty's come back from Knoxville, so I'm out of a job." She touched the gash on her forehead. "He just exploded and pushed me into the kitchen table." With a sigh, she added, "It's my fault. I piled too much on him at once."

"Quit saying any of this is your fault. He has you brainwashed. He is a grown man responsible for his own decisions, and you are *not* to blame yourself for any of his shortcomings." May Dean took Rennie's hand. "You're leaving him, right?"

Rennie shook her head. "I know he loves me, May Dean. It's just that he's under so much pressure right now, and he got all that bad news dumped on him in one fell swoop. Things will get better." She swallowed hard. "And how would it look for me to be a divorced woman living here in Spark? Nobody in the whole town is divorced. Not one. I'd give people even more to talk about."

"Divorce is more common than you think. And somebody's got to be the first, so why not you? I can guarantee you you're not the only unhappy wife in Cooke County, and maybe some scared, hopeless woman will look to you as an example. And I don't think things will get better with Tiny. He doesn't love you, Rennie, and I doubt he ever did. Someone who loves you wouldn't draw blood. You could have lost an eye." She paused. "Or worse."

"Please help me believe things will work out. Once Tiny is happier, our marriage will be back to how it was during the early times."

May Dean snorted. "I wouldn't wish for early times if I were you. His drinking is a big part of why you're in this mess."

"But we were happy, I swear. And we can be again." Rennie's voice trembled. "And if I'm blessed with another baby, one that is born healthy, then things are bound to be okay." She looked away. "If I leave, I'm giving up on the dream of having another child, and I'm not ready to do that."

May Dean's eyes widened. "Wait a minute. That cut on your neck a while back. Was that from Tiny?"

Rennie's admission was barely above a whisper. "Yes."

"Things are never going to get better, and no baby should be brought into such a stressful situation. Stop wishing for Tiny to start acting right, 'cause that's never gonna happen. What you need is an escape plan. Do you have any money saved?"

"I've been hiding five dollars every week in the lining of my mama's purse from my Blue Plate pay, but I can't exactly start a new life on that."

"Ev and I will give you money."

"No. Y'all have a baby comin', and I know how expensive that is."

"We'll figure this out, but I'd like to let Ev know what's going on." She rose and started for the kitchen "Would it be okay if I called him?"

Rennie shook her head. "Please let me try to fix this on my own."

"I'm sure he could help us." May Dean dropped back into her chair.

"I'll think about it, but don't say anything yet."

May Dean sat silently for a moment. "So you're not going to move out?"

"No."

"I can't make you leave him, but promise me this. Be prepared to go as soon as you feel unsafe." She tilted her head. "It'd be good to get that money out of your house. You can hide it here." She eyed her cousin. "Is there anything else you've been keeping from me?" May Dean's eyes narrowed. "If there is, you'd better tell me right this minute, no matter how small."

"There's only one more thing you don't know."

"Out with it."

"The dog I found, the one Tiny calls Spot. She didn't vanish like Tiny says. Her real name is Jane Austen, and I snuck her over to Ambrose's house. Tiny was going to kill her 'cause she's too old to guard the chickens."

A slow smile spread across May Dean's face. "I always thought Spot was a silly name. Good for you for getting her out of there. And good for Ambrose for helping you." She smoothed her dress. "In a way, he reminds me of Aunt Eugenia. They're from the same town, but he said they never met, right?"

Rennie nodded. "He said he'd never had the pleasure."

"He's too good of a catch to leave a bachelor." She tapped her chin with her finger. "There's got to be *someone* who deserves such a good man."

The jealousy that welled within her caught Rennie off guard. "She'd have to be pretty special. He's a wonderful man."

⌇

When May Dean brought her home around 4:00 that afternoon, there was no sign of Tiny, for which Rennie was grateful. Truth-telling was exhausting, and she welcomed the chance to gather her thoughts before she had to face her husband.

Rennie sat in her rocker on the back porch, thinking over the events of the day. She had been hiding how bad things were for so long and was relieved to have someone know the truth, but also afraid Tiny would figure out Rennie had broken that unspoken vow of silence and retaliate.

She reached for the old coffee can of sunflower seeds and sprinkled them into the plate for Poe, who was hopping about on the branches of a hackberry tree. As she waited for him to dive down for his snack, she massaged her aching knee and thought over May Dean's advice to leave Tiny. May Dean made living in a perfect world look so easy. Marry into the richest family in Spark, throw parties, travel, and live happily ever after. It only took a few minutes to reach May Dean's house from her own, but calculating the distance between their two lives would require May Dean's tape measure to the moon.

Poe's wings glowed in the late afternoon sun. As he lazily circled, Rennie saw a flash of something shiny in his beak. Would it be a watch spring or a nickel? Maybe another button. As she reached for her mug to deposit the treasure, Poe landed, his brown eyes appearing green in a shaft of sunlight. With a nod of his head, he dropped a thin gold chain with two entwined hearts onto the rusted enamelware plate before soaring into the sky.

CHAPTER 32

THE MAN CALLS HER STUPID, BUT WHAT SHE SAID TO *our girl was very wise.*

No two humans are smart in the same way, and their world is a stronger, more diverse place because of that. If they were all violins, they could never experience the beautiful music of an orchestra. Why is that so hard to understand?

There's only one way to be stupid, though—to be too thick-skulled to learn what the world is teaching you. And the ninnyhammer has the thickest skull of all.

Let him continue to think of her as lacking so he will not realize the power of her love.

CHAPTER 33

AS RENNIE GUIDED THE TRUCK TOWARD THE BLUE Plate, she made a mental note to stop for gas before she got too low. Guessing how much fuel she had left was like playing Russian roulette, and Rennie was no kind of gambler.

Arden was busy rolling silverware into napkins when Rennie let herself into the diner's back door. "Hey there," she called to Arden's back. "I came for my last check. I thought I should stop by early before you get busy."

"Hey, hon, it's in the drawer," she said as she turned around. Her smile vanished when she saw Rennie's battered face. She called out to her cook. "Betty, would you mind running down to the BuyMore to pick us up some more pork chops? You can put it on my account."

As soon as Betty closed the door, Arden pointed to one of the dining tables. "Sit down, Rennie. It's time I told you something."

Rennie hobbled to the seat, pulling her hair over the gash on her temple.

Arden took off her glasses and set them on the table.

"I was young and naive when I married my husband. His parents didn't approve of me and made no secret about that. They were rich and powerful and saw me as trash because I wasn't one of *them*. I had some romantic notion that we were star-crossed lovers, some kind of Romeo and Juliet thing. He was used to the best things in life and was a little immature, but I thought I could change him, help him be a better person." She looked upward and added, "Heaven help any woman who thinks she's gonna change a man. They get more like themselves every day, and the sooner a woman accepts that, the happier she'll be." She turned back to Rennie. "When the topic of a possible marriage first came up, his mother said marrying me would ruin her son, which flew all over me. *She* was the one who had ruined him, indulging him and thinking she could just throw money at all his mistakes. I informed her of such, which did nothing to raise their opinion of me but did a lot to improve my opinion of myself."

Rennie nodded, anxious to hear more of Arden's story.

"He'd proposed with his grandmother's enormous diamond ring and then threw a huge party to announce the good news to our friends, all before his parents got wind of our plans so they couldn't call it off. They'd never allow the humiliation of a broken engagement, so we married in the biggest church in town, packed to the rafters with every blueblood in Mississippi. I wrote wedding gift thank-you notes for four months straight." Arden shook her head. "I had enough fine china and sterling silver to last three lifetimes."

"Other than having in-laws who loathed me, I had a charmed life, or so I thought. We lived in a fancy house, and I had charge accounts at the best shops in town. I got my hair done every week and learned to needlepoint and play bridge. My only job was to volunteer with the right charities and make sure the house and I were always presentable."

"I can't imagine you as one of the beauty shop ladies."

Arden shrugged. "It was pretty easy to get used to, and after a while you think that's the way life is always going to be."

Rennie leaned in. "And it wasn't?"

"About a year in, he got caught stealing money from his employer's business. His parents hushed up the whole thing, but he got fired, which his parents retold at the country club as him quitting to start his own business." Arden shook her head. "No company would hire a thief, despite his last name. He hated that he got caught, and he took it out on me. It started off as some rough arguments, and then a punch or two. He always hit me where the bruises wouldn't show when we went to church."

"Oh, Arden. I'm so sorry that happened to you."

"I caught him cheating on me with a secretary from his old office. Apparently it had been going on the whole time we were married. She must've gotten tired of waiting for him to divorce me, because she resorted to leaving a tube of A Fair Affair lipstick in our bedroom." Arden shrugged. "I've always wondered if she actually wore that shade or if she bought it just so she could drop it on my Persian rug as a message from one girl to another."

Rennie shuddered. "How awful."

"When I told him I knew about his girlfriend and was going to divorce him, he beat me to a pulp. I passed out, and I guess he thought he'd killed me. He threw me into the trunk of his car and dumped my body in some woods. When I came to, I crawled to the highway, where a trucker picked me up and took me to the Biloxi hospital. I stayed there for almost two weeks recovering. After I was finally discharged, I told him now I was divorcing him *and* pressing charges. He'd concocted a story about me being in a car wreck to explain my absence, but I said I was going to tell the truth to anyone who'd listen. He laughed in my face and then said he was going over to his girlfriend's house until I calmed down."

"Oh, Arden," Rennie gasped. "How awful."

"The next day I got two phone calls. The first was from an elderly neighbor who asked me to stop by so she could return the blue plate I had used to bring her some cookies a few weeks ago, and the next one was from my in-laws, saying they needed to speak with me."

Arden got up and poured them each a glass of water. After setting the tumblers on the table, she continued. "I picked up the plate from my neighbor on my way to meet them. When I got to their house, they sat me down and said it would be easy to stop their son from being arrested, but they couldn't risk me running my mouth. They offered me the car I drove over there in and enough cash to make it worth my while to leave town, but put plenty of conditions on the deal. I had to leave that minute with only the clothes on my back, couldn't ever return or contact anyone from my past, and was not allowed to speak my husband's name ever again. I guess they did what I had accused them of always doing, throwing money at their problems, but I was smart enough to take the deal. My mother-in-law demanded I give her my engagement ring. I'll never forget her bony fingers outstretched toward me. She could have offered me a helping hand, but instead those red-tipped fingers snatched that diamond ring from me before I could even drop it in her palm." Arden rolled her eyes. "She didn't mind my keeping the wedding band since it was just store-bought, but she was gonna get her mother's diamond from me no matter what. After they got the ring, his father handed over a briefcase full of cash and the title to the car and told me to leave through the back door."

Arden nodded to the blue plate on the wall, the one whose brass prongs reminded Rennie of hands clutching a life ring. "I keep that where I can see it every day. It's a good reminder that I need to rely on myself and nobody else. That man tried to murder me, and I survived. Then his parents fixed it with the law so I couldn't get justice." Grimacing, she added, "They thought they'd bought me off, but what they'd really done was hand me a new life, where I was beholden to no one, and taught me the most important lesson I've ever learned—you're in charge of your own destiny." She took Rennie's hands in her own. "Take charge of *your* destiny, Rennie. Don't let Tiny kill you."

Rennie sighed. It made perfect sense, of course—don't let your husband kill you—but sometimes the simplest thing was the most complex. She was trapped and saw no way out.

CHAPTER 34

SHE HAS OFFERED WISE COUNSEL, TOLD WITH THE heart of someone who has lived the experience. The need for our girl to be near her is now clear.

Sometimes a human will recognize their own suffering in the eyes of another. She is a good woman, made strong by bad circumstances, and was sensitive enough to recognize the benefit of sharing her travails.

Our girl understands now, so she will act?

If only it were that simple. Her brain understands, but her heart has yet to relinquish the dream of a happy marriage and a child who will thrive, made possible by her union with that man.

Humans are forever nattering on about learning lessons, yet the universe is waving a red flag in front of her and she does not heed it.

No, it's not that she doesn't heed it; rather, she does not see it. She has a human brain, but she also has a human heart. We should rejoice that our own bodies are constructed with much more efficient hearts, for it is the human heart that is the single source of most suffering. They call it love, but it is anything but *that. It often takes years and sometimes decades for the human brain to repair what folly the human heart has caused. On occasion it fails to happen at all.*

So we are to wait for her heart to catch up to her brain?

Until she has a full knowingness of what she is faced with, yes, we must wait.

CHAPTER 35

RENNIE WAS MIXING EGGS INTO HER CAKE BATTER when the phone rang. Before she even reached for the receiver, she was already worrying. Had her uncle suffered another stroke? Was something wrong with May Dean or the baby?

"Hello?"

"Good morning, Rennie." Relief flooded her body when she heard her uncle's cheerful voice.

"Everything okay?"

"Right as rain. I wanted to let you know that I've asked Ambrose to drive me into Nashville. We may be a while, so there's no need to come by and check on me this afternoon."

"Do you have a doctor's appointment? I can take you."

"No, nothing like that. Just a little business to tend to. We're going to lunch at my favorite spot, Elliston Place Soda Shop, so I won't be hungry for dinner."

"Okay, thanks for letting me know. And enjoy your day."

She had been fretting about how she'd explain her bruises when she took her uncle his dinner. A bandage hid the gash, but the purplish-blue blotches covered too much of her face to conceal. And now the problem had solved itself, at least for the day. As she hung up the phone, Tiny walked into the kitchen.

"Who was that?"

"Uncle Dixon. He's going with, um, a friend to Nashville to take care of some business, so I won't need to go by there with his supper."

With a frown, Tiny asked, "What kind of business would he have in Nashville?"

"I didn't ask him."

"So you're free for the day." Tiny reached into his pocket and pulled out some cash. "I'm almost out of my Early Times. Can you go into Putney and pick me up some?" He handed her two bills. "You know where the liquor store is, right? We went there after one of your Nashville doctor appointments last year."

A poor sense of direction had plagued her all her life, and she *thought* she remembered but wasn't sure. With no interest in irritating Tiny any more than he already was, she nodded. "Oh, wait. What if they ask about my face?"

Tiny's laugh was harsh. "You think the liquor store boys haven't seen their share of cuts and bruises? They won't even notice."

"I'll need to wait until my cake is done. If I leave now, I'll waste the ingredients. I'll go right after I make your lunch."

Cooke County prided itself on being dry. Despite Tennessee's rich history of distilleries, both legal and not, no alcohol could be bought or sold in Spark. Consuming it, though, was another matter altogether, and the residents who cared had developed their strategies, driving into Nashville for serious stock-ups, or taking a twenty-minute drive into Putney in neighboring Caldwell County for a quick pint or boys' night in a bar.

As Rennie drove to the liquor store, Arden's story about her husband filled her mind. *"Don't let Tiny kill you"* was sage advice, and even though she appreciated the concern that prompted the story Arden told, one thing was keeping her from believing she was in danger—love. The love she shared with Tiny had conceived their son, and if her fervent prayer was answered, love would bring them another child.

Tiny'd had a run of bad luck and disappointments, and his temper often got the better of him, but deep down Rennie knew the man who had swept her off her feet was still in there, ready to soften his heart and make her feel cherished again.

The radio interrupted their program with a special bulletin: "The astronauts have just entered lunar orbit. Tomorrow they will be landing on the moon, a history-making moment for all the world. Can you imagine, folks, what the next twenty-four hours will bring?"

A sign made up of six enormous diamonds spelled out *Liquor*. She'd found the store without a single wrong turn. Rennie gratefully pulled into the gravel drive and parked as close to the door as she could get. She hobbled into the store, wincing when she put too much weight on her left leg. As Tiny predicted, the clerk didn't give the bandage or the bruises a single glance as she paid for the bottle of whiskey. Clutching the paper bag, she exited the store and climbed inside the truck.

As soon as she turned off the main road for Spark, she remembered her mental note to stop for gas. Ever since her uncle had cautioned her about the inaccurate fuel gauge, she'd done a good job of calculating when she'd need to fill up, but with recent events, she'd lost track. Turning around to go back to Putney seemed like a waste of what little gas she had remaining, so she'd just have to hope she'd make it. The next filling station on her route was Harold's on the outskirts of Spark. *I'll be there in five minutes, tops.*

Before long, the engine began to slow. She turned on her blinker and pulled to the side of the road, cursing her own stupidity. Why hadn't she remembered to fill the tank or carry a spare gas can in the truck bed? She could have kept a log of when she filled up or even made a habit of getting gas once a week, but she hadn't done any of those things, and now she was stuck.

Gingerly sliding out of the truck, she scanned the empty road, unsure of what to do. With her injured knee, walking to one of the distant houses was out of the question. She'd just have to wait for someone to come along.

After about twenty minutes, she spotted a dark truck heading toward her. Instead of thankfulness, a wash of panic passed over her. Fear pricked her spine, and she briefly thought of locking herself inside the truck's cab.

The truck slowed, then came to a stop directly in front of her vehicle. Two men got out, first looking at each other and then at her. A chill crossed her body and her throat was suddenly dry. Her instinct was to run, but she knew she couldn't get far.

The first man, about forty years old, spoke. "Lookee here, a damsel in distress."

The second man grinned. "Engine trouble, little lady?"

She gulped, then stood as tall as she could. "I ran out of gas. Any chance y'all have a spare can with you?"

The first man shot a stream of tobacco juice across her feet. "Nope." He jerked his thumb toward the truck. "But we'll give you a lift."

Rennie took a step back. "Um, I should stay with my truck. When you get to town, could you stop at the filling station and ask them to send somebody? The sign says *Harold's*."

The first man spoke. "Easier if you just come with us." The man took her arm and pulled her toward his truck.

A piercing sound startled all three of them. Her head swiveled toward the noise. Her uncle was pounding on the horn of Ambrose's truck, and Ambrose was rushing toward her, shouting, "Get away from her!"

The two men bolted for their truck and took off, tires squealing.

Ambrose's face looked like thunder. "My God, Rennie. Did they hurt you?"

She slowly shook her head. "I-I'm out of gas, and they stopped. I wanted to run, but my knee is messed up, and I knew I couldn't get away. I thought they would help me, but—" She burst into tears.

Before she knew what was happening, his arms encircled her. "You're safe. I'm here." His voice was low and warm, like clover honey ribboning off a spoon, and she instinctively nestled into his chest. She had longed to hug him when he agreed to take Jane Austen but hadn't dared. Now he was the one who was doing the hugging, and she thought she might faint. *Why does his heartbeat feel like home?* She stepped back, shaken.

"Thank you, Am-Ambrose," she stammered.

"We're friends. It's part of the deal." He stroked her hair, then stepped back. "Your face. That's a bruise." He touched it gently with his finger. "Did they do that?" Pausing, he added, "What happened? Those bruises have been there at least a couple of days."

"I tripped on a root, the one at Uncle Dixon's." She gave a little shrug and looked away. "You'd think by now I'd have learned to avoid it."

He pushed her hair away from her face and studied the gauze covering her wound. His shoulders stiffened. "I've got a spare gas can in the truck. Hold on and I'll get it."

After pouring gas into Rennie's tank, he opened the driver's door and helped her inside. "Dixon and I will follow behind you until you get home. As soon as you're inside, lock the door, then call Sheriff Ricketts and tell him what happened."

Her voice quavered as she answered, "I will."

When she pulled into her driveway, she waved at Ambrose and her uncle to indicate she was safely home. *Thank God they came along.* Seeing Tiny working on a piece of farm equipment brought something her uncle said to mind about the bee that alerted her to his fall. "*They understand love better than most people do. They know I love you and that you love me. When I fell I needed help, so they flew to get you.*" She tilted her head. Had the bees tried to tell her husband she was in trouble?

She crossed the field to speak to Tiny. "Did any bees bother you this afternoon?"

Tiny wiped his sweaty brow. "What a weird question. No." He looked at her empty hand. "Did you get my whiskey?"

"It's in the truck." She retraced her steps, thinking about what her uncle had said. *"Because you love me, you understood and came."* The bees couldn't fly all the way to Nashville to notify her uncle that she was in danger, but Tiny was at home while she stood on the edge of the road, stranded. The bees didn't go to him because they knew he wouldn't understand.

As she waited for Sheriff Ricketts to answer his phone, she touched her bruised temple and wondered why she was so sure Tiny loved her.

CHAPTER 36

HE DOES NOT LOVE HER, AND NOW SHE KNOWS IT.
    Her heart is finally catching up.
    The next turn on her path is too awful for her, and a solution is obvious. He is severely allergic to bee stings. Why can we not work as a collective to facilitate his death? She could not be blamed and would be spared what is ahead. Those who participate would gladly forfeit their lives if it meant he would lose his as well.
    Neither the council nor the queen would allow such interference, and even the suggestion would draw reproval.
    But we intervened when she was at the bottom of the creek bed by alerting Eugenia to her plight.
    She was not to perish by drowning, so we were aiding, not interfering. The Hall of Records does not list his death as anaphylaxis. He has his own future to adhere to.
    But we love her, and it would spare her so much. The sacrifice of some for the good of all is the essence of our existence.
    Our mission is to ensure that she fulfills what is written for her. We can provide succor and certainly will do so with every

beat of our wings, but impinging on his path would affect her own. It is delving into human emotions to indulge in the fantasy of eliminating him from her life, and such an act would be against all we stand for. We must instead be strong for her as she faces what lies ahead.

CHAPTER 37

RENNIE WAS SNAPPING THE HONEY MOON CAKE into its carrier when she heard May Dean beep her horn. A few seconds later, a car door slammed and May Dean walked into the kitchen.

"Happy Landing Day, Rennie! How's your knee?" She patted her rounded belly. "Sorry I'm late. I'm walking pretty slow these days." She fanned her face. "And it's so hot that I can't get very far without stopping to catch my breath."

"Happy Landing Day to you too. My knee's better. I'm taking aspirin and put ice on it, and that's helped."

"Is Tiny here? I didn't see his truck."

Rennie shook her head. "Last night he said he was going to Putney to watch a baseball game with some friends and never came home." She shrugged. "He'll turn up. Honestly, having some quiet time to myself is kind of nice."

"You deserve it." She checked her watch. "It's almost four. Are you about ready to go? I've got the iced tea, fried corn, sliced tomatoes, and fruit salad in the car. Ambrose is bringing the drinks, and Ev's over at Uncle Dixon's setting up the TV."

"Yep. If you'll grab the cake, I'll get the chicken casserole out of the fridge." As she lifted the heavy pan, she said, "Remind me to give you the purse when we get back."

May Dean frowned. "Shouldn't we get it now?"

"We're already running behind, and we don't want to miss touchdown. It can wait."

Ev and Ambrose were fiddling with the TV's rabbit ears when they walked in, while Uncle Dixon was arranging flowers in shades of red, white, and blue in a Mason jar.

May Dean set the cake on the kitchen counter. "Could you fellas help bring in the rest of the food? It can't sit out in that hot car for even a couple of minutes."

Ev started toward the door, but Ambrose stopped him. "You've almost got a clear picture. Keep working on that and Rennie and I will get it." He looked at Rennie. "If you're able to walk. If not, I'll bring it all in."

"I'll be okay. It's not too far."

As they passed by the root that Rennie claimed she tripped over, Ambrose opened his mouth and then shut it again. He lifted the casserole from the trunk. "Did you call Sheriff Ricketts?"

"I did. He took a description and said he would increase patrols in the area, but hopefully those two are long gone."

Before he could ask again about her bruise, Rennie grabbed the fruit salad. "We'd better get all this inside. Don't want to miss the touchdown."

Walter Cronkite was speaking. "Less than a mile from the moon's surface." The group gathered around the small television, transfixed as the module slowly descended, and then there it was. The rocket had come to rest. "Man on the moon," Cronkite said.

The idea of being completely separated from the earth was both frightening and exhilarating. Leaving every care and worry, existing in a brand-new place that had no connection to the troubles and challenges of daily living, was very appealing. As she looked around the room, though, she realized the moon was also a desolate place, with no loved ones, no bees, and no anchor to anything she had ever known or loved.

The voice of Neil Armstrong was next. "The *Eagle* has landed."

Walter Cronkite took off his glasses and wiped his eyes.

As Rennie looked around the simple room, she was overcome with a sense of well-being. Hope had always seemed such a vague notion, something you clung to despite daunting odds, but right in front of her was evidence that dreams do come true. Her own dreams—a good marriage and a healthy baby—felt possible for the first time since she had helplessly watched her son die in her arms.

"Hey, Rennie, you hungry?"

The surprising answer was yes, she was famished, and she happily joined in the supper they had all helped to create.

As Ambrose scraped the last crumbs of the Honey Moon Cake from his plate, he asked for a second helping. "This is the best cake I've ever had. You'd sell a million if you ever wanted to make a business out of your baking."

Ev chimed in. "At least a million. Darlene Prichard practically called me a liar when I told her this cake wasn't from a Nashville bakery." He grinned at Rennie. "You're bound to have a secret ingredient, but don't tell Darlene unless you want all of Cooke County to know about it."

"Arden had a customer come all the way from Nashville to try my food. That made me feel pretty good, like he could tell the love and attention I put into it."

Ambrose swiped a bit of frosting from his plate. "You really need to start believing everyone when they tell you you're a fabulous cook."

Rennie blushed. "Let's go sit outside where it's cooler until it's time for the moonwalk."

At 9:45 they came in from the porch and turned the television back on to watch Neil Armstrong walk on the moon. He climbed down the ladder and announced, "One small step for man, one giant leap for mankind." At that moment, the world had changed, and anything was possible. With know-how, planning, and effort, and maybe a little luck, any goal could be achieved.

The group was hugging and cheering, as was the whole world. The impossible had been done.

"I can't remember when I was out this late. It's almost eleven o'clock." May Dean pulled into Rennie's Beasley Court driveway. "Uh-oh. Tiny's home."

The jubilation from the landing was still in Rennie's voice. "I'm glad. Maybe that night away helped him gain some perspective. If we work together, we can get through this rough patch just fine." She opened the car door. "I want to talk with him about starting a baking business out of our kitchen. He might even be able to help me with deliveries." As she closed the door, she leaned into the window. "Thanks for the lift. I'll talk to you tomorrow. Drive carefully. There's probably people on the road who've been doing a little too much celebrating."

Tiny sat at the same kitchen table he had thrown Rennie into only a few days before, his face florid. In front of him lay her mother's black purse, with the silk lining torn from its insides like a slaughtered animal.

"I gambled last night and lost, and the fellas are pretty insistent I pay up. I remember seein' this purse in the closet, so I thought I'd check it for any forgotten money." He threw a wad of five-dollar bills onto the table. "And lookee what I found."

Both their heads turned when the screen door opened and May Dean stepped inside. "That's mine."

Tiny rose from his chair, towering over both women. "I'll thank you to go on home, May Dean. This is between my wife and me."

"That money is mine, Luther Hendricks, and you need to give it back. I've been saving up to get Ev some golf clubs for his birthday, and he's so nosy that he'd find the money if I hid it at my house, so Rennie is keeping it for me." She stepped forward and held out her hand. "Give it."

"You two was always thick as thieves, coverin' for each other."

Rennie turned to her cousin. "Go home, May Dean. I can handle this."

"No. That money is mine, and I want it back."

"Please, May Dean." Her voice shook. "Think of your baby and leave. I'll be okay."

May Dean touched her belly and then looked at Tiny. "You're stealing from me, and I'm going to tell the sheriff."

She moved to the door but turned back. "Rennie, I'm calling Sheriff Ricketts as soon as I get home."

Tiny watched from the window as May Dean's taillights disappeared into the darkness. He turned to Rennie. "I told you never to lie to me again or there'd be hell to pay." And then Tiny, who was dropped from his baseball team because he couldn't hit a barn door with a bass fiddle, connected with his wife's jaw with a hit as solid as any major league home run.

Rennie groaned and rolled onto her side. The kitchen was dark except for a yellowish glow by her hand. *It must be the moonlight.* She heard her aunt's soft voice singing. *"I see the moon, the moon sees me, the moon watches over us all, you see. There's love in the light and love in our heart, there's love all around us when we depart."* How had she never realized the song was about dying?

CHAPTER 38

Eugenia

May 1, 1951

HOLDING A STACK OF LINENS IN ONE HAND, EUGENIA paused before the door of what they had envisioned as a nursery when she and Dixon had first sketched out their home's floor plan. She had spent first months, then years trying to bless that room with a baby, but it wasn't meant to be. The irony of being able to right the wrongs in others' bodies while she was powerless to help her own was not lost on her. She had rocked a thousand miles in the chair her optimistic husband had made for their baby, trying to accept she would be childless even as she continued to concoct potions for herself that had worked so well for other women's empty wombs.

She opened first the curtains and then the window to air out the cozy room that had stood unused except for their niece's occasional visits. She adjusted the bright yellow marsh marigolds by the windowsill to more fully catch the sun's rays. Taking a crisp cotton sheet from the pile, she snapped it in the air, then settled it over the bed. She tucked the corners under the mattress and then smoothed the Honey Bee quilt made by her mother over the sheet.

Dixon strode in with a Mason jar of wood sorrel and set it on the nightstand. "Look how the oval petals are the same shape as the bee wings in your mama's quilt."

"A perfect match." Eugenia's smile was beatific as she plumped a pillow and laid it gently on the bed. "I've got everything ready for her."

A *caw* floated into the room through the open window, bringing a smile to Eugenia's face. She stepped to the window and said, "Meet me on the porch, Morrigan."

As Eugenia grabbed a coffee can from the table, the crow hopped toward her. Eugenia's voice quavered slightly. "I have something important to ask you today. I'll not be here much longer, and I would like you to watch over Rennie for me after I'm gone." Eugenia scooped a handful of seeds from the can. "The bees will be with her, of course, but will you also care for her? Your keen eyesight is one of your gifts, so will you use it to watch over her?"

A ray of sunshine highlighted Morrigan's cracked beak as she bowed to Eugenia. *I will.*

The crunch of tires floating through the spring air sent Eugenia scurrying to the driveway. A six-year-old Rennie hopped out of the car, carrying a paper grocery sack. Her mother waved briefly at Eugenia and Dixon, then drove away.

Eugenia hugged Rennie. "It's a day for celebrating!"

Dixon picked up Rennie and spun her in the air. "A whole weekend with our favorite girl!" He set her down and said, "Aunt Eugenia and I have lots of ideas for fun things to do, but we want to hear how *you'd* like to spend our time together."

A marsh marigold lay on the ground, having fallen from

the doorframe. Rennie picked it up and tucked it behind her ear. "I want to be with you. That's all."

Eugenia, Dixon, and Rennie filled their day climbing trees, watching a pair of hawks swirl over the tobacco fields, having a tea party in the bee yard, and wading in Flat Rock Creek. "I want to be this happy forever," Rennie had shouted as she arced into a bluebird-colored sky on the tire swing.

The setting sun tinged everything a warm pink and purple as Eugenia helped Rennie get ready for bed. As Eugenia gently brushed Rennie's long brown hair, she frowned. "You're looking mighty serious. Is something on your mind?"

Rennie's voice shook. "I want to ask you something, but I'm afraid to."

"Never be scared to ask me anything, sweet girl," she said as she buttoned Rennie's cotton nightgown.

"Cindy Carmichael sat next to me during milk break yesterday." Her lip trembled. "Cindy said you're a witch." Rennie turned troubled eyes to her aunt. "Is that true?"

Eugenia's voice was soft. "What do you think?"

"Witches are bad and try to hurt people. They ride broomsticks and are green and scary." Rennie studied the heart-of-pine floor. "You are nice to me, way nicer than Mama, and you're the prettiest lady I've ever seen."

Eugenia scooped up Rennie and carried her to the maple rocker Dixon had crafted by hand when they were still hopeful they would be blessed with a baby. Holding her close, Eugenia rocked for a moment, relishing the nearness of Rennie's rhythmic breathing. She took a moment to sync her own breath to match the child's and hoped their heartbeats were similarly paired. "I try to be kind and help people whenever I can." She stroked Rennie's soft cheek. "Tell me about Cindy Carmichael. Is she a nice girl and a good friend?"

Rennie shook her head. "She brags that she's the only one who has store-bought bread for her sandwiches, and she told Alice Ann Walker that she recognized the dress Alice Ann had on as an old one of hers from her mama's Goodwill box."

The rocking chair squeaked gently as Eugenia considered her answer. "It doesn't sound like this Cindy Carmichael is anyone you should pay any mind to."

Rennie looked up at her. "But is she right about you being a witch?"

Eugenia held out a pale arm for Rennie to inspect. "Well, for starters I'm not green, and I only use a broom to sweep the floors." When Rennie giggled, Eugenia added, "But I do understand the world differently than some people. I have been given special gifts, the same as we all have been. Cindy Carmichael should spend her time figuring out what gifts she's been blessed with instead of calling names." Eugenia's smile didn't reach all the way to her eyes as it usually did. "Did I answer your question?"

Rennie gave a sleepy nod. "The only broomstick around here is the one you sweep with."

Eugenia kissed the top of Rennie's head. "Are you ready to get into bed? I can turn off the light and you can fall right to sleep."

"Aunt Eugenia, sometimes I'm afraid to be left alone in the dark."

"The dark can be scary, but remember, the moon is always

with you, even when you can't see it. Just like I am. If you're ever frightened, remember this. Whenever there is moonlight, I am with you, just not always where you can see me." She stroked Rennie's hair. "Would you like me to sing you a song about the moon my mama used to sing to me?"

Rennie nodded, burrowing deeper into her aunt's arms.

"I see the moon, the moon sees me, the moon watches over us all, you see. There's love in the light and love in our heart, there's love all around us when we depart," her aunt crooned. As she tucked Rennie into bed, she said, "See the light slipping through that window? That's the moon keeping you safe even when I leave. None of us is ever alone with the moon in the sky." She had kissed Rennie's cheek and gently closed the door. Rennie fell immediately into a deep, restful sleep, comforted by the thoughts that her aunt was not a witch and that something had always been safeguarding her even if she hadn't known she was being protected.

CHAPTER 39

RENNIE'S HEAD WAS POUNDING. SHE WINCED AS SHE gingerly touched her aching jaw, then squinted at her watch. Eleven thirty. Some notion of May Dean saying it was past eleven o'clock when they pulled into the driveway rolled through her brain, so she hadn't been out long. *Tiny.* Was he lurking in the shadows, waiting to see if she was still alive? Arden's husband had dumped her body in the woods outside Biloxi, leaving her for dead. Was Tiny bringing the truck closer to the house to do the same to her? *The sheriff.* Didn't May Dean say she was calling Sheriff Ricketts? Straining to listen for any noise, she heard only the whirr of crickets.

A glow moved toward her. Not moonlight, but a bee. The shimmer in the black room was the same as something familiar. *What?* She squeezed her eyes shut, and when she opened them, she was back at the bottom of the creek bed, watching a crawdad scurry under a rock. A silver minnow flashed by, and then a pulsing light appeared, blinking like an SOS call. *Get out of the water. Look for the sunlight and follow it to the surface. Rise up.*

It's so pretty here. I'd like to stay.

You have a beautiful life waiting for you. There will be jagged days that will rend your heart, but you will be strong and brave. One day you will be a queen bee, living in a hive filled with all you've longed for, but you must get out of the water. Follow the sunlight. Rise up to save your life.

Her eyes opened wide as she remembered the light fading as the bee's body slowly sank to the creek bed. She had sacrificed her life to deliver that message. As her temple throbbed, she wondered about the bee's pronouncement. *"You will be a queen bee, living in a hive filled with all you've longed for."* She had thought they were promising her life, but was the beautiful hive actually heaven, and the promise was not of life, but of death? What she longed for was nothingness, a release from the pain screaming through her body. But then the bee's last words rippled through her brain. *"Rise up to save your life."* For a moment she was tempted to disregard that last admonition and allow her body to surrender to the darkness, but the bee's insistent beacon called her back to life.

Struggling to a sitting position, Rennie grabbed at her ribs. As she fought a wave of nausea and waited for the room to stop spinning, she watched the bee whose glow had roused her as it flew from her body to the door and then back again. She had to escape the house, the same way she had needed to get out of the creek all those years ago. Her life depended on it.

Taking hold of a chair, she pulled herself to a standing position and limped to the window to scan the yard. No sign of Tiny or the black Ford, but he could come back at any moment. *I have to hurry.*

Moonlight brightened the backyard, casting long shadows. Stumbling onto the back porch, she surveyed the property for any sign of her husband. Nothing. Her initial thought was to go to the place she felt safest, her uncle's farmhouse, but that would be the first place Tiny looked, and she couldn't risk putting Uncle Dixon in the path of Tiny's anger. Ev and May Dean would take her in, but her presence would put May Dean and her baby in harm's way. She couldn't hide anywhere Tiny might look. She choked back a sob. How could she get away? Her distinctive white truck might as well be a Hollywood searchlight, directing Tiny to her exact location if he decided to finish what he had started. The sheriff's office was about ten minutes away, but it would be deserted this late at night. Getting herself to a Nashville hospital was impossible in her condition. Ambrose would help, but if Tiny found her at his house, he would kill him first and ask questions later.

Sinking onto the grass, she put her head in her hands. *Think, Rennie.* The bee grazed her forehead with her wings. *Come home.* And then she knew where to go. The only truly perfect place in the world, her respite and her sanctuary, the bee yard.

The moonlight reflected off the Baptist church's white wooden siding. She parked in the back, taking the same spot she had the night she had given Jane Austen to Ambrose. She rested her head against the window, leaving a smear of blood on the glass, before opening the door and sliding to the pavement below. Her body screamed at her to close her eyes and rest, but she pushed herself to keep going. Using the door handle to pull herself up, she stumbled across the grass of her old house next door. She followed the path she'd taken a thousand times as a child, overgrown but still navigable. Once she reached the bee yard, exhausted from her efforts, she collapsed on the soft moss and let the darkness swallow her.

A slight humming noise awakened her. Warmth coursed through her body and the air was heavy with the scent of woodland phlox. A vibration filled the bee yard, buzzing against her skin. Her jaw was tingling, and when she raised her hand to gently touch it, her fingers brushed against several bees. Their needling was more of a quivering than a stinging, and the reverberation of beating wings reached to her soul. She slowly opened her eyes, looked around, and then closed them, sure she was hallucinating.

She opened her eyes to the same sight—tens of thousands of bees in a circle around her, pulsing like a beating heart. With each breath, she drew in their strength and ministrations. Sunshine filled her lungs and caressed her body, even as night cloaked the bee yard. Her tense muscles, aching from the attack and the effort it took to get to safety, loosened. She raised her head for a moment but then laid it down again on the soft moss and fell asleep, basking in the healing energy emanating from the ring of sonorous bees.

Her aunt Eugenia gently lifted her head and placed a few drops of a honey-like substance into her mouth and then dabbed a dark paste onto her wounds. She whispered soft words into Rennie's ear and kissed her gently on the cheek.

"Aunt Eugenia?"

"I'm here, Rennie."

She struggled to sit up. "Am I dead? Is this heaven?"

"You're not dead, sweetest girl. Remember what I told you? When you see the moonlight, I am with you, just not always where you can see me."

"I've been so scared."

"You've also been so brave."

Rennie winced. "He'll kill me if he gets another chance."

Aunt Eugenia's voice was smooth and strong, like the pipe vine she wove into a braid to support a tender plant as it grew skyward. "Don't give him that opportunity."

"I'm so afraid."

"Don't let your fear stop you from doing what's right."

"My head hurts, Aunt Eugenia."

She stroked Rennie's hair, matted with blood. "Shhh, sweet Rennie. The bees and I are here, and we'll not leave you until you are restored. Close your eyes and rest."

CHAPTER 40

WE SAVED HER LIFE.
She saved her own life. She knew to come home.
Will he try again?
Evil intentions are stirring, but humans' plans have a way of going awry, especially when animus is involved.

CHAPTER 41

"RENNIE!" A HAND GENTLY TOUCHED HER SHOULDER. "Can you hear me? Wake up!" Strong arms raised her upper body, and she opened her eyes to see Ambrose's leaf-green eyes filled with worry. "What happened?"

Rennie struggled to a sitting position and looked around. The ring of bees was gone, but about a dozen sat among the bee balm leaves beside her, keeping watch. "Tiny," she said. "I'd been hiding money from him, and he found it last night. May Dean tried to stop him, but he was so angry." She sat upright. "Is she okay? Did Tiny hurt her?"

"May Dean is fine, except she's sick with worry, like we all have been. After she left your house, she called Sheriff Ricketts. Ev got home shortly after that, and as soon as he heard what was happening, he rushed to your house. He and the sheriff got there about the same time, but there was no sign of you or Tiny. The sheriff drove to Dixon's house to look for you, and then Dixon called me." He gently smoothed some leaves from her hair. "We've been frantic, thinking he'd kidnapped you, or worse." He tilted her head up to his with his hand and searched her face. "You've got a bruise on your jaw, but I don't think it's broken. Do you think you can walk?"

She struggled to her feet but then faltered. "I-I'm not sure."

Ambrose lifted her into his arms. "Let's get you up to the house. Are you strong enough to put your arms around my neck?" Rennie nodded and nestled deeper into his chest.

As he passed through the arch of New Dawn roses, his body brushed against several blooms, releasing their fragrance. She closed her eyes, with the feeling washing over her that Eugenia was somehow present.

"Dixon! Ev! May Dean! I've got her," he yelled as he opened the door. May Dean and Ev rushed to her side, while Uncle Dixon struggled to stand.

Ev got to Rennie first. "How badly is she hurt?"

May Dean was close behind. "Praise the Lord!" She gently stroked Rennie's face. "Put her on the bed in the guest room. I'll call Dr. Grisham." She looked at her husband. "And then you call the sheriff."

After Doc Grisham pronounced Rennie "bruised but without any broken bones," he left, holding the door open for Sheriff Ricketts. The two men conferred for a moment, and then the sheriff went into the guest room.

He took out a notepad and sat in the wooden rocker. "Tell me what happened." He looked around the room and added, "I'm sure y'all understand this needs to be a private conversation, so I'll need you to step out."

As Rennie talked, the sheriff listened, taking only a few notes. He nodded a couple of times and frowned a couple more. Rennie touched her jaw as she finished her story. "So Ambrose brought me up to the house, and Ev called you."

Sheriff Ricketts closed his notepad. "Anything else?"

"No, sir, except that I was sure he was going to kill me."

"Right after you both went missing, I had a hunch I'd find Tiny at the Moonshine Lounge in Putney, so I drove out there. I was right. He gave me a different version of the night's happenings, but then again, he was drunker 'n Cooter Brown. I told him to go stay with his mama and daddy for a few days to cool off, so you're free to go back home." The sheriff rose from his chair, abruptly stopping the rocker's swaying with his hand. "I'll wrap up this investigation and get back to you with my findings." He tucked his notepad into his pants pocket. "I'll see myself out."

May Dean stepped away from the door as the sheriff exited. "Are you going to arrest Tiny?"

"Let's not get ahead of ourselves. I'll go talk to the boy now that he's had time to sober up and decide from there."

After the sheriff left, May Dean went to Rennie's side. "I heard what the sheriff said to you. He said step out of the room, not go far enough away that you can't hear the conversation, so it wasn't eavesdropping." She sat on the edge of the bed. "It sounds like he's not taking this too seriously."

Rennie nodded. "I get the same impression." Swinging her legs over the bed, she stood. "I think I'm going to be okay." Gesturing to her jaw, she added, "I'll have quite a bruise, but it could have been a lot worse." Her head swam for a moment, and a memory of bees caressing her face came back to her. She frowned, reaching for the memory. There were bees, thousands of them, tending to her wounds. And how was Aunt Eugenia there? She rubbed her hand across her forehead. Maybe she was the one with the concussion.

She immediately dismissed the idea, knowing her night in the bee yard was the most real thing she'd ever experienced, but one she'd keep to herself, at least for now. She moved to the door, steadying herself against the wall. "I'm gonna come out and talk to everybody."

All three men looked up when she hobbled into the den. "I gave the sheriff my statement. He told Tiny to stay at his parents' house for a few days so I can go back home."

"You're moving in with me." Uncle Dixon's voice shook. "I will not allow that man to ever be near you again. Ev or Ambrose can take you over there with a shotgun while you get your things, but then you're comin' straight back here." He rubbed his face with his hands. "Tiny could have killed you last night. He's not gettin' another chance."

She looked around the room at all the concerned faces and nodded her agreement.

Ambrose started for the door. "Come with me, Rennie. I'll drive you to your house so you can pack."

As they walked to Ambrose's truck, Rennie said, "We'll need to stop by your place first so you can get your gun."

Ambrose's eyes narrowed. "No need. If he so much as shows his face, I'll make sure he regrets it, and I won't need a gun for that."

Once inside her house, Rennie gathered up her belongings and stuffed them into a grocery sack while Ambrose waited on the porch. Last in the bag was the box containing her hickory stick doll. Reaching under the bed, she grabbed the Cotton Patch bag containing the black shirt she'd never had the nerve to wear. She tucked the broken entwined heart necklace into her pocket and went on the porch to join Ambrose.

Rennie closed the door gently behind her, wondering if she'd ever cross that threshold again. Ambrose had pulled his chair to face the Hendricks' property next door, and her heart flooded with gratitude. Safety was not an emotion she associated with the old farmhouse, but standing on that porch next to Ambrose, she was protected.

Ambrose took her two bags. "You ready?" he asked softly.

"Could I sit for just a minute? It seems strange considering why I'm leaving, but I need to say goodbye." She dropped into the wicker chair and reached for the mug containing Poe's buttons, screws, and paper clips. As she sifted through the objects, she said, "A lot happened here, good and bad. When we first got home from Boston, I was so grateful to be back in Spark, so hopeful we could have a happy life here." She shook her head. "It was obvious pretty soon that Tiny wasn't cut out to be a tobacco farmer. His first crop was a failure, and it's like he accepted *he* was a failure too. Everyone around him was making a living, maybe not a fortune, but enough to get by. His daddy helped him some, but he never got the knack for it, and I thought it was our lot in life to be just scraping by." She rose and walked to the edge of the small porch. "But then something wonderful happened, and I believed the good Lord was changing my life."

"Gabriel?"

She nodded. "Tiny blames me for Gabriel's death, and I'm not sure he's wrong. The Lord answered my prayer and sent me a child but then took him from me." She sat back in her chair. "I know it's wrong, but I'm not sure I've forgiven God for that."

A *caw* from the hackberry tree prompted her to take her coffee can from the windowsill. She poured out some seeds, paused, and then dumped the remaining food onto the plate. "Can I ask you something?"

"Sure."

"When we were picking blackberries that day, you told me you and God weren't on speaking terms. What did you mean?" She searched his suddenly tense face. "I'm sorry. That's none of my business."

"It's okay." He ran his hands through his dark hair. "It's not a secret, just something I don't bring up. When you meet someone, how do you drop into the conversation, 'I had a friend once, a best friend I loved like a brother, but he betrayed me, so I'm gonna keep everyone at arm's length because I can't go through that again'?"

"What happened?"

"He and I both went to the University of Kentucky. I met a girl and thought I was in love. Her daddy was a preacher with a big church outside Louisville. He said the Lord told him I was the man God chose to be his daughter's husband. We dated all four years of school. I had a bad feeling that last semester. Something was wrong, but I ignored it. My friend and my girl were spending a lot of time together, but I figured it was because we were graduating and about to go our separate ways."

A black truck appeared on the road, and they both watched warily as it approached, then passed the house without slowing.

"A week before we graduated, I proposed. She said yes, and I thought I had the world by the tail. I was going to marry her, bring her home to Travers, and take up farming." His eyes darkened. "My daddy didn't come to the graduation and gave me some story about not being able to leave the farm, so her parents filled in for him, taking me out to dinner and saying how perfect God's plan was and how I was already a part of their family. On graduation night I stopped by my buddy's dorm to ask him something, and I found my girl and my best friend together." He shrugged. "I guess the Lord didn't mention that part to her daddy. When I saw them in his bed, I gave up on anything or anyone claiming to be of God."

"That must have been horrible."

"It was. While I was loading my truck to go back to Travers, I got a visit from her daddy, who told me I was going to hell for breaking his daughter's heart. I pointed out that mine was the heart that was broken, and that out of the three people involved, I was the only one who didn't have to worry about going to hell." Ambrose cleared his throat. "On the drive home I promised myself I'd never have another friend who could get close enough to hurt me, and that I'd never let myself fall in love again." His eyes narrowed. "And to run far away from anyone claiming to be led by God." After a moment, he added, "When I got home that night I found out the real reason why my daddy didn't come see me graduate. He was sick and died about a week later. So I told whatever or whoever was calling himself God that he could kill my one remaining family member, have my best friend steal my girl, then have me be told I was going to hell, but that I refused to have anything to do with him or his church from then on." His face was pale. "No wife and no friends was how I was planning on living my life."

The wicker rocking chair squeaked softly. "I thought we were friends."

"We are."

"But you said—"

She could feel his eyes searching her face. "If I explain, you're going to think I'm crazy."

"I doubt that."

"It's the bees. About a year ago, I was in our bee yard, feeling pretty low, when a bee landed on my shoulder. I had asked her why all this had happened to me, when the bee put a single word into my head—*love*."

Rennie sat up. "What?"

"She didn't use words, but I could understand her just the same. She said I was never going to find love with those two, either the love of a friend or the love of a partner, and losing them both was the best thing that ever happened to me." He grinned. "You sure you don't think I'm crazy?"

She thought back to the glowing bees that had interceded on her behalf more than once, and how they had conveyed messages when she needed them most. "Nope."

"So I asked why they didn't give me a heads-up about my girl and my so-called friend. The answer I got was very plain. Even a scout bee couldn't fly all the way to Lexington. I was too far away for them to warn me."

"What did you do next?"

"I asked was I ever going to have a true friend or a true love, and she said I would have both." He looked at Rennie. "But I needed to go to Spark to find them."

Poe flew down to his plate and began pecking at the seeds. The rapid *tap, tap* of his beak hitting the metal plate matched her own thumping heart. The crow lifted his head and watched Rennie as she thought through her next question.

"Those bees, Ambrose. Where did your family get them?"

He looked at her. "From your aunt Eugenia's hive."

CHAPTER 42

SUNLIGHT STREAMED INTO RENNIE'S BEDROOM AT her uncle's house, waking her. She flipped on the radio to check on the progress of the astronauts, due to splash down that morning.

"NASA reports that all systems are go for a safe return to Earth at 10:50 local time, less than three hours from now," the newscaster announced. "The splashdown site is approximately one thousand miles southwest of Honolulu. Nine navy ships are standing by to retrieve the men from the ocean."

Rennie entered the kitchen where her uncle was enjoying his coffee. "It's almost time for splashdown. I'll be so glad to have them back on Earth."

"Me too. That's what people are forgetting. President Kennedy called for us to land men on the moon but also to return them safely to Earth. That last part is the trickiest of all."

Rennie pulled out the cast iron frying pan. "Would you like one egg or two?"

"One's plenty."

"How'd you sleep last night?"

"Like a top, and I hope you did the same."

"So you're feeling all right?" She had been living with her uncle a little less than a week and was reaching a new understanding about the depth of his frailty. There was a big difference between appearing fine for a few hours while she visited and seeing the unvarnished truth of how he really was, and she was worried.

"Never been better, sweet girl. How's that egg coming along?"

She got the message and let it drop. After sliding the egg onto a chipped yellow-and-white plate, she buttered the toast and set the food in front of her uncle, then gently placed the Mason jar full of honey beside him. He stared at it, watching the morning sun sparkle in the rich amber liquid.

"So much work for me to have a sweet taste to my breakfast. We surely don't appreciate those bees enough for all they do for us humans." He tapped the jar with his finger. "Did you know a bee makes one-twelfth of a teaspoon of honey in her lifetime?"

Rennie's eyes widened. "Only that much?"

"I love those bees, same as they love me. I'm glad Ambrose is taking such good care of 'em."

"We're lucky to have him as a neighbor."

Uncle Dixon gave a little nod. "He's an honest man, which is hard to come by these days. Now look at me, and remember I said this." Uncle Dixon put his right hand on Rennie's shoulder and gave a little squeeze. "If Ambrose tells you something, then it's the truth. You got that, Rennie? The truth."

"Of course. Ambrose is an honest, truthful man, and I'll

believe every word he says." Uncle Dixon studied her face, like he was trying to make sure she had really heard him. "I'll remember. I promise." She nudged a glass toward him. "Can you finish your orange juice?" Hoping to ease the sudden tension in the room, she added, "It's got potassium in it, and I read that's supposed to be good for stroke victims."

Uncle Dixon answered softly, "I've never been a victim in my life. My brain's just gotten a little fuzzy, so I've got to make some adjustments in how I get along, but that's not being a victim. Matter of fact, my stroke is a blessing. When the good Lord reminds you your time on earth is limited, you go ahead and do things you'd been meaning to get to one day. This stroke has gotten me closer to my time to be with my wife, and it's helped me spend more days with you." His eyes crinkled above his smile.

"I'm not sure I'd ever think a stroke was a blessing, but I'm glad you can see it that way." She checked the clock in the kitchen. "Sheriff Ricketts is coming by at nine o'clock to talk to me about pressing charges against Tiny."

"I hope he's ready to do the right thing." Uncle Dixon surveyed her bruised jaw. "The bee salve is really helping."

Rennie sat at the kitchen table. "When I came to the bee yard that night, I was badly injured, but when Ambrose found me, it seemed like my wounds were mostly healed." She thought back to the circle of bees, the odd vibration in the air, and her conversation with her aunt. "Something magical happened that night. Aunt Eugenia and the bees saved my life."

He nodded. "Love is the strongest power there is."

A sharp rapping on the door startled them both. "Rennie," a voice called from the porch. "It's Sheriff Ricketts."

Uncle Dixon struggled to his feet. "I'll go out to the porch and give you some privacy, unless you want me to stay with you."

It was tempting to have her uncle's reassuring presence as she discussed prosecuting Tiny, but it was high time she managed on her own. "I'll meet you out there when we're done."

Rennie opened the door and let the sheriff in. "Let's sit in the den."

The sheriff perched on a chair, then cleared his throat. "Tiny has given me his statement. He said you two got into a fight because he found you'd been hiding money from him."

"That's one way to put it, but it was my money."

"He also said May Dean Bradford was present and claimed the money was hers." His stern look chilled Rennie's heart. "Is that true?"

"She was trying to protect me."

"That's not what I asked." His eyes narrowed. "Do I need to remind you how serious it is to give a false statement to the law?"

Rennie looked down. "No, sir, it wasn't true."

"What we've got here is a domestic situation. A wife lied to her husband after he caught her concealing money. Then another female, your cousin, lied to him to try and cover it up. Tiny got angry and smacked you." He stood, suddenly looming larger than life as he was silhouetted against the screen door. "I'm not filing charges. I suggest the two of you kiss and make up." With his hand on the door, he added, "Don't lie to him again, Rennie. You know how his temper is."

Rennie sat on the sofa, stunned. Any thought she had of the sheriff locking Tiny up and throwing away the key vanished. Her husband had nearly killed her, but *she* was the one getting a lecture from the law. She needed to look elsewhere for help. She corrected herself. She needed to look *within* for help. No man, no person, was going to save her. She had to do it on her own. She could accept help from those who loved her, but the power that would save her had to come from somewhere within her own fractured soul.

Uncle Dixon looked up when Rennie stepped onto the porch. "Is he going to arrest Tiny?" His gaze seemed to pierce through to her. "Never mind. I see my answer."

"I'm going down to the hives for a few minutes if you'll be okay here for a little while."

"Sure." Lewis Carroll looked up from his spot on her uncle's lap. "We're just enjoying the morning." He rubbed the cat's ears as he looked over his farmland. "I have a favor to ask you. The next time you're in town, would you buy me some envelopes at the Emporium? The smallest box they have. I only need two."

"Sure. Should I get stamps?"

"Nope. Just the envelopes. And be sure to take some cash outta the drawer to pay for them."

The sunlight on his face highlighted the deeply etched lines on his cheeks, and his eyes, once the color of the rich Tennessee earth he had farmed for decades, were cloudy. "Don't you worry, Rennie. All I have will be yours soon. This is just a rough patch. You and Ambrose will be fine."

Tears filled her eyes as she made her way down the familiar path. Her uncle's confusion was getting worse by the day, and now he was mixing up Tiny and Ambrose. She and

Tiny were definitely *not* going to be fine. Hedge parsley waved in the breeze in its late July glory, and the air was filled with the call of juncos and cardinals, but all Rennie could see was the sheriff's face, and all she could hear was his voice saying her beating was a squabble. She sank onto Eugenia's bench and sobbed.

"I should have known the sheriff would take his side." As she cried, she watched the bees moving in and out of their hives. Their survival depended on them working together. A single bee would die if alone, and their only chance at thriving was becoming a part of the collective. A dead leaf, pushed by the wind, tumbled across her foot, and she watched it disappear from view. She needed to abandon the pipe dream of repairing her marriage and think about her own survival. The idea of giving up the possibility of another child left her soul in tatters, but she was not willing to risk her life returning to Tiny in exchange for that possibility. There was no money for a divorce, but maybe she could live like Arden did, married on paper but living an independent life.

She walked to the hives, passing over the soft moss that had cushioned her when she slept the night she had stood in death's doorway. Had her aunt and the bees mended her body only for her to return to a shadow-filled, less-than life with Tiny?

Placing a hand on the roof, she felt the rusted nails and rubbed the bit of faded black cloth between her fingers, put there the day Uncle Dixon lost the love of his life. No. Her aunt wouldn't have done that, and neither would the bees. Energy surged through her as she was filled with the understanding she was meant for more.

But how could she conjure a different life, one where she could take care of herself? *Think, Rennie.* What was she good at? A current of electricity ran from her fingertips as the answer formed in her brain. Of course. Baking. She could turn her cakes into a business. *Her* business, a way to become independent and maybe even save enough to divorce Tiny. Spark wasn't big enough to support a cake business, but she could sell to the diners and meat and threes in Nashville, with a clientele like Arden's, and slowly become self-sufficient. The Blue Plate customers loved her desserts, and there had to be dozens of similar restaurants with hundreds of like-minded customers who would do the same in Nashville. And there was a business card from a Nashville restaurant in the Blue Plate's drawer, proof that her cooking was good enough to impress a professional.

She sat on Eugenia's bench and touched the rose medallion that had become a kind of talisman. A baking business, where she could be her own boss and provide for herself for the first time in her life. Her family—Uncle Dixon, May Dean and Ev, and their new baby—would surround her with love as she rebuilt her life, experiencing the thrill of living on her own. She leaned back and lifted her face to the sun. Closing her eyes, she let her mind wander to what she could see ahead for herself. A business filled with love and honey. She smiled to herself. A life filled with love and honey. Of course. Her new business would be called Love and Honey.

With renewed hope, she returned to the house. Checking her watch, she said to her uncle, "It's almost time for splashdown. Let's go watch it, and then I want to ask your advice about something."

Dawn was breaking over the Pacific Ocean, and the newscasters were discussing the heavy cloud cover. A countdown clock was running. Rennie's stomach was doing flips, first for the safe return of the astronauts, but also for her own safe return to life. Finally, she could envision herself happy, independent of Tiny.

Cronkite's voice was steady. "Hot dog. There they are." Sunlight burst through the clouds as he said, "*Apollo 11* has made it." Rennie and Uncle Dixon hugged.

"Right on target," said Cronkite.

"They're back from the moon," another announcer said.

Uncle Dixon's voice shook. "President Kennedy must be so proud. His dream has come true." He rubbed his eyes. "I imagine he'll call for a ticker-tape parade through Washington."

Rennie frowned. "You mean President Nixon?"

"No, the president. Mr. Kennedy." He reached over and switched off the television. "What did you want to talk to me about? You mentioned something about advice."

Rennie turned away to hide her worried expression. "It can wait."

―

While Uncle Dixon napped, Rennie pulled out the ingredients for her Honey Moon Cake and started baking. She had always found solace in the measuring and stirring, but now her brain began to consider what else baking could provide for her. When Arden offered her the temporary job at the Blue Plate, she had been surprised, but now she was comprehending that her food could be a ticket to freedom.

As she added a bit more honey to the batter and gave it a final stir, she realized her next step. After she slid the pans into the oven, she made two phone calls.

Arden looked up from her ledger when Rennie opened the Blue Plate's door, cake carrier in her hand. "I'm glad to see you, Rennie. Your phone call was very intriguing." She eyed the faint bruise still visible on Rennie's jaw. "If you'd prefer privacy, we can go somewhere else."

"Here is fine." Rennie set the carrier on an empty table. "Like I mentioned on the phone, I'm hoping for some business advice." She unsnapped the lid. "I've come up with a new cake, and people really like it. I brought you one to try."

"Let me get a knife and a couple of plates, and let's see what you've got." After cutting two slices and handing a plate to Rennie, Arden took a bite. Her eyes widened and she took a second taste, pulling the fork out slowly from her mouth.

Rennie was watching Arden's face anxiously. "I call it a Honey Moon Cake. I'd like to start my own business selling them in Nashville, but I don't know how to start." Rennie knit her brows. "If you think it's good enough to sell, that is."

Arden set down her fork. "That is the best cake I've ever put in my mouth. You could build whatever type of business you'd like around this one cake, or you could have it as the centerpiece of a collection. Tell me what you've got in mind."

The relief in Rennie's voice was palpable as her plan

gushed out. "I was thinking of selling to Nashville meat and threes. Your customers really liked my cooking, so I figure the same could happen for restaurants like yours in Nashville. I could take samples to a dozen or so and see if they'd be interested in ordering from me. My first stop would be that diner in Nashville, the one whose owner left me his card. I thought I'd add up the cost of my ingredients and then add about 10 percent for my labor." Rennie shrugged. "That's as far as I've gotten."

Arden looked at Rennie. "You're right about calling on that restaurant owner who liked your cooking so much. His place is a lot nicer than a diner, though, one that would be perfect for your new business. I like the idea of selling to Nashville restaurants, but not the diners part. Places like mine are limited as to how much they can charge. I raised the price of my chocolate meringue pie by a nickel and customers had a fit. I had to drop it back down. Sell to the fancy restaurants, Rennie, and charge a fortune." She took another bite of cake. "This flavor is unlike anything I've had before, and honestly, it would seem a little out of place on a menu alongside what I offer, cobblers and such. Pitch it as gourmet, a delicacy, and you'll be successful."

"Would restaurants really pay a high price for just a cake?"

"Never call it that. It's not *just* a cake." Arden's voice changed, and Rennie got the impression she wasn't just talking about business anymore. "You teach people how to treat you. If you walk in with your head high, confident in what you're doing, people will take you seriously. But if you've got your shoulders slumped and you're apologizing before you even say why you're there, they'll see you as somebody not worth their time, and they'll dismiss you as an amateur." She took Rennie's hands. "Know your worth." Arden gave her hands a squeeze. "Here's what we'll do. I'm closed on Mondays. Let's you and me go into Nashville for a little reconnaissance mission. We'll go to the three or four high-end restaurants for dessert. We'll check out the prices and exactly what our competition is and then move on to phase two, pitching this fabulous cake."

"I'd like that."

"Meet me here Monday morning at eleven and we'll do it."

A customer walked through the front door. "Am I too early for lunch, Arden?"

"Not at all, hon. Have a seat and I'll be right with you." Arden rose from the table. "If you'll let me, I'll be your first customer and buy the rest of that cake." She walked over to the till and opened it. Taking out a ten-dollar bill, she handed it to Rennie. "I'm putting it on the chalkboard as a one-day-only special for twice what I charge for any other dessert." She winked. "It's all about marketing."

After slipping the bill into her purse, Rennie checked her watch. "I've got an appointment with Raddy Tisdale to talk about getting a divorce."

"That's great news." Arden beamed at Rennie. "Tell you what. After your meeting with Raddy, come on back here and I'll buy you a celebratory lunch."

Raddy Tisdale's waiting room was filled with Tennessee history memorabilia, and his knowledge about the Volunteer State was legendary. He had hand-drawn maps from when the state was still a territory, a leather pouch said to belong to Davy Crockett, and even a framed letter from John Sevier, the state's first governor. He'd published a book through a nonprofit historical society called *My Tennessee* and taught a unit about the state to the Spark Elementary fifth graders every spring.

Mr. Tisdale emerged from his office to shake Rennie's hand. "I'm glad to see you, Rennie. How's your uncle getting along?"

"Pretty well. Thank you for seeing me on such short notice."

"Always glad to help out one of my best students." While most of her classmates had taken advantage of a week off from their regular teacher by goofing off or cutting class, Rennie had sat spellbound as Mr. Tisdale spoke of Tennessee's early history. "Your paper on the diversity of our agriculture is still the best one I've ever had the pleasure of reading." He gestured to a wingback chair. "What can I help you with?"

"It's my, well, um, I-I . . ." She closed her eyes for a moment, summoning the strength that imbued her in the bee yard. "I want a divorce."

The lawyer grabbed a legal pad. "You're married to Luther Hendricks, correct?"

"Yes, sir."

"You don't need to go into too many details right now, but why are you seeking this divorce?" When Rennie didn't answer, he said gently, "Has he put his hands on you?"

"He's always had a bad temper, but things got a lot worse after he got dropped from the baseball team and we moved back to Spark. He beat me the night of the moon landing, and I tried to file charges, but Sheriff Ricketts called it a squabble and said we just needed a few days apart so he could cool down." She studied the brocade fabric of the chair before looking up at the lawyer. "I'm afraid he'll kill me next time."

"Domestic violence is not a squabble; it's a crime, and Mike Ricketts needs to do his job." Mr. Tisdale jotted several notes onto the legal pad. "I have two precious daughters, and I cannot imagine either of them staying in an abusive relationship. I'd be glad to take your case."

"Thank you." Rennie twisted the wedding ring still on her finger. "My main question is how much will it cost? On the phone you said I could talk to you for free, but a divorce is bound to take a lot of money."

Raddy leaned back in his chair. "It does, usually. But let me tell you a little story. My oldest daughter, Jeanie, was sick with recurring bouts of fever when she was a baby. The doctor had no explanation and said she'd outgrow it. One night she was burning up, and her temperature was 105. She was too weak to even cry, and my wife and I were terrified. I went to your aunt Eugenia." He reached behind him and grabbed a photo of two smiling girls from his credenza. "That's little Jeanie on the right, with her baby sister, Cheryl Ann," he said, pointing to a girl of about five in pigtails. "Anyway, your aunt broke that fever, and Jeanie made a full recovery." He set the frame back on the credenza. "She's been healthy ever since and is even getting married this fall."

"My aunt was a healer. I'm glad she could help your daughter."

"I offered Eugenia money, which she would not accept. But I can take your case pro bono as a way to repay that debt I've long owed."

"What's pro bono?"

"It means I won't charge you for my work."

"I'll always be with you, even when you can't see me." Rennie leaned forward in her chair. Could it be that easy?

Mr. Tisdale continued, "I've known the Hendricks family for years. Tiny was a nice enough kid, but ever since he came back to Spark, he's turned into his daddy. Wayne and I have had some dealings, and let's just say the apple doesn't fall far from the tree. I'd be glad to help you be shed of Tiny. There will be court costs I can't do anything about, but that should be only fifty dollars or so."

Rennie slumped back in her seat. She hadn't even started her business, and who knew how long it would take her to make fifty dollars profit.

After a moment, she lifted her chin. This divorce was her chance at freedom, and she'd do whatever it took to have that chance. The ten dollars Arden paid for the Honey Moon Cake was a great start, and she'd get to work right away calling on those restaurants until she had the money. With a determined voice, she answered, "Thank you, Mr. Tisdale. I really appreciate your offer to help me for free." She rose from her seat. "I'll need to save up for those court costs, but as soon as I have the money, I'll come back."

"I'll walk you out. I'm meeting Mrs. Tisdale at the Blue Plate for lunch."

"I'm headed there myself," said Rennie. The pair walked for a moment, but as soon as the Emporium's bright awning came into view, Rennie excused herself. "I almost forgot. I need to pick up something for my uncle. Thank you again, Mr. Tisdale."

The bell on the Emporium door jingled. As she stepped through the door, Grady Neal greeted her. "What can I get for you, Rennie?"

"Hey, Grady. Just need your smallest box of envelopes."

"Sure thing. Let me go get them."

A baby's cry came from behind a curtain, and for a half second, Rennie thought it was Gabriel. A young woman emerged from the office, shushing the fussy infant. "Hi, Rennie. I hope Lottie isn't bothering you. She's teethin' something awful."

"She's not bothering me one bit, Hannah."

"Hon," Grady called from the back. "Could you come help me a sec?"

Hannah looked at Rennie. "Would you mind holding her?"

Rennie's knees nearly buckled from the mix of pain and joy at having a baby in her arms. The baby's soft, downy head nuzzled against Rennie's breast, rooting. If she closed her eyes, she could imagine it was Gabriel she was holding, alive and healthy. She gently swayed back and forth, reveling in the child's warmth and Ivory soap smell. The baby grasped her finger and squeezed with a strength that startled her. "I see the moon, the moon sees me," she crooned softly. As the baby looked up at her with eyes as blue as a clear morning in June, Rennie closed her own, drinking in every second of this moment.

Grady emerged from the back with the envelopes, followed by Hannah. "Thank you, Rennie." She took her daughter from Rennie's grasp, and Rennie had to fight the instinct to reach her hands back toward the baby. After paying for the envelopes, Rennie stumbled out of the store, eyes welling with tears, and sat on the bench outside the Emporium.

She had lost so much when Gabriel died, and with the divorce, she was about to give up her chance at another baby. As much as she hated to relinquish her dream, she feared she wouldn't live long enough to have a second child if she stayed married to Tiny. He had been a failure with baseball, investing, and farming, but she couldn't shake the feeling that he would find the success that had eluded him when he promised to end her life.

Tears slipped down her cheeks as she rested in the sun for a few minutes. Then she wiped her eyes and headed for the Blue Plate.

CHAPTER 43

"THERE YOU ARE." ARDEN BUZZED OVER TO RENNIE. "Were your ears burning? Nancy Tisdale just had a slice of your Honey Moon Cake and wants to talk to you."

Rennie walked over to the booth where Raddy Tisdale was sitting with his wife. She nodded to the plate scraped clean of every crumb of cake and dot of icing. "I'm glad you enjoyed my dessert."

"It was fabulous." Mrs. Tisdale tilted her head toward her husband. "Our daughter is getting married in October, and I haven't been able to find a cake worth having until I tried this." She pointed to her empty plate. "Will you make Jeanie's cake for her wedding?"

"Oh, I-I've never made a wedding cake before."

Nancy Tisdale glanced at her watch and jumped. "I'm late for my appointment at the Curly Q. I don't want Evangeline mad at me." She laughed. "When a woman takes scissors to your hair, you want her in a good mood." As she picked up her purse, she pointed her finger at her husband. "Raddy, do whatever you have to do to convince Rennie to make our cake."

As the Blue Plate's door closed behind Nancy Tisdale, Raddy motioned for Rennie to take a seat, a huge grin across his face. "My wife has been to every bakery in Nashville sampling wedding cakes and has complained about each one. I've been listening to her moan for weeks. She's even been threatening to drive to Atlanta to start looking there." He took a slow sip of his iced tea. "If I can make my wife happy and get you out of a marriage to Tiny Hendricks at the same time, then we've got what I call a win-win on our hands."

Arden approached the table with a plate in her hands. "I promised Rennie some lunch, so I'll drop this off and let you two talk." Arden removed the dirty dishes from the table and returned to the kitchen.

Mr. Tisdale watched Arden walk away, and when she disappeared behind the swinging doors, he quietly said, "You don't have to decide anything right away, but I would be honored if you baked my daughter's wedding cake, and I'll put down a deposit of, let's say, fifty dollars if you agree."

"I don't need any time to think about it. I accept and will make the best cake you've ever had. When's the wedding?"

"October 25th."

Relief flooded her body at the thought of her freedom. It couldn't come fast enough. "How long will it take for the divorce to be finalized?"

Raddy frowned. "If he doesn't contest, sixty days, but if he wants to go to court, he could drag it out for months, even years." He paused. "I have a judge friend who owes me a favor. If Tiny will assure me he's not contesting the divorce, I might could get it done in thirty days."

The anger Tiny would display when he heard about the divorce scared Rennie, but the thought that she might not survive the next beating scared her even more. She wasn't sure how to tell him, but she'd find a way.

"We should talk in a more private location. After your lunch, can you come back to my office? I need some background information. The date you were married, that sort of thing."

"Absolutely."

CHAPTER 44

A DAY TO CELEBRATE.

Indeed.

That an act of kindness from twenty years ago is helping today has amazed our girl.

She does not yet fully realize love is eternal, without obligation to human constructs as mundane as time.

Humans are so linear, and everyone knows the world is round.

Rennie will always be enveloped by that love, from Eugenia and so many others.

Including us.

Especially us.

CHAPTER 45

ON MONDAY MORNING AT 11:00 A.M. SHARP, RENNIE pulled into the Blue Plate's parking lot and touched the hearts on Eugenia's necklace for luck. This was the beginning of her Love and Honey business, and she wanted to feel her aunt and uncle were with her as she began what could be a whole new start. Tiny had broken the clasp when he yanked it off her neck the afternoon of her birthday party, and even a few years ago she could have taken it to her uncle and received it back good as new. Now his hands could barely manage the buttons of his blue flannel shirts, so Rennie made do with a wire bread tie snaked through the misshapen links.

Arden came out of the Blue Plate's back door and waved at Rennie as she opened the passenger door for her. "Nancy Tisdale is pleased as punch that you're making her daughter's wedding cake, and she's telling the good news to everyone she knows. Wedding cakes could be a second revenue stream for you, or if you decide against selling to restaurants, it could be another option for a business model." She got in the driver's side and started the Oldsmobile. "You were smart to say yes, even if you hadn't planned on offering wedding cakes. Always keep your eyes and ears open. You never know when a great opportunity will come along."

Rennie turned to face Arden. Time to say it out loud. "I've taken your advice and I'm going to divorce Tiny. You were right. I need to leave him before he kills me."

"I'll give you whatever money you need." Arden's face was grim. "And don't say no. The whole point of having money is for getting what you need, and you *need* this divorce."

"Thank you, Arden. That means a lot to me, but I've found a way to pay for it."

The traffic was light, and soon they were approaching downtown Nashville. As Arden turned onto West End Avenue, Rennie said, "Can I ask you one more thing?"

"You don't need permission—just ask."

"I'm thinking of taking back my maiden name. It would help me heal and set me on a path to feeling like my old self again, before I ever took up with Tiny. Like I could close the book on that part of my life and be ready for whatever is ahead." She looked at Arden. "Did you ever think of dropping your married name?"

Arden smiled. "Gatewood *is* my maiden name. When I crossed the Mississippi state line and entered Tennessee, I left everything behind, including that family's name."

"But you wear a wedding ring."

She waved her left hand. "Nope. I bought this for myself in Memphis to keep any man at a safe distance. My wedding ring is somewhere near the *Welcome to Tennessee* sign by the highway." She grinned. "I bought myself a little house and enjoy my peace and quiet without a soul around. I see people all day long at the diner, but when I'm at home, I am just with me, myself, and I, and I wouldn't have it any other way. I will *never* remarry, and that is a guarantee."

A few minutes later, Arden pointed to a converted private home on the outskirts of downtown with white pillars and a wide front porch. "Here's our first stop." A wooden sign said: *Welcome to Roscoe's Kitchen. Serving Nashville Since 1947.* "The same year I moved to Spark. How about that? They have a solid reputation for steaks and seafood." She handed her keys to the valet. "I thought we'd have a light lunch first, then get started on our dessert tour."

The hostess seated them and handed the women leather folders with menus printed inside. After looking at the offerings, Rennie closed the folder. "I don't think I can afford to order any lunch and dessert too. I'll just eat some of the bread in this basket." She looked up. "It's free, right?"

"It is, but today is my treat," Arden said. "It brings me a lot of joy to help you launch your career. Order whatever you want."

After enjoying delicious crab cake salads, both women studied the dessert menu, printed on heavy cream-colored paper. Crème brûlée, Chocolate Decadence Cake, and bananas Foster were listed, each with a mouthwatering description. Rennie's eyes popped at what they were charging. "A slice of cake is four times what you charge at the Blue Plate."

"Yep. This is why I want you to target upscale restaurants."

When the waiter came to their table, Rennie said, "Can I have the Chocolate Decadence Cake?"

Arden ordered the crème brûlée, then after the waiter

left, said quietly to Rennie, "You are the customer. They are here to serve you. Don't ask for permission. Just tell them what you want." She shook her head. "We women are taught to always be quiet, not make a fuss, and apologize even when we've done nothing wrong." She looked at Rennie. "Would Ev order like that? He's polite, and his mama raised him right, but would he ever ask permission to eat a piece of cake in a restaurant?"

Rennie considered the question and then answered, "I have a lot to learn."

"And I'll help you all I can," Arden answered.

"Those dessert prices were so high. I still can't believe people pay that much," Rennie whispered.

"Absolutely they do. Businesspeople bring out-of-town clients here to impress them. Part of the experience is having the client see how much the host is spending. It all goes on an expense account, so the host can be the big deal he so desperately wants to convince the client he is." She nodded her head to a table where a plate of bananas Foster was being flambéed tableside. "Putting on a show is part of running a successful business. This restaurant knows their customers and is givin' 'em what they want."

The waiter brought their desserts, and Arden poked at the crème brûlée. "Pretty good presentation, with a nice thick coating of caramelized sugar." She took a bite. "It's good. They use real vanilla and cream."

Rennie examined her cake. "They give a big portion, and the swirls of chocolate sauce under the slice make it look fancy." She tilted her head. "I could do the same thing with honey for my cake, and not just have the drizzle on top."

Arden nodded. "Now you're getting the hang of how this works. Does it taste as pretty as it looks?"

An explosion of chocolate hit her taste buds. "It's delicious. Rich and dense, without being dry."

"You can see why they've been in business for decades. An excellent meal."

Le Bijou de Tennessee was next on the list, located on Broadway in downtown Nashville. Towering ivy topiaries flanked the large wooden door and a gas flame flickered from a black wrought iron lantern.

They had a seat at the bar and looked over the menu. The prices were even higher than at the previous restaurant. "This isn't even in English, Arden. I can't see them putting something called a Honey Moon Cake on the menu."

"Nonsense. They'll just call it whatever *honey moon* is in French. Never self-reject. You've got a good product, and any restaurant would be happy to carry it. Maybe they'll say no, but let *them* say it, not you."

When the waiter came to their table, Arden handed him the two closed menus. "Bring us your two most popular desserts."

Rennie turned to Arden. "How did you learn so much about running a business?"

"My in-laws. They were efficient and effective." She shrugged. "I learned a lot from them, even when they treated me like last week's leftovers. Handle a problem right away, be decisive, open with your best offer, and make it clear you're not negotiating—so many lessons."

After receiving their desserts, she continued, "Trial and error is a good teacher too. If I wasn't sure how to handle something, I picked what I thought was the best option and tried it. Sometimes it worked, sometimes it didn't, but either way, I knew more at the end than I did going in." She took a bite of her lemon mousse and made a face. "Freezer burn."

Rennie tried her crepes Suzette. "This seems a little stale." She pushed the plate toward Arden. "See what you think."

Arden chewed thoughtfully. "Margarine." She looked at Rennie. "Still think you couldn't compete with the Nashville big dogs?"

"Nope." Rennie grinned. "My cake is better than either of these."

"I agree. Let's pay the bill and get out of here."

When Arden pulled into the next parking lot, she said, "This is Alan's. The owner is the one who's already a fan of your food. We're incognito this time, but at your next visit, you'll come with your cake and I predict he'll be your first sale."

Rennie studied the building, located in a tony part of town. Mature boxwoods flanked the flagstone walkway leading to the front door.

A waitress greeted them as they entered. "Welcome to Alan's. Two for lunch?" she asked, looking at Arden.

"No, thanks. We're just here for a couple of desserts."

"Great. Would you prefer a booth or seats at the bar?"

"The bar, please."

Rennie ordered apple pie, while Arden chose Baked Alaska. After a few bites, Rennie pushed her plate away.

Arden put her fork down. "It's okay but not great. I can't tell what's missing, though. Here, you try it."

"The meringue is chewy and the ice cream is good, but the pound cake seems a little bland."

Arden got up from the bar. "Excuse me, Rennie, I'll be back in a bit." She took her purse and headed for the sign marked *Restrooms*.

A man refilled Rennie's water glass and glanced at her plate. "Was the pie not to your liking?" he asked.

"Oh, it's, um . . ." She paused, searching for a nice way to say what she thought. "I think if the cook had used Granny Smith apples instead of Red Delicious, and brown sugar instead of white, it would be better. And a little more cinnamon."

He gestured to the Baked Alaska. "Did you try that?"

"I did."

He cocked his head. "What did you think?"

"Mostly good, but the cake was a little . . ."

"Tasteless?"

Rennie nodded. "Exactly."

The man leaned closer to Rennie. "Are you a baker?"

Arden had cautioned Rennie that this trip was only for research, but she also told Rennie to take advantage of unexpected opportunities. This was *definitely* an unexpected opportunity. She straightened her shoulders and answered, "Yes," then added, "I'm launching my new baking business, Love and Honey, for Nashville restaurants with my signature dessert, what I call a Honey Moon Cake. I use local honey and eggs from my home in Cooke County." Clasping her hands together under the bar to stop them from shaking, she said, "I could bring some samples in for you all to try if you think the owner might be interested."

"I *know* he would be." The man grinned and put out his hand. "I'm the owner, Alan Carter."

Rennie shook his hand. "I'm glad to meet you, Mr. Carter. I'm Rennie King Hen—Rennie King."

Alan tilted his head. "Cooke County? Any chance you're with the Blue Plate? I had one of the best lunches of my life there a few weeks ago."

Rennie blushed. "That's me, Mr. Carter."

Alan picked up the bill the waitress had left by the plates and put it in his pocket. "Call me Alan. I'm looking forward to trying that Honey Moon Cake, Rennie King."

Jane Austen's whole back end was wagging as she approached the truck. Rennie hopped out and knelt to the ground to hug her. "Hi, sweet girl. I'm so glad to see you."

Ambrose came from the back of the house, wiping his hands on his jeans. "Here to see the best girl in the world?" There was that dimple again.

"I am." Rennie tried to slow her jumping pulse. She was married and Ambrose was just a friend. "Has she put on a little weight since last week? She looks a little heavier."

His eyes sparkled. "My mama told me never to discuss a lady's age or weight, but Jane Austen's a big fan of her second breakfasts. Can you come sit on the porch for a few minutes?"

"I'd like that." She patted Jane Austen's head. "Come on, girl, let's go inside."

Ambrose squinted at Rennie. "You've got a scratch on your neck. Let me see." He gently moved her hair aside and brushed his thumb against her skin. Her breath caught in her throat at his touch. "There's a drop of blood, but it doesn't look like a bug bite." He smelled like hay and sunshine and honey. Rennie stumbled a bit, and Ambrose steadied her. "It's your necklace. There's some kind of a wire."

"I, um, it got broken and I wanted to wear it today. I tried to fix it, but . . ." She blushed.

Ambrose untwisted the bread tie and held the necklace in his hand. "This was Eugenia's, the one Dixon gave you for your birthday."

Rennie nodded.

"I'll take it to my workbench in the barn. You go on the deck with Jane Austen and let me see if I can fix this for you." He started for the barn. "I'll just be a minute."

She'd never been alone in his house and couldn't resist a peek at his bookshelf. Her eyes widened when she noticed a well-worn copy of *Jane Eyre*.

She stepped onto the deck and was looking through his telescope when he returned. "Here you go." He slipped the delicate necklace around her neck, fastening it as Rennie breathed in his scent. "I tapped the bent links back into place with my tack hammer and was able to repair the clasp with needle-nose pliers."

"Thank you." Rennie touched the intertwined hearts. "That was really kind." She gestured to the telescope. "This is pretty fancy."

"My dad got me interested in the stars when I was a kid. This was his. I've really gotten into the constellations lately. The stories behind them are amazing. Take Orion, for example. Some people think the pyramids in Egypt are aligned with his belt, but . . ." He grinned. "Sorry. I get a little carried away sometimes with my hobby."

"I looked at your bookshelf on my way out here and noticed you and I share a hobby, reading classic books." She stifled a smile. "You're a fan of *Jane Eyre*?"

Ambrose laughed. "Don't look so surprised. I may be a tobacco farmer, but I'm not a total rube. *Jane Eyre* is one of my favorite books, partly because of Charlotte Brontë's courage. Even though women were not considered capable of being serious authors, she decided not to hide behind her male pen name and revealed herself as a female to her publisher, who was very surprised indeed to meet Charlotte Brontë, not Currer Bell."

Rennie was both mortified and intrigued that Ambrose knew more about Charlotte Brontë than she did.

"Did you know she also wrote a novel called *Shirley*? It's about a financially independent woman who makes savvy business decisions and who marries for love, all uncommon in her day." He smiled. "Even more reason to admire her."

Rennie shook her head. "I had no idea."

"I minored in English in college. It won't really help me be a better farmer, but I think books can make us better people. It's a good way to learn about the world without having to go do it all yourself."

A sharp *caw* caught Rennie's attention. She looked up and spotted a large crow circling overhead. "There's my friend Morrigan," said Ambrose. Reaching for a dented Twining's Irish Breakfast tin, he added, "I bought her some mealworms at the feed store."

The crow landed by Rennie, who saw the bird's chipped beak when he turned to look at her. "Poe? I've missed you."

It was Ambrose's turn to be surprised. "You two have met?"

She nodded. "He brings me gifts in exchange for peanuts and sunflower seeds. I was growing him some before . . ." Her voice trailed off. "I should be going. Thank you for fixing my necklace." She bent down to pat Jane Austen. "I'll come see you again real soon." Gesturing at the telescope, she said, "It's supposed to rain tonight, but I hope the forecast is wrong so you can see your constellations."

"It's not going to rain. The bees said so."

"Interesting. They've never discussed weather with me."

"Not like that. Bees can't fly in rain, so before bad weather moves in, they work especially hard gathering nectar because they'll be cooped up in their hives until it clears off. They were no busier than usual today, so no rain for us." He walked alongside Rennie as she headed for her truck. "Good to see you as always, my friend." He stopped. "I'm headed back to Travers first thing tomorrow for a few days. I'll be back on Sunday. Would you mind checking on Dixon's bees for me? Everything should be fine, but I'll feel better knowing someone who loves them is lookin' in on 'em."

"Sure, no problem," she said weakly before climbing into the cab of the truck, startling herself with how much she would miss him while he was gone.

CHAPTER 46

RENNIE WORKED AT HER UNCLE'S KITCHEN TABLE, calculating the cost of making a Honey Moon Cake. Until her trip to Nashville with Arden, she had not considered adding more than minimum wage for her time, but now that she knew the Nashville dessert prices, she realized she had been undervaluing her labor. How many cakes would she need to sell to be able to support herself? Hard to know, but at least she was on her way to opening her business. And making Jeanie Tisdale's wedding cake allowed her to explore a second revenue stream. She smiled at her new vocabulary. *Just like a real businesswoman.* For the first time since she buried Gabriel, she thought that, just maybe, her life could be beautiful again. She glanced at the Kit-Cat clock with its rolling eyes and swishing tail, then tiptoed into the bedroom to check on her uncle. He'd still been asleep when she'd gotten up that morning, not rising till after nine. He hadn't touched his breakfast or lunch and had called her Eugenia twice. Her brain was telling her his time was near, but her heart refused to listen. She was only now beginning to enjoy life again, and the thought of living in the world without her uncle was unimaginable.

Rennie slipped down to the bee yard to sit by the hives for a moment. The hum of the bees, usually so soothing, sounded like a dirge, while the colorful flowers looked garish instead of cheerful. Tears pricked her eyes and a slight headache throbbed in her temples.

As she sat in the sun, her mind filled with memories of her aunt and uncle. They loved one another deeply, and although he had never said the words, Rennie knew her uncle's world became bleaker the day his wife died. And now, in the bedroom they shared, with the walnut dresser watching over him as he had wished, he was preparing to receive his most fervent wish, to be reunited with her.

"And I'm sitting here feeling sorry for myself," she said to the hives. "I should be rejoicing." As she touched the bench's rose medallion, she whispered, "I'm not ready to say goodbye to him. I'm a human, so that's understandable, but I need to be thinking of him, not myself." She walked to the first hive and studied the faded scrap of mourning cloth. "I will miss him always, but please help me focus on his joy and not my sorrow."

When she returned to the house, he was still sleeping, with Lewis Carroll curled up beside him. A slight smile graced his lips. His pale skin looked paper-thin across his cheekbones, and his eyes were sunken. Was his breathing shallow, or was it her imagination? Rennie curled up in the maple rocker next to him and pulled out a book she had found on a shelf. She read a few pages but then stopped. Reading allowed her to visit anywhere on the globe and beyond, but at that moment her whole world was within that simple bedroom and she was exactly where she wanted to be.

After a few hours, she slipped out to the kitchen for a drink of water. As her glass filled under the tap, she resisted the urge to stop the rhythmic tail of the Kit-Cat clock. Rennie disregarded the dial in its round stomach that insisted it was 7:00 p.m. The way a day was measured had changed. Nothing mattered but Rennie and her uncle, and something as ordinary as time had no place in their home that day.

She returned to her uncle. No change. He slept on, and she willed herself not to adjust his quilt or smooth his hair. He didn't like hovering. She thought about calling the doctor, or Ev and May Dean, but didn't. An ambulance and bright lights and noise were not what he would want. He was reuniting with his beloved wife, and she wasn't going to selfishly try to make his body linger in Spark when his whole heart was already in heaven.

As the sun slipped behind the barn, she stood on the porch. She and her uncle had enjoyed so many talks out there, her in the swing and him in his willow rocker. The rounded top was smoothed by fifty years of his hand touching it as he sat or rose, and she gently caressed the slick wood, making the chair move slightly. Her eyes filled with tears at the thought of never seeing him rocking an afternoon away, looking out over his backyard again. As darkness fell, she went back inside.

She tiptoed into her uncle's room and was surprised to see him sitting up in bed, wide awake. "Hey there, Rennie girl. How are you getting along on this beautiful night?"

His voice was weak, and she could barely hear him. "Could you tell me today's date?"

"It's Wednesday, July 30th." She bent to smooth the quilt over his small frame.

He nodded. "The end of July." Rennie tried not to panic at the finality of his tone. "If you would, please open the bottom drawer of Eugenia's dresser for me and pull out the two envelopes. Can you set them there right on the top? Remember, that dresser is yours now."

She laid both envelopes on the wood, not trusting herself to look into Uncle Dixon's eyes.

"Can I get you some food or a glass of water?"

"Some water sounds perfect. Thank you for always taking such good care of me. Ambrose is a lucky man to have you as his wife."

When she got back to the room with his water, he was asleep. She tucked the double wedding ring quilt around him and returned to her chair beside his bed. Lewis Carroll was by his feet, sleeping peacefully. After a few minutes, her uncle woke up and said, "It's beautiful there, Rennie. Colors we don't have here, and music. So peaceful and filled with love. I don't want you to feel bad for me. Not one whit."

Tears stung her eyes. "I love you, Uncle Dixon." *What will I do without him?* She had a moment of selfishly wanting him to stay, despite the talking-to she had with herself earlier. "Any chance you feel up to telling me one of your stories?"

For the first time ever, he turned her down. "I'm sorry, sweet girl, but I don't feel quite able right now." His eyes looked over her head, and he nodded slightly, then turned his attention back to Rennie. "You were precious to me,

Rennie King, I thought my days of being happy were long past, but then you came home again. I loved every minute of our days together."

She was alarmed at how he started speaking in the past tense. "I hope I still *am* precious to you." She tried to keep the panic out of her voice. "And we'll have lots more days to share."

"My time is through, but yours is just starting. You have such wonderful things coming your way. Listen to the bees, and try to remember how it was."

Her voice caught in her throat. "I don't want you to go."

Uncle Dixon was whispering, and it was an effort for him to talk. "I'm a bee in July, Rennie, not worth a fly, but remember, you're my bee in June." He closed his eyes and drifted off again.

Rennie was quiet, with tears slipping down her face as she watched his irregular breaths making the faded quilt rise and fall. The time between breaths grew longer. Lewis Carroll had woken and was watching him too. "And you're *my* bee in June, Uncle Dixon."

She sank into a chair and fell into a fitful sleep. When she woke, pink streaks of the sun streamed into the east-facing window over the dresser. She looked over at her uncle and saw his sweet face, still smiling. He had one hand outstretched across the quilt, and Rennie desperately hoped Eugenia had taken that hand as she guided him home.

CHAPTER 47

THE MOST PRECIOUS REUNION.

To witness the power of love between Eugenia and Dixon is an honor.

With them both with us now, the universe feels more complete.

She is so sad, though.

A loss being a gain is a challenging concept for humans. She will still feel their love, made stronger by their being reunited.

She will need that love for what is ahead.

Indeed. Love is the most powerful force on earth, and she will need every ounce of that power for her next challenge.

She has been through so much already. Can we not delay what is ahead until she is stronger?

It has already begun.

CHAPTER 48

EV STOOD IN UNCLE DIXON'S BEDROOM, FROWNING over the two envelopes. "They're labeled *Open When I've Died* and *Open Before the Funeral*, so that's what I'll do." He tore the first envelope and read with a shaky voice.

Dear Family,

I have made all my final arrangements with Crick Phillips at the funeral home. I am paid up, and Crick already has my suit down there to put me in. I wore it to marry Eugenia, and I'll wear it to be with her again. He's got my obituary for the paper too. I want the visitation to be at Crick's, then the service to be outside by my grave at Cedar Hill. Brother Cleave tried to convince me that my soul would get a better sendoff from his pulpit, but I consider God's green earth to be my church, so don't let him go back on that. No store-bought flowers, please. All I want is whatever is in Eugenia's gardens. Please cut some blooms from around the house and down by the hives. I know May Dean is allergic to cats, so Rennie, could you also see after Lewis Carroll for me? I figure there's something I've forgotten, so use what's in the drawer to cover whatever I left out. I love you all, and please do not be sad for me. I am with Eugenia in Paradise and will watch over you all with much love.

Dixon King

May Dean dabbed at her eyes and said, "I'll go out to the kitchen and call Mr. Phillips and Brother Cleave." When she returned, she said, "They're on the way to pick him up. Brother Cleave said we could have the funeral on Saturday if we don't mind doing it later in the day. He's officiating at a wedding in Tullahoma but can be back by three." She shrugged. "I was thinkin' we'd have a noon service with dinner after, but I guess we can make it an early supper."

A soft knock on the front door about thirty minutes later signaled the arrival of the funeral home people. Ev checked his watch. "May Dean, if we don't leave right now, we'll be late for your doctor's appointment."

Rennie spoke up. "Y'all go on. I can handle things from here."

May Dean picked up her purse. "I'm sorry we have to go, but we'll be back in the morning. We can go over the details of the service and read that second letter."

The funeral home workers lifted his body and gently placed him on the stretcher, but they were going to take him outside with only a sheet covering him. "Hold on a minute. He hates to be cold." She grabbed the double wedding ring quilt from his bed and tucked it around him. "Okay, he's ready." She bent down and kissed his hollow cheek and then, with tears streaming down her face, watched him being wheeled out to the waiting hearse.

She pulled the Cotton Patch blouse, the only piece of black clothing she owned, from her drawer and carried it to Uncle Dixon's kitchen table. Smoothing it free of wrinkles, she spread the sleeves across the wooden boards. The scissors made a rhythmic sound as she cut three squares of fabric. Rennie gathered up the squares and placed them in her pocket.

She searched for Lewis Carroll as she trudged to the barn. No sign of him. Opening the barn door, she admired the hand-carved latch her uncle had opened and closed countless times. The sight of the rows of honey resting on wooden shelves, neatly labeled with the harvest dates, brought a catch to her throat.

Uncle Dixon's workbench was meticulously organized. She unscrewed the mayonnaise jar with its rusted blue lid and shook a few nails into her palm. Choosing three the same size, she added them to her pocket. With Uncle Dixon's hammer in her hand, she followed the path to the hives.

Eugenia's bench was warm from the summer sun. Bees darted about and a gentle wind stirred the leaves and flowers. A nuthatch warbled in a nearby tree as a mourning cloak butterfly landed on a thistle. On the surface everything seemed right with the world, but in reality nothing was as it should be. Her uncle's body was at the funeral home waiting to be dressed in the blue suit he'd owned for at least forty years, a preacher was composing his eulogy, and a crew of men was digging his grave in Cedar Hill Cemetery.

She fingered the soft black cloth, dreading the task in front of her. Saying it out loud made it true, and she didn't trust herself to be able to form the words. Her uncle had told her, though. *"Tell them everything, whether joy or sorrow. Say the truth the best way you know how."*

Rennie approached the first hive and knocked three times on the roof, then did the same with the other two. Swallowing hard, she began. "Beloved bees, Uncle Dixon died this morning. There's a visitation at the funeral home on Saturday at 3:00 p.m. Then we'll drive out to Cedar Hill Cemetery to lay him to rest next to his wife. After the burial we're going to have supper at May Dean and Ev's house."

A few bees crawled around the entrance to their hive, but most of them were still, perched on the edge of their hive, listening.

"Uncle Dixon loved you all. He said bees were some of God's best work, and he was right. Did you know he called me his bee in June?" The buzzing became more intense. "Uncle Dixon told me it grieved him terribly to come down here and tell you all his wife was gone, and now it's my turn to be brokenhearted. He is finally back with Eugenia, so we should be rejoicing, but that's too hard right now, at least for me." She lovingly stroked the edge of the landing board. "I brought you some black cloth so you all can have a proper mourning. We'll grieve for him and remember always how good he was to us. We are his bees, and there is no greater honor."

She drew a nail and the piece of the shirt out of her pocket and arranged the black square directly over the faded, tattered threads of cloth left there years ago by her uncle. She positioned the first nail so it would stand next to the one her uncle drove into the roof so many years earlier, as sharp and straight as a sentinel guarding a treasure.

Replicating his movements brought her a strange comfort as she brought down the hammer. She repeated this same action two more times so that all three hives could have their mourning cloth.

She sank back on the bench with the rose medallion digging into her back. The bench had always offered her comfort, but on that day the iron petals felt like the nails she had just hammered, piercing through her skin and directly into her heart.

She began gathering a mix of blooms, being sure all the colors were represented. After carrying them up to the house, she placed the stems in a metal bucket to take to the funeral home. A jar of honey sparkled on a shelf by the stove. She picked it up and set it beside the flowers.

The familiar screen door made its usual *thwap* as it closed behind her. She started for her usual seat, the swing, but then stopped. Uncle Dixon's weathered green rocker was empty, of course. She gently stroked the frayed, braided wicker of the arm, setting the chair in motion. A sob choked her as she sat in the chair.

Uncle Dixon had told her so many wonderful stories from that spot, like the one about Uncle Bertrand, who accidentally proposed to the wrong identical twin because of a moonless night but was too much of a gentleman to correct his error. And of how he came to own Ernest Hemingway, a mule that had been abused by a neighbor. He had an uncanny way of recognizing when a soul needed help, whether human or animal. "Just part of the magic that was Uncle Dixon, I guess," she whispered.

She sat on the porch until it was too dark to see. Making the effort to rise from the chair was overwhelming, but the thought of needing to give Lewis Carroll his dinner finally pulled her from the seat. She searched the house, calling his name, but couldn't find him. She checked under the beds and on top of the refrigerator, but no cat. *Oh, Lord.* Could he have been run over by either the hearse or Ev's car? Dashing to the driveway, she scanned the gravel. Nothing. She searched the barn. No cat. She shook the kibble in his dinner bowl, always a sure bet, but he had vanished.

She paced back to the house from the barn, calling for the cat with each step. Turning on every light in the house before she went to bed, she listened for Lewis Carroll as she dozed.

The next morning Rennie awoke to a heavy fog that shrouded the hills and dampened her as she searched the house, barn, and property again. Still no sign of the gray cat. Rennie took her morning tea onto the porch and sat in her uncle's chair. The slight southern breeze blew across the Solomon's seal surrounding the porch, lifting their scent into the air. "Bees? I need your help. Can you help me find Lewis Carroll? I've looked everywhere. Is he hurt? Did he run away?" A sparrow tutted in the distance, and the wind chimes clinked out a few tinny notes. She glanced around for a bee pulsing out which direction she should go to find him. Nothing. She called his name, but even as she did, her heart understood she would get no answer.

Losing Lewis Carroll was almost more than she could bear. Her uncle had asked her for only one thing, to care for his cat, and she had failed him. A huge loss and a small one combined brought Rennie to tears. How foolish she was to ever think that life could be beautiful.

CHAPTER 49

EV OPENED THE SCREEN DOOR OF UNCLE DIXON'S house and said, "Rennie? We're here."

Rennie came in from the porch. "How did it go at the doctor's yesterday?"

May Dean took Ev's outstretched hand as she stepped inside the house. "Everything's good. He was a little worried about my weight gain, but now he thinks I'm just having a big baby. He's certain it's a boy." She patted her stomach. "Everett Stallings Bradford Junior."

Ev picked up the second envelope from the dresser. "Y'all ready for me to open this?"

Rennie nodded.

He opened the envelope and read aloud.

Last Will and Testament of Dixon King
I leave to my niece May Dean King Bradford my daddy's gold watch, which can be found in the top left-hand drawer of Eugenia's walnut dresser. I also want her to have the maple rocker by my bed for her to rock her sweet baby girl. (Eugenia told me, so I have no doubt you

are having a daughter.) I made it with my own hands for what I thought would be my own baby someday, and it gives me joy to know you will be rocking yours in it.

To my other niece, Roberta Irene King Hendricks, I leave Eugenia's wedding ring, which is in a box beside the gold watch. I also leave to Rennie the dresser itself, as a reminder of all the family stories I told her.

A few weeks ago, I sold the farmland, house, and barn to Ambrose Beckett, who is now the sole owner. You all can take anything you want from the house or barn, but the buildings and land belong to him. Please give whatever you all don't want to a charity that helps people less fortunate than I have been.

Ev looked up from the paper. "That's it, except for his signature and the date." He shook his head. "This is a real shock, but it's definitely Dixon's handwriting."

A tense silence filled the room. Rennie was the first to speak. "Could you repeat that last part about the farm?" she asked slowly. Surely she had misheard.

Ev read from the document again. "I don't know what to say, Rennie. He sold it to Ambrose Beckett."

May Dean sank into the rocker, now hers. "I always thought he'd leave the farm to you, Rennie, and then you and Tiny could have your own place." She looked up. "Ambrose basically stole it from you. Did Uncle Dixon ever say anything about this?"

Rennie shook her head. "Uncle Dixon called me one day to tell me not to come by because he and Ambrose had some business in Nashville to take care of. I assumed it was something medical he didn't want to discuss." She sat on the bed, not trusting her legs. "He always told me the farm would be mine, and said it again just a couple of weeks ago, but he was pretty mixed up toward the end. Something must have changed." Her voice was weak. "I guess I just assumed what he told me was true, that I'd get his farm."

May Dean's body stiffened. "It *was* true, until Ambrose showed up."

The day she met Ambrose came back to her mind. He had laughed at her motives when she brought him the cherry pie. *"That's why you came, right? To check me out. Your uncle is feeble and owns the most desirable farmland in Cooke County. A stranger shows up and they're instantly good friends. Seems suspicious to me too."* This whole time, her first misgivings had been right. He'd heard about her uncle's farm from someone in Travers and decided it would be easy to trick an old man and a couple of country bumpkins out of the best farmland in Spark.

May Dean's face was blotchy, and her voice shook. "Everybody knew he was leaving the farm to Rennie. Why would he sell it to Ambrose?"

A gasp caused all three to look up. Darlene Prichard stood in the doorway, her eyes as big as the lid of the casserole dish she was holding. "I knocked and then yoo-hoo'd, but no one came to the door, so I let myself in. Crick Phillips called Dewey yesterday to make sure Dixon's obituary made it into this Friday's *Gazette*, so I heard about his passing." She looked at the dish in her hands. "I-I made a chicken casserole for you." She backed up. "I can see that, um, y'all are busy, so I'll just put this in the fridge and go." She stopped for a moment. "I'm so sorry. He-he was a wonderful man."

No one said a word until the screen door closed behind Darlene. Ev spoke first. "The whole town's gonna hear about Ambrose owning the farm in about fifteen minutes."

"I say good," snapped May Dean. "Everybody needs to know we've got a con artist livin' among us. He had us all fooled, although I should have figured him out when I invited him *twice* to come to church with us and he said no both times." She narrowed her eyes. "He was probably worried he'd burst into flames the minute he crossed the threshold." She turned to Ev. "Will you drive me over to his house? I want to give him a piece of my mind."

"He's not home," Rennie whispered. "He told me a couple of days ago he had some business to tend to in Travers and wouldn't be home until late tonight. He asked me to look after the bees until he got back."

"Probably busy bilking another family out of their inheritance." May Dean crossed her arms. "Guess he wanted to make sure his bees didn't die while he was gone."

Rennie opened the dresser drawer and pulled out the gold watch. "If he says you're having a girl, then you are, but you can save this for a son if you ever have one." She pointed to the rocker. "Can you take this too? I'd like to think of it already in your nursery, waiting for her to come."

May Dean said, "We're in my convertible, so the rocker'll fit if we put the top down." She took the watch from Rennie's hand. "What about Eugenia's ring? Don't you want to get that?"

She looked down at her wedding band, which hadn't left her finger since Tiny had placed it there. "Not yet," she said.

After Ev and May Dean left, Rennie sat in her uncle's

chair on the porch, stunned. He would make vague references to her keeping up Eugenia's garden after he was gone or maybe adding on a bedroom once their family outgrew the small house, but there had never been anything formal. She grimaced. Until Ambrose Beckett came along and hoodwinked her uncle into selling it to him. She should have trusted her first instincts and called him out for what he was, a thief. During their very first conversation, she had sensed an uneasiness about him when she asked why he moved to Spark. He had stammered a bit and then fed her that tale about his grandmother knowing Eugenia. Was any of his story true?

"I doubt it," she whispered, as she rocked herself in the chair.

She had given Jane Austen to this man and trusted he'd care for her. Rennie went by often to see her, and the dog always seemed happy and well fed, but now everything was in doubt. Maybe he took in Jane Austen as part of the con to convince everyone he was a nice guy, a dog lover glad to help out a friend. *A friend.* Rennie searched through what she remembered about their conversations. How much had she revealed to Ambrose about her life, her marriage? She cringed when she remembered how she felt so safe as he stood guard while she packed her belongings to move to her uncle's house.

Where was she going to live? Returning to Tiny was unimaginable. The thought of calling off the divorce horrified her, but what else could she do? The farm she had thought would be hers was someone else's property. Ev's sister from Atlanta would be moving in as soon as her husband left for Vietnam, and the baby was coming, so their house would be too full for a cousin afraid of her own husband. She didn't have enough saved up to rent somewhere, even if she postponed the divorce. Arden had told her more than once how much she treasured her solitude, and although she would take Rennie in, it would be temporary. She stared off into the distance, rocking herself gently in the chair as she searched for options. With a heavy sigh, she stilled the rocker. There was no other solution. As abhorrent as the idea was to her, would she have to reconcile with Tiny?

A bee landed on her arm. Rennie watched as she waggled her body like a head shaking *no*. "Uncle Dixon told me bees dance out a map to a new home when it's time to start a new hive. Are you planning on leading me to a new place to live? Or maybe you're here to warn me, just like you did when I first went to meet Ambrose. Oh wait, you didn't do that, the same as you didn't stop me from marrying Tiny to begin with." She shook the bee from her sleeve. "I believed my uncle's stories, so I guess that's my fault, but don't expect me to listen to any more Appalachian magic bee nonsense." Tears choked her. "If this is your idea of a beautiful life and having all I've longed for, I wish you'd left me at the bottom of the creek."

The rocker squeaked slightly as she reevaluated her relationship with the bees. Her uncle had understood and loved the bees, just as they understood and loved him. He had tried to make her feel special by telling her the bees cared for her too, but that was just one of his tales, or maybe his way of compensating for the lack of love from her parents. She thought the bees were guides, lodestars helping her along her path, but she was wrong. They allowed her to marry Tiny and to befriend Ambrose, the first and second man to betray her. She bristled. The bees had even failed her uncle, the man they supposedly loved. They permitted him, weak and confused at the end of his life, to be conned out of his farm. Those bees were there to produce honey for humans, no more than the chickens that laid eggs or the cows that gave milk. Humiliation washed over her as she realized how foolish she had been, believing insects could offer her solace, wisdom, and protection.

Her aunt and uncle were both gone, her so-called friend had duped her, and her husband had beaten her within an inch of her life. Even the cat had abandoned her once Uncle Dixon had died. She had never felt so alone in all her life. Putting her head in her hands, she sobbed.

CHAPTER 50

SHE HAS LOST THE LAST SCRAP OF HER FAITH.

We cannot blame her for that.

But we are right here beside her. How is it she cannot see us or sense our presence?

It is that human brain of hers. It cannot see what she will not believe.

What if we reminded her that one day she will be a queen bee, living in a hive filled with all she has longed for? Surely she could hear that.

She did not believe those words as she lay on the bottom of the creek bed, and she would not believe them now. We must wait until she can consider that these things are even possible.

CHAPTER 51

RENNIE'S ARMS WERE OVERFLOWING WITH FLOWERS when she approached the funeral home's wide double doors. The service was scheduled for later that afternoon, and she wanted every blossom and leaf to be perfectly placed before anyone arrived. From her wrist hung a bag containing a jar of honey. Even though she was mad at the bees, she knew they needed to be represented.

Crick Phillips held the door for her. "You can take those into the kitchen in the back. Would you like some help arranging them? Our Enid always does a good job with floral arrangements."

"Thank you, but I'd like to do them myself."

"Understood. We've got every kind of vase you could want in there. Help yourself." He paused. "I wasn't sure about the quilt, Rennie. Do you want us to bury him with it, or would you prefer to take it back home? It's folded in my office right now, but I can do whatever you'd like."

"*When I'm gone, I want you to use it.*" The words her uncle spoke to her about the quilt were too sacred to share with

Mr. Phillips, so she thought of a plausible response. "That quilt was on his bed since the day he moved into that house. It doesn't seem right not to return it to where it belongs. I'd like to take it home with me."

"Yes, ma'am. When you're finished with the flowers, come to my office and I'll give it to you."

When Rennie returned to the farmhouse, she clutched the double wedding ring quilt in her arms. She didn't want to let it go, as it felt like letting go of her uncle all over again, but she eventually smoothed it over the bed, running her hands along the cotton fabric to ensure not a single wrinkle was present.

The funeral home's lot was already full when Rennie arrived for the service. She parked, grateful not to see Tiny's black truck.

When she walked through the door, the people clustered around Darlene looked up and immediately stopped talking. Who needed the *Gazette* when they had the editor's wife to bring everyone up to speed?

May Dean took her by the hand and pulled her into an empty room. She shut the door and turned to face Rennie. "Didn't you tell me Ambrose said he never met Aunt Eugenia?"

Rennie nodded. "That's right."

May Dean's eyes narrowed. "Well, Mrs. Holloway, who lived next door to Aunt Eugenia's family growing up, just arrived from Kentucky to pay her respects. She told me the sweetest story about the week Eugenia McDonald and her mother spent nursing *Ambrose Beckett* back to health after he received terrible burns in a bonfire when Ambrose was about seventeen. She and her sister carried food over to them, as Eugenia and her mother were both so busy nursing *that sweet young man* back to health after his terrible accident." May Dean's eyes were flashing. "Mrs. Holloway went on to say that she spent an afternoon over there after she dropped off one of the meals, talking with Eugenia and Ambrose about how happy Eugenia and her husband were on their fifty-acre farm, which she found to be the prettiest, most fertile land she'd ever seen."

"*What?*"

May Dean nodded. "He learned about their farm *years ago* and made up his mind to get it one way or another."

Arden opened the door. "There you are, May Dean. Everyone is asking me questions about dropping off food, and I don't know the answers. Could you come out here and talk to them?" Arden turned to Rennie. "I am just so sorry for your loss. Your uncle was a fine man, and it was an honor to know him."

"Thank you," she said dully. "If you'll excuse me, I need to check on the flowers."

Bunches of delicate white Solomon's seal were in sprays around the casket, along with blue flag iris and wild geraniums. Yellow lanceleaf coreopsis nestled next to lavender spiderwort, with downy wood mint mixed in. The jar of honey glowed amber in the single ray of sunlight that had penetrated the dark curtains, and Rennie was glad to have a contribution from the bees there. She bent down to position the jar more fully in the sunlight.

"Rennie?"

Ambrose was standing in the doorway. He came toward her, arms outstretched for a hug.

"Stay away from me, Ambrose Beckett. I know what you did. *All* of what you did." She gestured toward the lobby.

"Thanks to Darlene, the whole town's gotten the news that you bought Uncle Dixon's house out from under him, and thanks to my aunt's old neighbor, we know you spent a week recovering at Eugenia McDonald's house, hearing about her farm, the best in Cooke County." Her eyes were sparkling. "That would be my *aunt* Eugenia, the woman you swore you never met."

Ambrose shook his head. "You've got it all wrong, Rennie."

"No. Finally, I've got it all right. You are a liar and a swindler and certainly not my friend!" Her voice rose. "Taking advantage of a weak and confused old man to get his property is as low as it gets." Tears filled her eyes. "I actually believed all that nonsense about that girl breaking your heart and how the bees told you to come to Spark." She shook her head. "That's what I get for thinking I could actually trust somebody."

Ambrose took a step toward her. "Please, let me explain."

Rennie shook her head. "I do not want to hear one word from you ever again."

Tiny strode toward Rennie and put his arm around her. "You're upsetting my wife, Beckett."

Rennie recoiled at the sound of Tiny's voice, and the touch of his hand sent gooseflesh across her body.

Tiny thrust out his chest. "Leave our family in peace."

She wanted to push his arm away, but the thought of having to reconcile with him stopped her. As much as it nauseated her, she took a step closer to her husband.

Ambrose looked from Tiny to Rennie and bowed slightly, then left, leaving Rennie with tears of frustration stinging her eyes.

May Dean trounced over to Tiny. "You've got some kind of nerve acting like the protective husband while our uncle lies cold in his coffin just a few yards away. I know what you did and who you really are, and I will never—"

Ev slipped his arm though May Dean's. "Sweetie, some of Dixon's friends from Nashville want to offer you their condolences," he said before gently pulling her away.

Tiny stepped forward to take Rennie's arm. She swallowed hard and took his beefy hand in hers.

⌒

August afternoons in Spark were typically miserable, but that day the air was pleasant, and the slight northerly breeze that blew across the cemetery was cool. Chairs were lined up in neat rows beside the open grave, with four chairs making up the first row. Rennie sank into her seat, flinching when Tiny dropped down beside her. *Better get used to it*, she told herself.

Brother Cleave appeared slightly uncomfortable as he shifted his feet in the grass. A bead of sweat dotted his upper lip despite the near-perfect weather.

Rennie tuned out Brother Cleave only a few sentences into the eulogy, as she realized he had warmed up the same service he had given for a farmer who had died a few months ago. Maybe he was annoyed that Uncle Dixon had declined to be preached over in a church, or maybe he had been so busy with the wedding he had performed earlier that he had no time to think of kind words to describe her uncle. Or maybe, Rennie thought, understanding a man like Dixon King was beyond the limited capabilities of someone like Brother Cleave. Uncle Dixon considered his simple bee yard to be more magnificent than any cathedral, and he viewed helping a neighbor to be more godly than sitting in your assigned pew every Sunday at 9:00 a.m.

Movement in the long row of verdant hydrangeas bordering the cemetery fence caught her eye. She looked, and then, like the night she had taken refuge in the bee yard, she had to look again to confirm what was before her.

The lush bushes bowed to the ground with the weight of thousands of bees resting on their blooms, branches, and leaves. Uncle Dixon's bees. All of them. She nodded to acknowledge their presence, prompting a scowl from Tiny, who angrily snapped his head toward the preacher.

"Uncle Dixon," a six-year-old Rennie had asked one summer as they sat in the Elliston Place Soda Shop enjoying hot fudge sundaes, "how far can bees fly?"

"Why don't you ask them?"

She had giggled. "That's silly."

He'd raised his eyebrows and asked, "Are you sure? Maybe you should try it." Her uncle added, "Since we're in town and they're at the hives, I'll answer for them. They fly as far as they have to. If they've got good flowers and plants to visit, they don't need to go any farther than their own bee yard. I once heard a beekeeper speaking at the agricultural center say scientists have measured tagged bees flying as far as six miles from their hive when food is scarce." He grinned. "But Eugenia makes sure food is never scarce."

Cedar Hill Cemetery was a good ten miles from the hives. Her uncle had said bees would fly as far as they needed to, and Rennie knew they needed to be at the funeral, the same as she or May Dean did. The bees' symbiotic relationship with her uncle had always seemed natural to her, but once in school, she had realized how unusual her uncle's hives were.

"We're doing a unit on insects in Mrs. Quimby's class, and she showed us a film strip about beekeeping that didn't make any sense to me," a young Rennie had said one afternoon. "The beekeeper was in this suit with a hood and was puffing smoke into the hives. Mrs. Quimby said the smoke made the bees sleepy so the keepers could open the hives, and the suit was to protect him from any bees that didn't get enough smoke."

"Mrs. Quimby is a mite confused. When bees feel they're in danger, they alert the other bees with a scent. The smoke masks the smell so the other bees don't know danger's brewing. Smoke scares bees. Just imagine thinking your home is on fire, so dark you can't see to escape. I'd never do that to bees I was tending." He shrugged. "I've always thought bundling up in a suit and blowing smoke around was for putting on a show, not for the bees' well-being. If the keeper would just work on building a good relationship with the bees instead of doing like they think they're supposed to, them and the bees would both be better off."

Brother Cleave's intonation changed as he wrapped up, and she briefly looked around at her neighbors. She caught sight of Ambrose standing at a distance, head bowed. As friends approached her to give their *so sorry*'s and hugs, she felt pity for them. They had all attended an uninspired service, while she and the bees had been part of a sacred thanksgiving.

After the service, Tiny turned to Rennie. "I'm starving. I imagine half the town has brought food to May Dean and Ev's house, so thank God I don't have to eat her slop. Let's go."

Rennie shook her head. "I'm going to visit Gabriel first. And besides, we each have our trucks, so you can go on without me."

"You think I'm walking into that house without you beside me? May Dean was shooting daggers at me the whole funeral, and I'm in no mood to give her the opportunity to have a go at me before you get there. You heard her at the funeral home."

"I'm going to see my son first. If you're too scared of a five-foot-nothing pregnant girl, that's on you. I'll get there when I get there."

She walked across the cemetery, passing a lichen-covered stone angel before arriving at her son's grave. Kneeling to brush a leaf off the limestone square, she pressed her hand, palm outstretched, on the flat marker already showing signs of weathering.

Gabriel King Hendricks
May 10, 1969

"Please, Uncle Dixon, find Gabriel and watch over him for me," she whispered into the air. A good five minutes passed, with Rennie staring blankly at the stone before she slowly rose and paced back to her truck.

May Dean's kitchen counter and table were barely visible for all the bowls, plates, and platters. Fried chicken, sliced ham, turnip greens, Jell-O salads, green beans, and pecan pies covered every surface. Funerals were the number one opportunity for people to gather, eat, and swap stories. Not every family had a wedding or a new baby, but funerals didn't discriminate. Everybody had their turn, and on that day, the Kings were up.

Rennie had heard some of the stories about her uncle but not all of them. She listened to Shorty Strickland tell about the time Uncle Dixon pulled Shorty's car out of an icy ditch with his truck and about how her uncle quit entering his honey in the state fair to give the other farmers a chance at the blue ribbon. One man told a decades-old story that he could barely get through without crying. After four solid days of rain had washed out the roads, the man's father had called the Kings late one night, begging Eugenia to come. Dixon had carried his wife through knee-deep water all the way to their home to safely deliver a baby, the man now recounting the tale.

Around dusk, May Dean and Rennie found themselves in the kitchen. Dirty plates, glasses, bowls, and silverware lay in stacks by the sink. Rennie said, "You go rest, May Dean. I'll clean this up."

"That will take you hours. I'll help."

"I need to keep busy. Walking back into that empty house is more than I can bear right now." She slipped on a pair of rubber gloves. "Go lie down."

May Dean rubbed her back. "I'll take you up on that. My feet are so swollen that I'm not sure I can even get my shoes off." She looked around the kitchen. "Where's Tiny? I want to make sure he's behaving himself."

"I saw him eating in the dining room when we first got here, but that was hours ago." Rennie shrugged. "He'll turn up. He always does."

CHAPTER 52

IT WAS CLOSE TO NINE O'CLOCK WHEN RENNIE FInally headed for home. She grimaced as she drove. *Home for now, anyway.* She parked the truck in its usual spot and tossed the keys onto the dashboard. She cocked her head, puzzled. Lights were on inside Uncle Dixon's house. In the distance, she saw a light on in the barn too. She had left for the funeral home right after lunch because she wanted to add a few more bishop's-caps to her arrangement and hadn't left any lamps on. She had searched the barn last night for Lewis Carroll but remembered pulling the string to the one bare bulb as she left. A chill skittered up her spine.

Taking the path to the house, she caught a glimpse of a black truck pulled up behind the barn. It looked like it was meant to be hidden, but a shaft of moonlight bounced off the chrome bumper, giving her enough of a view to see it was Tiny's. Why in the world would he be at Uncle Dixon's? Her stomach clenched as she approached the house.

Turning the doorknob slowly, she regretted not locking the door on her way out that afternoon. She paused on the threshold for a moment, afraid to step into the room that had always, until that moment, been so welcoming. All of her senses, still raw from losing Uncle Dixon, were screaming at her. The ticking of Uncle Dixon's Kit-Cat clock was as loud as thunder. Its eyes swept the room, the tail twitching with nervous anticipation, as if to tell her to search every corner.

Furniture was knocked over, papers were scattered everywhere, and cabinet doors were flung wide open. Sofa cushions had been sliced open, and stuffing was strewn over the wooden plank floor. The curtains had been torn from the rods, and Uncle Dixon's cheerful yellow plates were in shards around the kitchen floor. A red metal gas can she recognized as belonging in the barn sat on a chair.

She crept down the hall, still not comprehending what was in front of her. Was Tiny here? Why was a gas can in the house? Nothing made sense.

She stepped into Uncle Dixon's bedroom and gasped. Tiny stood by her uncle's bed with an ax in his hand, his breath ragged and his eyes blazing. Eugenia's dresser was in splinters. Each drawer had been hacked apart, and the contents were scattered across the room. One of the hand-carved knobs had rolled into a corner, and Eugenia's Bible was ripped into pieces. The quilt Rennie had smoothed across the bed that morning was in a heap on the floor.

"Where is it?" Tiny was snarling, and she barely recognized his voice. She had witnessed his anger before but never like this. His face was flushed a deep red. "You little bitch," he growled. "Where is the money?"

She backed away from her husband, fumbling for words. "I-I don't know, Tiny. I was as surprised as everybody else about him selling the farm."

"You made sure you were his favorite, acting all like you cared about him and his crazy ways. Where is it?"

"The only place I know he keeps money is his kitchen drawer."

"There was thirty-four dollars in there, so he's got himself another hiding place, and you know where it is."

She froze, trying to decide if she should make a run for it or stand up to him. When she should have been scared out of her wits, she suddenly felt both brave and calm. Uncle Dixon was there, not frail, the way she knew him, but young and strong, ready to take on a bully. Her uncle, the strong, handsome man from the photograph, was standing beside her. She couldn't see him, but like she didn't need words to talk with Jane Austen or the bees, she didn't need her eyes to know he was there.

Her voice was strong. "I do not have the money, and I don't know where it is. Get out of this house."

"I've searched every inch of this place, starting with that dresser you always talk about. I figured the money'd be taped to the back, but it's not."

The sensation of having Uncle Dixon protecting her vanished as quickly as it had come, and she started quaking. She had been puzzling out what Tiny's plan was, but then it came to her in a flash. "You want to steal the money for yourself and take off." She clenched her fists to still their shaking.

Tiny smirked. "Look at you, so smart. Everybody knew he was leaving the farm to you, and I figured I didn't have long to wait to get my hands on it, especially after his stroke. I started off mad, like the rest of you, that he sold it, but then I realized he'd just saved me the trouble."

She backed up toward the door. "Was your plan all along to steal the money and leave town?"

Tiny shook his head. "At first I thought we could be happy together, try for another baby, with the sale of your uncle's farm giving us enough money to live off of. But then my pa started pressuring me to pay the rent, and I got swindled out of my signing bonus." His eyes shone. "After I found out he sold it, I realized I could still have the money. All I had to do was find it."

A chill passed through her. "Aren't you worried I'll go to the sheriff?"

"My plan was to get the money and then wait for you to come back from May Dean's. There was going to be a tragic fire with you trapped inside. I'd be a widower with a pile of cash everybody thought burned up in the blaze. I'd be so torn up about losing you that I'd decide I couldn't stay in Spark." He shrugged. "I couldn't find the money, but the rest of it suits me fine. Can't leave a witness to all this," he added, gesturing to the ransacked house.

Rennie bolted for the front door, but Tiny seized her arm with a grip so tight she yelled in pain. He flung her against the wall, and then her world went black.

CHAPTER 53

A GENTLE BUT URGENT VOICE WAS IMPLORING HER TO wake up. Black smoke and pungent gasoline fumes choked her, and the bedroom was filled with the acrid smell of burning wood. She somehow got to her feet and staggered to the door, sputtering and gasping for breath. Flames licked the walls of the hallway between the bedroom and the front door, blocking the exit. The room spun, and she fell to her knees.

A bee flew to Rennie's side, quivering. Her minuscule wings fanned the smoke from her face, allowing her to draw a deep breath of sweet air. *Fly with me.* Was the bee sent to take her to heaven? The thought of being an angel, soaring to Gabriel, filled her with joy and she nodded to the bee. *I'm ready.* She closed her eyes and waited, but instead of a choir of angels, she heard, *Fly with me to the window.* Rennie stumbled to her feet, unsure of what direction to go. A pinpoint of light emanated from the bee's body, a beacon in the swirling smoke. She followed the light but was stopped by the burning remains of the dresser. She tried to reach across the dresser to the window, but the flames were too high. A second bee appeared, glowing with a light that reminded Rennie of a full moon. *The drawer, Rennie, use the dresser drawer.*

She grabbed the long front piece of the shattered drawer and set it on her shoulder, then swung it as hard as her husband playing in the most crucial game of his life. The window exploded, showering glass like drops of August dew onto the floor. A gust of wind blew through the baseball-sized opening, stoking the flames now consuming the dresser. She gulped in the fresh air but was still blocked from reaching the window. She sank to the floor, begging Gabriel to come for her.

A young Eugenia was kneeling beside her in the bedroom, stroking Rennie's hot face with her cool hands. She wore the dress from the county fair photograph, and her hair was plaited into that same braid. Then the Uncle Dixon from the photo appeared and calmly joined his wife beside Rennie. A warmth, different from the heat generated by the flames that danced around them, filled her body, reminiscent of the night the bees encircled her while she slept in the bee yard. Grateful to be escorted to heaven by the two people she'd loved all of her life, she waited for death to claim her.

My quilt, Rennie. Her eyes shot over to the splintered remnants of her uncle's bed. Beside it, on the floor, lay the double wedding ring quilt Eugenia's mother had made as a wedding gift. She recalled his words. *"When I'm gone, I want you to use it."*

She snatched it up and laid it across the dresser, covering the shards of glass. Heaving herself onto the dresser, she reached for the window. She gasped for air and her lungs filled with smoke.

A bright light filled the room and a breeze caressed her face. The thick smoke cleared, and she could see two bees hovering by the hole in the glass panes. *Follow us.*

The two bees flew to her, then toward the driveway. Rennie glided in their wake, the way Poe effortlessly floated on an air current as he waited for Rennie to prepare his seeds. Once safely away from the house, the pair of bees rose toward heaven, their still-visible light slowly fading as they soared into the sky. She understood that she was not to join them and instead landed on the grass, which was oddly cool with all the flames around her. She shut her eyes in gratitude.

A scream pierced the blackness, and she sat up, bewildered. A second scream, coming from the house. She scrambled to her feet, scanning the darkness punctuated periodically by flashes of fire. First she saw the bells of Ireland by the porch being eaten alive by the blaze, while the blossoms the color of Eugenia's eyes turned to ash. Then she spotted Tiny. His body was framed in the window, frantically pulling at the door, which was blocked by a fallen piece of wood.

She ran toward the house. "Tiny! Break the window!" The knobby root of the oak tree tripped her, and she tumbled to the ground.

When she woke up, Ambrose was kneeling beside her.

"Rennie!" He lifted her from the grass and put her

in the passenger seat of his truck. "We're going to the hospital."

She struggled to open her eyes. "Tiny's in the house."

Ambrose's eyes widened. "What?"

"Tiny's trapped inside."

"Shit!" Ambrose ran for the house, bright with flames.

CHAPTER 54

A YOUNG WOMAN WITH A WHITE CAP PINNED TO HER hair leaned over Rennie. "You gave everyone quite a fright last night," she said.

Rennie looked around at the stark room. "Where am I?"

"The hospital in Nashville. You have some lung damage from smoke inhalation, and the doctor thinks you might have a slight concussion from hitting your head, but nothing too serious. Thank the good Lord your neighbor saw the flames." She checked a bag of fluid hanging on a pole. "Your husband has some burns to his hands and part of his face, but he's going to be okay too, although he's hurt pretty bad." Smiling at Rennie, she added, "I asked about having you all moved to a room together."

Tiny. "No." Rennie squeezed her eyes closed, which did nothing to erase the image of him leering at her before he threw her against a wall. The memory of inhaling gasoline fumes and choking on heavy black smoke crowded her aching brain.

The nurse shot her a sharp look. "They said we couldn't

do that. Because of his injuries, he has to stay in the burn ward." She shook a thermometer. "Let's get some vitals, and then you should rest. Someone will be in a little later with your dinner." She gently placed the thermometer in Rennie's mouth and placed a blood pressure cuff on her arm. "You're a lucky lady to have survived. The doctors have said no visitors for a few days while they fully assess your internal injuries." She started for the door. "I almost forgot. Someone came by to see you, which we couldn't allow, but he left you this." The nurse pulled a copy of *Shirley* from her pocket. "What an odd gift. Most people bring a card or fashion magazines, but maybe it's about Shirley Temple." She scrutinized the cover. "Doesn't really look like her, though." After setting the book on the bedside table, she jotted a few notes in her chart. "Try to get some rest," she said with her hand on the door. "You've been through so much."

When Rennie woke, she began sorting through her memories, trying to make sense of the last twenty-four hours. Sweet Uncle Dixon had been laid to rest beside his beloved wife. The bees had traveled farther than the scientists had said possible in order to pay their respects. While everyone was at Ev and May Dean's house, Tiny had ransacked her uncle's house, searching for the money from the sale of the farm.

A chill passed through her. He had set a fire, trying to kill her. How had she escaped? She knit her brows. The bee. A bee had told her to go to Gabriel. She shook her head. No, the bee fanned the smoke away with her wings and guided her to the window. Wait, there were *two* bees.

Smoke confused bees. Had the fire reached the hive and two disoriented bees had flown into the fire instead of away from it? One bee had instructed her to use a board from the dresser to smash it open. But Aunt Eugenia was there, wasn't she? And Uncle Dixon? Or was that a dream? She sat up. They were the bees. She rubbed her head. A concussion could make someone confused, she remembered Tiny saying. But somehow that memory was more real than anything she'd ever experienced. She closed her eyes and slept.

When she awoke, she began assessing what she had lost in the fire. The dresser that held so many of her uncle's memories, and her own, was gone. The Bible, the county fair photo, Eugenia's wedding band—they were all gone, along with the rest of the house. She had thought about taking the gold ring from the drawer but hadn't. And now it was too late. Her hickory stick doll was gone too. Tears stung her eyes. At least May Dean had taken the rocker and watch for her baby. She fell into a fitful sleep.

⌒

May Dean slipped through the door. "Praise the Lord, you're finally well enough to have visitors. I've been calling the nurses' station every day to check on you, and when they said I could come, I zipped up here as fast as I could. How are you?" She bent down to peck Rennie on the cheek. "They say you'll be released in a few days. Ev and I have decided you're coming to live with us. The whole town has been praying for you." She handed Rennie the paper in her hand. "You made the headline of the *Gazette*."

Newcomer Saves Rennie and Luther Hendricks from Blaze!

Only a few hours after local farmer Dixon King was laid to rest, a fire broke out at his home on Creekside Road, trapping Rennie and Luther "Tiny" Hendricks inside. Spark newcomer Ambrose Beckett, who recently bought the old Sawyer place, rescued the pair. In an exclusive interview with the *Gazette*, Mr. Beckett was asked how he came to notice the blaze.

"My hobby is stargazing, and I was on my deck looking at the constellations when I noticed something unusual off to the east. I turned my telescope from the sky to Mr. King's house and saw the smoke through the darkness. I jumped in my truck and drove over there."

The *Gazette* pressed Mr. Beckett for more details, and he only said he was glad he could help.

Rennie threw the newspaper on her bedside table. "I was wondering how he saw the fire."

May Dean folded her arms. "I hate that we're indebted to that thief, but I am thankful he saved you." She smoothed Rennie's hair. "And Tiny, I guess."

Rennie rubbed her stiff neck. "Ambrose found me on the ground. As he was putting me in his truck to come here, I remember telling him Tiny was trapped inside. I guess Ambrose went into the house and somehow got him out."

"So he saved Tiny? You mean you would have been a widow, shed of Tiny Hendricks for good, if Ambrose hadn't wanted to be a hero?" She sank into a chair. "I hope the Lord isn't too upset with me, but I'm sorry Ambrose didn't just drive you straight to the hospital and leave Tiny in that house to burn." She suppressed a smile. "I'm going straight to hell for this, but I told Ev I hoped Tiny was left as crispy as a piece of Arden's fried chicken."

Rennie grabbed her side. "Don't make me laugh, May Dean. It hurts." She grinned. "I imagine the Lord might have been hoping for that too."

May Dean turned her head, but not before Rennie saw her smile. "Maybe so, but I think I'll stop by the hospital chapel on my way out to ask for forgiveness." She picked up her purse. "I can't wait to have you home."

A light knock on the door interrupted Rennie's thoughts. "Come in."

Ambrose stood before her holding a Mason jar of flowers in his hand. Both anger and gratitude flooded through her at the sight of him.

"I hope you don't mind my coming by," he said. "I have a lot to tell you, starting with Lewis Carroll. The morning after the fire, I found him curled up beside Jane Austen on the sofa."

Rennie forgot her anger for a minute as relief washed over her. Lewis Carroll was safe. "I thought he was gone."

"The bees are okay. I've been checking on them every day. He put the jar on her bedside table. "I've been checking on *you* every day too. The nurse on the phone said this morning you could have visitors." He gestured to the blooms. "I gathered these while I was down there about an hour ago, thinking they might cheer you up a little bit. I took the blazing star and wood lilies from around the hive, but the meadow beauties came from the path to the house."

With a voice still hoarse from the smoke, she said, "I am furious with you about buying the farm, but I am very thankful you saw the smoke and saved me." She swallowed hard. "And Tiny."

"I didn't see any smoke."

"So your interview in the *Gazette* was a lie? Do you even know *how* to tell the truth?"

"There's a lot I need to explain. But yes, I lied to Dewey because the truth was none of his business." Ambrose sat in a chair. "It was dark outside, and I was on my deck with Jane Austen at my feet, thinking about your uncle. A bee landed on my hand, glowing like a lightning bug. She flew toward your uncle's house and then flew back to me. *Go to Rennie* is what I heard. *She's at Dixon's. Go now.* By then I smelled the smoke, and I drove as fast as I could to your uncle's house."

Rennie shook her head. "You mean you drove to your *own* house. The one that used to be my uncle's."

"That's some of what I need to explain. It's true the house is mine, but it's not what you think. It was all your uncle's idea. He sold it to me for a dollar so—"

Rennie's raspy voice rose. "My *uncle's* idea?"

"Yes, but—"

She struggled to sit up. "As soon as I can, I am coming to your house one last time to get Jane Austen and Lewis Carroll, and then I will thank you never to speak to me or even look in my direction ever again."

The door swung open and a gray-haired nurse marched in. "Land sakes! I can hear the yelling from clear over to the nurses' station." She pointed to Ambrose. "Leave this room, young man. Visiting hours are long over, and you are upsetting my patient." When Ambrose didn't move, she pointed to the door. "Out!"

Ambrose looked from the nurse to Rennie, both glaring at him, and quietly slipped out the door.

꒰꒱

May Dean was sitting by her bed the next day when the doctor came in. "Mrs. Hendricks, your recovery has been nothing short of remarkable. I am discharging you, with instructions to follow up with your local doctor as soon as you get home. If you don't have any complications, we won't need to see you again." He shook his head. "It's a real miracle how you were not more seriously injured. My colleagues and I are amazed." He was still shaking his head as he left the room.

May Dean gently lowered a shirt over Rennie's head. "I couldn't decide if a pullover or a button-up would be easier for you to get on, so I bought them both," she said as she straightened the collar. "Lean on me while you pull up the skirt. It has an elastic waist."

Rennie gingerly slid herself off the bed and stepped into the skirt. "I've never had such pretty clothes. I hope they weren't too expensive."

May Dean waved her hand. "Don't worry about it. Castner Knott is always having a sale. You have a whole new wardrobe waiting for you back at the house." She grabbed her purse and opened the door. "My guest room is our next stop. I bet you're ready to get out of this place."

"Not quite." Rennie swallowed hard. "Before we go, I want to stop by Tiny's room."

"Do you want to give him *another* chance to kill you?" She pushed the elevator button. "Absolutely not."

"No more chances for *anything*. I've got a few things to tell him, including the fact that I'm filing for divorce."

The elevator door opened, then closed, as May Dean paused for a moment. "Wait for me on this bench, and I'll go ask his room number."

When she returned she pushed the button again and said, "He's on the fifth floor, room 503."

When Rennie and May Dean stood in front of Tiny's door, May Dean squeezed Rennie's hand. "Don't be scared. I'll be right beside you."

"I love you for wanting to stand by me, but I need to do this alone." Rennie's stomach was fluttering and sweat prickled her armpits. The image of Tiny sneering at her as he explained how she was going to die and he'd be left a rich widower flashed in her mind. "This won't take long. Why don't you bring the car around to the lobby, and I'll meet you down there."

May Dean looked doubtful. "He literally has made a habit of trying to kill you, Rennie. You shouldn't be alone with him."

"I'll be okay." Rennie wasn't sure if she was trying to convince her cousin or herself. "I promise."

"I'll leave." May Dean pointed to the nurses' station. "But yell for help if you need it."

Rennie watched May Dean waddle to the elevator. After she disappeared from view, Rennie stared at Tiny's door. *I can do this. I'm stronger now.* She wiped her sweaty palms on her skirt and knocked. After a gruff "Come in," Rennie opened the door to see Tiny staring at a wall. A machine beeped rhythmically, and a seemingly endless tangle of wires protruded from his body. The right side of his face was bandaged, as was his right hand. She hesitated for a moment, then took a step toward him. The pair locked eyes. Pain, grief, and anger burned through Tiny's sharp gaze.

Rennie cleared her throat, still raw from smoke inhalation. "I'm filing for divorce as soon as I can get to Raddy Tisdale's office."

Though scratchy, his voice had an unfamiliar tenderness. "Listen to me, sweetheart. I'm a changed man and can make all this up to you. I swear. If you cancel the divorce, I'll treat you like a queen." His blue eyes followed her as she paced the room. "We were once so good together, and we can be again. I'll make sure you never regret it if you just give me another chance." He offered a weak smile. "What do you want? Just name it. A ring from Tiffany's?" He caught her eye and lowered his voice. "Another baby?"

She stared at the still-handsome man, the one who had made her knees weak and her palms sweaty during their courting days. The man who made her feel so special because he'd chosen *her*.

"There's only one thing I want. A divorce."

He answered in a thin, raspy voice. "What if *I* don't want a divorce?"

"Everything is always about you, isn't it? If you don't agree to a divorce, I'll go to Sheriff Ricketts and tell him the truth about what happened. He may have let you off for beating me, but even *he* can't ignore attempted murder."

Tiny struggled to sit up, causing one of the machines to beep in protest. "Mike Ricketts will declare the whole thing an accident after I tell him you left some food on the stove when you left for the funeral, consumed with grief and all." He coughed, wincing as he held his side. "I'm gonna tell him I saw the smoke and rushed in to save you, then got trapped myself." A smile snaked across his lips as he added, "Mike isn't gonna do a damn thing, just like last time." He lay his head on the pillow and grimaced in pain.

Rennie felt a surge of power, like the one that had gotten her out of the burning house. "Maybe not. But the state's fire marshal will get involved as soon as I tell his office to check for traces of gasoline, and he doesn't know you from Adam. The sheriff may change his tune after the fire marshal starts talking about felonies. Are you really going to take the chance that Mike Ricketts can get you out of this?"

She stepped closer, with Raddy Tisdale's words echoing in her brain. *"If Tiny will assure me he's not contesting the divorce, I might could get it done in thirty days."*

"Listen closely to this part, Luther Hendricks. *I'm* the one who can get you out of this. You're not going to contest the divorce. Instead, you're going to leave Spark and never return. If you ever set foot in this town again, I'll claim that my concussion kept me from remembering you tried to kill me, but the sight of you was such a shock that I remembered what happened and will be ready to file attempted murder charges, for which there is no statute of limitations."

Tiny sneered. "You think that'll work?"

"Are you willing to risk the rest of your life in prison that it won't?" The look of defeat that crossed his face gave her the answer.

Tiny fumbled for the water glass, wincing as he reached toward the table. "Give me the damn water glass. My throat is killing me."

Rennie instinctively moved toward the glass, then stopped. "Get it yourself. Or if you're too weak, ring for a nurse. My days of waiting on you are over." She lifted her eyes to meet his gaze. "It's time for you to do what *I* say for a change. Go to Raddy Tisdale's office as soon as you get out of the hospital and tell him you're not fighting this divorce."

His hand dropped back onto the bed as he shot her a withering look. "Lawyers cost money. If I get a bill, I'm sending it to you."

"Don't you worry," Rennie snapped. "The bill's my business, not yours."

Tiny was silent and then said, "I guess you can afford it since you've got your uncle's money squirreled away somewhere. That farm was worth a fortune."

"There's no fortune, Tiny. Ambrose Beckett bought my uncle's farm for a dollar."

Tiny's laugh was more of a choke. "Looks like you got swindled too."

As May Dean drove Rennie back to Spark in the convertible, Rennie spotted the *Welcome to Spark* sign in the distance.

Rennie unrolled her window. "Could you slow down a minute?"

"Sure."

Rennie twisted the thin gold band from her finger and heaved it toward the sign.

CHAPTER 55

MAY DEAN CARRIED TWO GLASSES OF LEMONADE TO the terrace and handed one to Rennie. "It's been two weeks since you told Tiny you were filing for divorce, and we haven't heard a word about what he's doing about it. Is he contesting? You never did tell me what you all talked about in his hospital room."

"Let's just say he won't be a problem." She set her drink on the wrought iron table. "Mr. Tisdale went by and saw Tiny last week. He got Tiny to sign something that says he won't object. He thinks he can call in a favor and have me divorced in thirty days."

"I'll say a prayer, actually several prayers, it's even quicker." May Dean frowned. "It's too pretty a day to talk about your soon-to-be ex-husband. Let's change the subject." Her face brightened. "How fabulous about Mr. Carter ordering cakes from you. Two a week! You were so smart to take him a sample with your business card on it."

"It's generous of you to call that scrap of paper a business card, but it *is* exciting to have a standing order. Love and Honey is already turning a profit. I'll be able to save enough to rent a place for myself, Jane Austen, and Lewis Carroll. Then I can take care of them and me, and also work on growing my business."

"Don't be in such a rush to move out, Rennie. You need to build your strength back." May Dean shifted in her chair. "Ambrose Beckett keeps calling and coming by the house, desperate to talk to you." She tossed her hair over her shoulders. "He said to tell you he's taking good care of Jane Austen and Lewis Carroll, that they're getting along great, and that he will keep them until you're settled in your new place." Her voice took on a chilly tone. "I thanked him because that's the Christian thing to do, but then I told him I never wanted to set eyes on him again and sent him on his way. I don't know many swear words, but I used all the ones I could think of." She looked at Rennie with troubled eyes. "I hope you understand about us not being able to have your pets here. It's already hard to breathe with the baby pressing on my lungs, and if I'm inhaling pet hair, well . . ."

"I understand. Nothing is more important than keeping you and the baby healthy. And it sounds like they're happy living with Ambrose for now." Rennie sighed. "I still can't believe I thought he was my friend."

The phone startled them both. "Probably Ev, wanting to know what to bring home from the Blue Plate for dinner." She waddled toward the house, returning a moment later with a huge grin on her face. "It's Alan Carter. He needs to speak with you."

Rennie went to the kitchen and picked up the receiver. "Hi, Alan. How are you?"

"In a bit of a pickle, honestly. I just took a call from a good customer of mine who has the restaurant booked for a private party on Tuesday. We have fifty-four people coming for lunch. The whole event's been planned for months, but here's the thing. She was in last week and tried your Honey Moon Cake and is insisting on serving it to her guests instead of what she'd already chosen. I told her I'd have to check with the baker. Can you possibly manage making me five cakes by Tuesday?" He paused. "I know it's a lot to ask, but would it help to know that her daughter-in-law writes a food column for the *Nashville Banner*? This could be your big break."

Rennie struggled to keep her voice calm. "I'll be glad to make five cakes for you, Alan. Would delivering them at eight o'clock Tuesday morning work for you?"

"You're the best, Rennie."

May Dean was standing in the doorway. "This is fantastic, but my kitchen can't handle five cakes going at once. And I'm down to two jars of Uncle Dixon's honey."

Rennie dropped into a chair. "Let me think a minute. The Blue Plate's closed on Mondays, so I'll ask Arden if I can use her kitchen." She rubbed her neck. "The hard part will be going to Uncle Dixon's to get the honey from the barn. I'm not sure I'm ready to see, well, to see everything."

"Ev will be glad to do it."

"I've been putting it off, but I need to go over there and say goodbye to the land, and especially to the bees." Rennie sighed. "Seeing what's left of the house will make it all too real."

The sharp smell of smoke still lingered in the air, nearly three weeks after the fire. Heaps of charred wood lay in random piles, only hinting at the structure her uncle had built for his bride so long ago. The metal kitchen sink lay beside a pile of ashes, its pipes protruding into the air like spidery legs. The chains to her porch swing were coiled like a snake, marking the spot where she had whiled away two decades of sunny afternoons. Her uncle's wicker rocker was gone, a mound of ashes she could find only by the charred bells of Ireland she knew grew beside it.

She walked to what used to be her uncle's bedroom, surveying the remnants of the window she had crawled out of. She had no way to understand it, except that she knew it to be true—her aunt and uncle came to her as bees and had used magic or enchantment, or maybe even love, to transform her into a bee so that she could fly through the window and soar to safety. *Thank you for rescuing me.* She pulled her shoulders straighter and started for the barn to retrieve the honey she needed for her cakes.

The leather cord to the barn door latch was soft in her fingers. Her uncle had carved the hasp from a hickory limb, expertly creating the sturdy closure that held the door against all the storms the world could hurl at it.

The interior of the barn was dark and quiet, a contrast to the bright sunlight and noisy nuthatches and cardinals calling in the trees.

The workbench was smooth to her touch. Her fingers dipped into the grooves made from decades of repairing farm equipment, and she fought back tears as she recalled her uncle working where she stood, hammering a bent saw or sanding a rusty hinge.

Glowing with a light that reminded her of the bees that had come to her during critical moments of her life, the honey jars seemed to pulse on their shelves. She reached for one and held it up to the window, recalling her uncle telling her a bee made only a few drops of honey in its lifetime. In a way so insignificant, but in another the culmination of her allotted time on earth. She gathered the jars into one of May Dean's shopping bags, then closed the latch of the barn and slowly walked to her truck.

After securing the shopping bag on the floorboard, she turned toward the bee yard. Following that familiar path for the last time wrenched her heart like nothing else, even saying goodbye to her uncle as he was lowered into the ground.

As she crossed under the arch of New Dawn roses, she pushed from her mind the night Ambrose brushed against them when he carried her to the house, releasing their heady, comforting fragrance. She had seen Ambrose as a friend and the strength she didn't have for herself, someone to be trusted. His swindling her uncle out of his farm was the end of their friendship and more evidence that Arden was right to wield a gold ring against the men in Spark the way villagers used garlic against vampires in movies.

The bench welcomed her, and she gratefully sank down, reaching to touch the rose medallion, warm from the afternoon sun. Her energy level was returning, but fully regaining her strength would be a slow process. The hum of the hives comforted her, and she focused on her breathing, drawing in the healing air that always seemed to restore her.

After a few moments of rest, she rose and walked to the first hive, knocking gently on its roof, then did the same for the other two hives. She returned to the bench and bowed her head for a moment, then began to speak. "Precious bees,

I am here to ask forgiveness and to say goodbye. I doubted you and accused you of being no more than livestock. I thought because I had made mistakes in my life, who I married and who I trusted, that was evidence that you did not guide me. But in that fire, I understood it all. You love me, just as Aunt Eugenia and Uncle Dixon did."

At the mention of her aunt and uncle, wind stirred in the wild geranium.

"I'm still not sure if you conjured them or if you *were* them, but I know my life was saved that night by forces other than my own. I am grateful and am going to try to be worthy of this second chance."

"I've started a cake baking business with a secret ingredient, your honey. It's doing really well, and I am going to be able to take care of myself because of it. And I'm divorcing Tiny." She touched her now-bare finger. "I don't think he's going to bother me anymore."

She walked to the edge of the bee yard, standing by the spring that burbled into Flat Rock Creek. The apology came easily because it was her own shortcomings that had necessitated it. The next part, telling them she wouldn't be able to see them anymore because they were now owned by Ambrose Beckett, was harder, because it was his actions, not her own, that created the circumstances.

She returned to the bench, caressing the rose medallion in a gesture of farewell before sinking back onto its warm latticed seat. Instead of words, tears came. She closed her eyes, searching her brain for a way to explain that she would never see them again.

"Rennie?"

Her eyes flew open. Ambrose. She sat up and, in as icy a

tone as she could manage, said, "I apologize for trespassing, but I came here to say goodbye to your bees." She rose from the bench, intent on going back to her cousin's house.

Ambrose's voice was low. "They're not my bees." He took a step toward her.

She held up her hand to stop him. "Yes, they are. Bought and paid for with a whole dollar. You admitted that yourself."

"Buying bees is the same as buying trouble, and selling bees means selling your luck. Nobody sold these bees, and nobody bought them. They're your bees and have been since Dixon died."

Rennie returned to the bench. "That doesn't make any sense."

"I've been trying to explain, but between the nurses and your *very* protective cousin, I haven't been able to." He took another step and then stopped. "I have so many things to explain. May I sit with you?"

She paused. Would she regret allowing Ambrose so close to her? A bee landed on the bench's curved arm and was soon joined by a second bee. The county fair photograph flashed in her mind.

"All right," she said warily.

Ambrose sat, turning his body toward hers. "I lied to you. I *had* met Eugenia before, but I didn't want you to know."

"Why on earth would meeting my sweet aunt be a secret?"

Ambrose closed his eyes for a moment, then looked at her. "Because of where we were."

"Why would I care about that?"

"It was the night of the bonfire, the night I got burned. Eugenia helped me."

Rennie rolled her eyes. "She helped *everyone*, Ambrose.

So what? Someone carried you to her house and she tended your burns, and you had to lie about that?"

His face was solemn. "No one took me to her, because she was already there." He gazed into Rennie's confused face. "At the bonfire. She was celebrating Beltane, same as me."

"What is Beltane? And why would my aunt be celebrating it?"

"Beltane is an ancient Celtic ritual, like what people know now as May Day, the welcoming of summer. There's dancing, lots of food, and bonfires. We decorate doors and windows with yellow marsh marigolds to symbolize letting the sun into our homes. We celebrate Beltane as part of our connection to nature and as a way to honor the sacredness of our planet." He took Rennie's hands. "Some who practice witchcraft also celebrate Beltane."

Rennie's face grew angry. "You stop right there. Are you saying my aunt was a witch?" She glared at Ambrose. "And you are too?"

He raked his fingers through his curls. "Maybe I need to back up a little." Rubbing the scar on his hand, he continued, "Growing up, I knew things I shouldn't have. One December I told my aunt next year's Christmas would be so different with the twins, and she looked at me like I had sprouted wings, but that's exactly what happened—she gave birth to two little boys in November. I stopped my mother one time as she was leaving for town, telling her she shouldn't go because she was about to get an important call. She scolded me for telling lies, but then the telephone rang. Her mother had fallen and broken her hip. My parents thought my predictions were from the devil, so I learned to keep everything to myself about who I really was."

"So who are you?"

"I'm a man with a deep appreciation for the sacredness of the earth, the wisdom of the universe. I feel a connection to the stars I watch with such wonder on my back deck. Some people who don't understand my respect for Mother Earth and the interconnectedness of all living things might call me a witch." He shrugged. "In simpler terms, I'm like your aunt."

"Quit including my aunt in this wild story of yours."

"The bees she gave my parents thrived under my care, and people drove from miles away to buy our family's honey. I could nurse any dog or horse or cow back to health, and for a while I wanted to become a veterinarian because the animals understood what I could do and were grateful, not judgmental. I'd heard talk about a woman who was like me, your aunt, but she'd already moved away. But then I heard she'd come back to visit her parents, and I was determined to talk to her."

Wind blew through the lindens' leaves, giving Rennie the feeling she was surrounded by hearts. The beehives seemed to pulse, and a peacefulness settled over her soul. Could all this be true? She thought back to her night in the bee yard, when her aunt and thousands of bees had saved her life. "This is starting to make sense."

"I went to Beltane that night hoping to meet her. Someone accidentally knocked me into the bonfire and I was badly burned. She rushed to help me. My parents had forbidden me to explore my gifts, so I knew I couldn't go to them. I told Eugenia this, and she took me to her house, where I stayed for a week while she and her mother nursed me back to health."

Rennie knit her brows. "So you don't come home for a full week and your parents didn't question that?"

"Eugenia said I had to tell them I was safe, that a mother would worry. I called and said I'd gone off to Nashville with a buddy to sow some wild oats. *That* they were fine with. My mama said, 'Boys will be boys. Just come back when you've had enough.'"

Rennie recalled all the times her own mother seemed annoyed by her very existence, and how Eugenia could set everything right with just an embrace or kind word. "I understand that."

He hung his head. "At first I didn't want you to suspect, for *anyone* to suspect I was different, so I lied about the moon water you saw on my railing and how I just *happened* to guess that May Dean was having a girl who'd be born on Halloween." Rubbing his neck, he continued, "We were becoming friends, and I desperately wanted to tell you the truth." He nodded toward the field just beyond the bee yard. "But that day we picked blackberries, you said how much it hurt you for people to say your aunt was a witch. I didn't want you to know I'd met Eugenia through Beltane, something associated with witchcraft, because then you might think less of her or think she *was* one of those storybook creatures with cauldrons and broomsticks. You love her so much, and I didn't want to tarnish that love in any way."

She eyed Ambrose suspiciously. "So you can't cast spells?"

He grinned. "If I *could* cast spells, I would've put one on Tiny a long time ago."

She suppressed a giggle.

Ambrose continued, "All the things you loved about your aunt, the way she cared for you and cured sick people, the way she was so wise, so connected to the earth and all its gifts, that's what I have too. It's just a way of living close to nature. We experience the joys and disappointments of walking through this world just like everybody else. It's more about understanding things about your life, about other people and situations." He frowned. "Not everything, though. It turns out some things we have to figure out on our own, like my fiancée and my so-called best friend."

"So you can't just, like, check some book and see what your whole life will be like?"

He smiled. "Nope. Knowing things sounds pretty good, but it can be heartbreaking. Like your aunt understood she'd never have a biological child, but she tried every potion and powder to help her conceive, even though she knew it was no use." He took her hand. "She considered you to be her daughter, just not one she had given birth to."

The love she felt from her aunt enveloped her body like a warm quilt, fresh with the scent of sunshine from the clothesline. *I will always be with you, even when you can't see me.* "She was more of a mother to me than my own."

"Eugenia had a premonition of her death and had gone back to Travers to tell her parents goodbye. She also knew there was someone she needed to meet, which turned out to be me. She taught me a lot that week I lived with her family. The last thing she ever said to me was that the bees held my truth and to always let them guide me."

Rennie's eyes studied the three hives. "It always comes back to the bees." She looked at Ambrose. "Keep going."

"Your uncle recognized me as soon as we met, of course." He grinned. "It was my eyes that gave me away, the same color green as Eugenia's."

"So let me see if I've got this right. You know things and can help people, the way my aunt did."

He nodded solemnly. "Correct."

"And May Dean's having a little girl on Halloween?"

"Guaranteed."

"And she'll be healthy?" Rennie's voice trembled. "Not like Gabriel?"

Ambrose squeezed her hand. "Yes. A healthy little girl."

Rennie bristled. "Wait a minute. What about buying my uncle's farm for a dollar?"

"Your uncle loved you very much." His eyes watched the two bees still on the bench's arm. "And he still does. He knew May Dean was well cared for, but he worried about you. That's why he wanted you to have the farm, to give you security." Ambrose sighed. "But the rules of this world were made by men. When he saw how Tiny had changed, or no, actually, once he saw how Tiny was becoming who he really was deep down, Dixon realized Tiny would steal the farm from you. He'd sell it and take the money for himself, and as a woman, you'd have no legal recourse against your husband."

A buzzing filled her ears. Was she going to faint, still weak from the fire, or were the bees ensuring she was listening with her whole being?

Ambrose continued, "Dixon came to me with a plan. If I would buy the farm for a dollar, then Tiny couldn't get his hands on it. Then *I* could sell it back to *you* for that same dollar." He flashed that dimple at her. "But not the bees. He specifically excluded them from the sale. Don't you remember him saying you never buy or sell bees?"

"I *do* remember," Rennie said, slowly nodding.

"Dixon said for me to tell you they are a gift to you for the love you have shown them, and him, all these years."

Rennie blinked back tears. "But if you sold the farm back to me, Tiny would just take the farm and the bees then."

"Dixon knew you were going to divorce Tiny, but it wouldn't be while he was alive. He trusted me to keep the farm safe for you until the paperwork was finalized."

"I filed for divorce right after I got home from the hospital. Tiny told Mr. Tisdale he wasn't contesting the divorce, so he was able to call in a favor from a judge and make it happen faster. I have seventeen days left."

"Then I'll sell it back to you in eighteen days."

"How did Uncle Dixon know I was going to divorce Tiny?"

"I told him."

Rennie sat up. "*You* told him?"

He nodded. "Remember, I know things." Beads of sweat dotted his brow. "There's something else."

Rennie bit her lip. "Good or bad?"

"Good, I hope." He rose and paced to the closest hive, placing a hand on the shingled roof. He stood for a moment with his eyes closed and then returned to the bench. "Dixon asked me to do something else."

She looked at him quizzically. "What?"

He blushed. "Dixon fussed at me a little. He said that the bees had already told me something, and it was high time I told you." Ambrose returned to the bench and took her hand. "The day I took you to pack your things for Dixon's house, do you remember when I said my bees told me to move to Spark?"

Rennie nodded. "You said they told you that you would find a true friend here, and a wife. Am I the true friend?"

She smiled. "I thought our friendship was over, and I'm glad to be wrong."

He searched her eyes. "I left off what else they told me." Ambrose ran his hands down his pant legs. "They said it would be the same person. My true friend would become my true love."

"Why didn't you tell me any of this?"

"For one, you were a married woman at the time, and even if I didn't approve of or even like Tiny, he was still your husband. Second, I didn't want you to think I was crazy." He rubbed the back of his neck. "If you don't want anything to do with me because of what I've told you, I understand. I'll sell you the farm back for that dollar and I'll leave you in peace. But I want you to know this." He touched her cheek. "At first I didn't understand who the bees meant when they told me my true love was here. But your uncle did. He didn't say anything until much later, but he had it all figured out right away. That's why he sold me the farm. He knew how it was all going to go."

"Wait, did *he* have a book? Did he know things too?"

"No, he was just a man who saw another man hopelessly in love."

"I'm confused again. In love with who?"

He put his finger under her chin and tilted it toward him. "You, Roberta Irene King." His petticoat-green eyes were sparkling. "I am in love with you."

Rennie whispered, "You are?"

Ambrose nodded. "And I have been since we met up in the church parking lot when you brought me Jane Austen. I was determined to stay all night and into the morning to wait for you, even if I had to explain to the good reverend when he came to open up the next morning that I wasn't leaving until a small woman with a large dog arrived, because I had told her I would be there, and I wasn't leaving until I had fulfilled that promise. I paced around that entire parking lot about a hundred times, and it was during one of those laps I realized I was in love."

"Ambrose, I-I don't know what to say."

"That's okay. I've known all this for a while, but it's all new to you." He searched her face. "There are two things I really want to do right now, but I need to wait seventeen more days. But on day eighteen, I look forward to doing both." He flashed that dimple she had such a hard time resisting. "You know how May Dean made that moon landing countdown calendar and put it on Dixon's fridge? I'm going home to make my own calendar before I forget I'm a gentleman." He stood and pointed to the bench. "Will you meet me back here in eighteen days at noon? No, wait, make that sunrise."

Her brown eyes sparkled. "I will."

CHAPTER 56

RENNIE THOUGHT THE DAYS LEADING TO HER DIVORCE would drag, but she found just the opposite was true. Love and Honey Cakes took off faster than that *Apollo* rocket to the moon and had consumed most of her time. After the luncheon at Alan's restaurant and the glowing article in the *Nashville Banner* food column a week later, orders poured in.

Rennie tried to bring up moving to a place of her own, but May Dean wouldn't hear of it. "I *need* you, Rennie. Ev's at work all day and there's no orders for his sister's husband to leave for Vietnam yet, so you'd be doing me a big favor to keep me company."

She and May Dean fell into a routine, with Rennie baking in the mornings and the two of them delivering cakes in the afternoon, with an occasional side trip afterward to boutiques and children's stores to shop for the baby.

"Let's throw a divorce party, Rennie," May Dean said as she and Rennie sat on the terrace. "Later this afternoon you'll be a free woman, and that's worth celebrating. Tiny's appointment with Mr. Tisdale is at 3:00, and then you go at 4:00?" When Rennie nodded, she said, "It was nice of Mr. Tisdale to schedule y'all's appointments at different times so you won't have to see Tiny." The phone rang in the kitchen. "Would you mind getting that? It's getting harder each day for me to get out of a chair."

Rennie picked up the receiver. "Hello?"

Tiny's deep voice boomed across the line. "I've got something important to tell you, Rennie. Can you meet me at the Blue Plate at 3:30?"

She hesitated but then said, "I'll be there."

May Dean objected immediately when Rennie told her what she was doing. "He's already proven he'd rather be a widower than a divorcé. Absolutely not."

"Arden will be there, not to mention the other customers. Even Tiny isn't that stupid."

When Rennie walked through the Blue Plate's front door, Arden buzzed over to her. "I told him to get the hell out of my restaurant, but he said he was meeting you here. I wouldn't even give him water until I checked his story." She looked over her glasses. "Is it true?"

When Rennie nodded, Arden walked Rennie to the table, scowling at Tiny as she dropped two menus on the table. Rennie handed them back to her. "We won't be here long enough to eat. How about two iced teas?" After Arden left, Rennie slid into the booth opposite Tiny, whose face was still bandaged from his burns. "How are you, Tiny?"

He shrugged. "Gettin' by. You look good."

"My recovery is going well, and I'm staying busy." She

took her tea from Arden, who was still glaring at Tiny. "What's so important?"

"I had a lot of time to think, laying up there in the hospital. When I was in high school, I was the best there was. Everybody told me so, and I believed them. I was good-looking and strong and could hit a ball like nobody else. I was gonna be a star, even bigger than my brother. It all went to my head, and pretty soon I believed all the hype. Then I headed off to play ball professionally." He bowed his head. "I took you along as my wife, and I regret that. You were so sweet, always telling me I was great and would achieve my dreams, no matter how big they were. *You* believed in me, which made *me* believe in me. Anytime I got a little scared, you were there to lift me up, to help me believe in myself again. You were my cheerleader, my good luck charm, and my security as I left Spark for the big time. Off we go, and guess what, everybody in the ball club was the best in their hometowns too. I went up there thinking I was God's gift to baseball, but I got humbled pretty quick. My whole identity was tied up with being the golden boy, and when reality came crashing down on my dream, I couldn't handle it." His voice broke. "I'm sorry for messing up so bad."

"Trying to kill me is not exactly *messing up*."

He grimaced. "I deserve that." A coughing fit overtook him, and he gulped his tea. "Still havin' a little trouble with my lungs." After another swig from his glass, he said, "Here's the big news I wanted to tell you. A buddy of mine has offered me a job announcing minor league baseball games outside Atlanta." He gestured to the bandages swaddling his head. "The perfect face for radio, huh?" Without waiting for a response, he continued, "Anyway, I figure it's the perfect chance for us to have a fresh start. We can cancel the divorce and move to Georgia together. I signed those divorce papers 'cause Mr. Tisdale laid out what would happen if I didn't, and I don't have the money to fight you in court, but *you* haven't signed yet. We can go to his office together and tear them up. I'll have a steady job, and here's what's so exciting: I'm gonna start a private baseball coaching business, working with kids who are where I was, talented but green. We can have another baby and, just like in those books you're always reading, live happily ever after."

Rennie stared at him, her voice incredulous. "You want to give our marriage another chance?"

"Yeah. I thought you'd be excited." He pouted. "I've changed, and we can start over, leave Spark and all its bad memories behind." Shrugging, he added, "I nearly died, Rennie, but I didn't. Instead, I realized how wrong I was. I'm offering you a whole new life, you and me together. I have become a better person and am ready to prove that to you." He threw his shoulders back and added, "Pretty big news, if you ask me."

For an instant, Rennie caught a glimpse of the boy she had fallen for, so proud and strong, trying to act humble when he knew he was hotter than the surface of the sun. How had she mistaken his arrogance for confidence, something she had not one thimbleful of, but longed for with all her heart? So much had changed since those early days. Tiny claimed to have grown, but she understood she was the one who had changed, and the words she would have given almost anything to hear only a few short months ago now fell on an indifferent heart.

"You nearly died because you trapped yourself in your own fire. The one you set to kill me." She picked up her purse. "I think moving to Atlanta is a great idea. For you. In fact, I insist you do that. But never come back, Tiny. I meant every word I said in the hospital. If you so much as set a pinkie toe back in Spark, I'll have you arrested." She slid out of the booth. "You were right about one thing, though. I will have a new life, so much better than the one I endured with you."

Tiny stood, grabbing his baseball cap resting on the vinyl seat beside him. "I've no doubt." He jammed his cap on his head and stared at her with flashing blue eyes. "Goodbye, Rennie."

The sparkling front window of the Blue Plate gave her the perfect view of Tiny walking to his battered black truck and climbing in. She tried to pay for their iced teas, but Arden wouldn't take her money. "I didn't drop a bill on your table because there isn't one. I don't know what you said to him, but I could see it all over his face. You finally fixed his wagon, and I'm proud of you." She came around the counter and gave Rennie a big hug. "Now go get divorced."

With a smile on her face, she walked to Raddy Tisdale's office and sat in the same chair she had occupied weeks ago when she came to ask about getting a divorce. Pen in hand, she looked up. "May I sign it Roberta Irene King? I'm taking back my maiden name."

"We'll need you to sign the divorce decree in your married name, but as soon as that ink is dry, you can legally start using Roberta Irene King again."

"Thank you for handling this pro bono and helping me to earn the court costs with your deposit for the wedding cake. I'm very appreciative."

He chuckled. "I got the better end of the deal, I assure you. I finally get to repay an old debt, not to mention my wife read that *Banner* column about you and has been bragging to everyone she knows that she hired you *before* you were famous."

CHAPTER 57

THE *GAZETTE*'S WEATHER COLUMN ALWAYS LISTED the sunrise and sunset times for the week. Sunrise the next day would happen at 6:10 a.m. At 5:50, she slipped out of Ev and May Dean's house, leaving them a note that she'd be back soon, and headed for the bee yard.

She parked in her usual spot in the driveway, making sure to avoid the tree root that had a habit of tripping her. Glancing at the charred remnants of her uncle's house twisted her heart, but she reminded herself that he was where he wanted to be, with his beloved Eugenia.

The air was warm and humid, and as she walked toward her bees, the sunlight shone on the grass, damp with dew. Flowers burst from every corner, scenting the air with a heady fragrance.

As the rising sun touched the rooftops of the beehives, Rennie could see Ambrose standing by the bench, with Jane Austen and Lewis Carroll beside him, waiting for her to make her way down the path. The first towhees were stirring, calling, *Drink your tea*. Bees were darting among the starry campion and buttonbush.

"Good morning." She gave him a shy smile.

He answered, "It's the best morning of my life. Is your paperwork finished?"

"Yes. I'm officially divorced."

Ambrose grinned. "As I mentioned eighteen days ago, I have two things I want to do, but I'm not sure which should come first."

She ducked her head. "You've got a real problem there."

"Indeed, I do."

"My uncle was a very wise man. He always told me to trust my gut, that it would never steer me wrong."

"Sage advice." He stepped forward. "When Tiny proposed to you on your graduation day, you were put on the spot, in front of at least a hundred people." He waved his arm toward the hives. "We've got about eighty thousand spectators, but I hope it feels different. The last thing I want to do is make you uncomfortable. The bees are here, of course, because this is their home. It's your home too, Rennie, and I hope it will also be mine." He paused. "Do you want me to stop, to give you some time?"

She looked up and saw Poe gliding through the sky, the sun glinting off a piece of metal in his beak. His presence felt like an omen that everything was as it should be. She answered Ambrose. "When Tiny proposed that afternoon, I was caught up in his emotions, his excitement about being scouted. The whole room was cheering, and I let them drown out my own misgivings. Here in this bee yard, I know I am among only those who love me." She hesitated. "But I do need that time you mentioned to focus on myself. I want to live on my own and find out who I am after all I've been through. I want to be independent, to think and act for myself. I have a new business to grow, a new life to discover, and a lot of healing to do. I want to do that free of any commitments."

Ambrose nodded slowly. "That makes sense."

She tilted her head. "One of those things I want to explore is a relationship with you. I'm not in a strong enough place to make promises, but I would like to spend some time together." She tucked a strand of hair behind her ear. "Maybe we could start with a picnic here in the bee yard to celebrate my divorce."

"Are you asking me on a date?"

A smile crossed her face. "I am."

"I accept." Ambrose moved close to Rennie. "And now for that second thing I've been wanting to do." He gently put his hands on either side of her face and tilted her head up toward his. "May I kiss you?" When she nodded, he lowered his mouth to hers. His kiss was warm and urgent. Rennie wrapped her arms around Ambrose, then stood on her tiptoes to more fully reach him to return his kiss. Her knees buckled and he held her closer.

Bees were crowding the landing board, while more settled on the nearby grass. Poe came to rest by the bench, his offering encircling his beak. "Another pop top ring," Rennie said, "like the one I got the day the bees told me to go to Uncle Dixon." With a shake that looked like a *no*, the bird dropped a gold ring at Rennie's feet.

She bent down. "What in the world?" Peering inside the band, she read, *To EM from DK. ALWAYS*. "Aunt Eugenia's wedding ring." Her voice shook. "I thought it was lost in the fire."

Poe, hopping nearby, watched her intently as she looked

at him with amazement. "How did you ever spot this tiny ring in all that ash and rubble?" Poe bowed and then flew into the linden tree. Rennie took Ambrose's hand and opened his palm. "Why don't you hold on to this for me, and give it back to me later?" She hesitated. "It may be at our wedding, or it may be the day we part ways, but it will make my heart glad to know you've got it."

CHAPTER 58

One Year Later

THE JOY OF THIS DAY WILL BE PASSED DOWN TO OUR descendants, who will all know the story of this moment. How it came to be that these two humans—

Don't you mean these three humans?

Shhh, let them tell it. It's their news.

Ambrose stood by the hive, holding Rennie's hand. "Would you prefer I say it, or you?"

She bent down to rub Jane Austen's grizzled ears as Lewis Carroll twined around her legs. "Let's do it together."

Ambrose knocked on each of the five hives. "Beloved bees, Rennie and I are here to notify you of the happiest news. Just as your family expanded when we brought my two hives here to the bee yard, our little family is also expanding. We are expecting a baby. We hope that you all will guide them the way you did with Rennie and me. Please help us to raise a child who is wise and kind." Ambrose smiled at Rennie. "Your turn."

Rennie caressed the hive's shingled roof. "We wish for our child to have strength, resilience, and joy, and know that with your help, it will be so."

We accept with joy the task of helping to raise a fine, compassionate human. We will, with all our hearts and assiduity, provide protection, counsel, and, most of all, love for all of their days.

"It makes my heart happy to know our child and Gabriella will play down here together, just like May Dean and I did. We need to make sure he or she does not ever lose the magic of the bee yard. I did, and it almost killed me." She smiled as she noticed the crow sitting on a linden tree branch. "I'm glad Morrigan was here to share this moment." She rose from the bench. "Shall we go see how the house is coming along? I want to peek at that fancy oven and check the pantry dimensions again. Alan is keeping me busy with the cakes, and I want to make sure I have enough storage room for all my supplies. And I'd like to see if the nursery is finished yet for little Eugenia or Dixon." She patted her belly. "I wonder which it will be." She stopped and looked at Ambrose. "Wait a minute. You know, don't you?"

He grinned. "Yes, Mrs. Beckett, I do."

She laughed. "Don't tell me, Mr. Beckett." A cloud passed over her face as she softly asked, "Will the baby be healthy?"

"Yes, we're having a beautiful, perfect, healthy baby."

A new queen in a new hive, beginning the generations that will tell her story of survival and triumph. As they live their lives and eventually grow old, they will come to this bee yard with first their children and then their grandchildren, basking in the love that surrounds them.

And our descendants will be alongside this family, sharing in their joys and offering our love and guidance as they flourish.

We did a fine job.

Yes, and so did they.

With Jane Austen and Lewis Carroll beside them, Ambrose and Rennie walked hand in hand up the path, passing through the arch of New Dawn roses as they made their way back home.

Author's Note

Several years ago, I was scrolling social media when I saw that my friend Evelyn Allen had posted a newspaper article from the *Danville Bee* dated June 4, 1956, about a swarm of bees that had attended their keeper's funeral. If I were making this up, I would have named the newspaper something other than the *Bee*, but this story is true. John Zepka, of Adams, Massachusetts, was described as a man who "had a way" with bees. I don't doubt it, as thousands of bees gathered for his burial to honor him one final time.

I was curious about this event and discovered the ancient tradition of "telling the bees." When a keeper dies, the bees must be informed of the passing. After knocking on the hives three times, the new keeper delivers the news. Black cloths are affixed to the hives and the bees are assured their care will continue. Failing to adhere to this custom invites disaster in the form of the bees' departure, their inability to produce honey, or even their death.

I had been toying with a story about a young woman named Rennie whose world was pretty bleak. The one bright spot in her life was her uncle Dixon, a man who embodied all the folk wisdom soaked into the Tennessee hills I love so much. I had a plot I was happy with, but I knew the story was lacking an element that could transform it into something more powerful than a tale about a tobacco farmer and his niece. Uncle Dixon became a beekeeper who knew all about telling the bees, and the result was *Bees in June*.

Thank you, Evelyn, for posting that article, and thank you to all the beekeepers who work tirelessly to nurture the magical bees that are so important to our planet.

One of my cousins, Susan Webster Bailey, was raised on a tobacco farm in rural Tennessee. I asked her to tell me about the old days, and one of the stories she shared with me became a cornerstone of this book. When she was a child, she played beneath a walnut tree on their property and loved that tree like a friend. She cried when the tree eventually had to come down. Her father built a china press from the wood of that tree and gave it to her as a wedding gift. It has graced her dining room ever since. I changed the china press to a dresser for the purposes of this book but kept the love it symbolizes.

Thank you, Susan, for sharing your beautiful story with me. Below is a photo of Susan's beloved china press.

Acknowledgments

Writing is largely a solitary experience, but it takes so many people to turn typewritten pages into a book. Thank you to my family, who always give me the space and time to work and who are willing to help me think through any plot point or character trait.

Thank you to the members of the Nashville Writers Alliance for their insightful critiques and suggestions in our weekly meetings.

Thank you to Wanda Clark, a master gardener, who I turned to for advice about the flowers and trees I knew would be an integral part of this story. She introduced me to GroWild Nursery in Fairview, Tennessee, where the owners graciously allowed us to roam their property, studying their vast array of native plants.

Evelyn Allen posted a newspaper article about a swarm of bees who attended their keeper's funeral. That article led me to discovering the ancient tradition of "telling the bees," which I discuss more in my author's note. Thank you, Evelyn, for that post. I probably should have been working when I was scrolling social media instead, but the result was *Bees in June*, so it all worked out.

Susan Webster Bailey told me a story about a china press her father made for her from a fallen walnut tree. That china press became a dresser in this book and serves an important role in the story. Thank you for sharing your story with me, Susan, and inspiring Eugenia's beloved dresser. I give more details in my author's note about her gift from her father.

Thank you to my agent, Kathy Schneider at Jane Rotrosen Agency, for her unwavering support and expert guidance. I am grateful for you every day, Kathy.

Thank you to Becky Philpott, whose input helped to whip this story into shape.

Thank you to everyone at Harper Muse who works so tirelessly to bring beautiful books to readers. I am honored to be a part of your publishing family.

My last thank-you is to my editor, Becky Monds. She made me a better writer and always had just the right word or idea when I got stuck. I will be forever grateful she pulled *The Empress of Cooke County* from her slush pile. You're a bee in June, Becky.

Discussion Questions

Attention, book clubs! Interested in having the author chat with your group via Zoom? Contact her through her website, www.elizabethbassparman.com.

1. What role does the lunar landing play in the novel?

2. How are Tiny and Rennie alike? Compare Tiny's investment in the bar to Rennie's commitment to her marriage.

3. Rennie is very troubled about telling lies to Tiny. Can you think of any other lies she told?

4. Did Tiny ever love Rennie? Did Rennie ever love Tiny? How do Rennie's feelings evolve regarding Tiny?

5. Dixon, Eugenia, and May Dean each married the right person, but Rennie did not. Did the bees let Rennie down?

6. What do Rennie and Eugenia have in common? How are they different?

7. Rennie is helped by both the bees and humans. How are these two groups similar and how are they different?

8. Dixon possesses folk wisdom while Ambrose and Eugenia have more magical capabilities. Is there a difference?

9. What are the ways the author shows who is connected to the earth and who is not? Where does Rennie fit in this continuum?

10. What is the role of the crow? Throughout the story Rennie calls the crow Poe, but at the end she calls the crow Morrigan. What changed?

From the Publisher

GREAT BOOKS
ARE EVEN BETTER WHEN THEY'RE SHARED!

Help other readers find this one:

- Post a review at your favorite online bookseller

- Post a picture on a social media account and share why you enjoyed it

- Send a note to a friend who would also love it—or better yet, give them a copy

Thanks for reading!

LOOKING FOR MORE GREAT READS? LOOK NO FURTHER!

Illuminating minds and captivating hearts through story.

Visit us online to learn more:
harpermuse.com

Or scan the below code and sign up to receive email updates on new releases, giveaways, book deals, and more:

@harpermusebooks

"I couldn't have loved it more." —Fannie Flagg, *New York Times* bestselling author

Featuring two strong women, mother-daughter tension, beauty parlor gossip, and one shocking turn of events, *The Empress of Cooke County* will transport you to a small town in the 1960s with the one woman determined to rule it all. Perfect for fans of *Fried Green Tomatoes*.

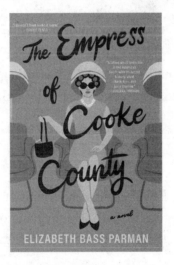

AVAILABLE IN PRINT, E-BOOK, AND AUDIO

About the Author

Photo by Jackie Arthur

Elizabeth Bass Parman grew up entranced by family stories, such as the time her grandmother woke to find Eleanor Roosevelt making breakfast in her kitchen. She worked for many years as a reading specialist for a nonprofit and spends her summers in a cottage by a Canadian lake. She has two grown daughters and lives outside her native Nashville with her husband.

Elizabeth can be found at
www.elizabethbassparman.com
Instagram: @elizabethbassparman